P9-AEU-434

The Way We Were

THE

Arthur Laurents

WAY WE WERE

1817

HARPER & ROW, PUBLISHERS

NEW YORK · EVANSTON · SAN FRANCISCO
LONDON

To Lorry and Millard Kaufman,
to James Mitchell,
and to Anita Ellis

one

SHE NEVER COULD sit on the sidelines. Nevertheless, she certainly could be sitting out front instead of standing here in the wings, sinking, drowning, clutching at the lifeline of her long string of beads.

Stash stopped applauding just long enough to slap her fingers.

"I don't chew gum at night any more," she explained, but stopped torturing the orange and yellow beads.

Out on the stage, the folk singers were still bowing. She tried to applaud along with Stash and Vivian, but her hands were icy with fear: she had a flash vision of her fingers snapping off like skinny icicles. She grabbed at the beads—she had found them unstrung in a thrift shop on Bleecker Street—and closing her eyes, concentrated on willing the audience to applaud the folk singers into another encore. They hadn't done "Joe Hill" yet, nobody had, why didn't they do "Joe

Hill"? They launched into "Joe Hill": the instant bore-
dom out front was so tangible, it ricocheted into the
wings and hit her in the pit of her sinking stomach.
She would have to follow that.

Behind his thick eyeglasses, Stash's merry eyes
squinted in exaggerated pain; his chubby cheeks became chubbier as he mimed throwing up. It was all to
relax her, so she smiled, or hoped she had. She looked
at Vivian, with her Mexican silver earrings and another
of her peasant blouses yanked lower than it was cut.
Katie wanted to punch her. With all those breasts,
Vivian couldn't have the flu. And her bangs were
fluffed so perfectly (over the lines in her forehead),
she must have washed her hair last night and then
stuck her head out the window and screamed to make
sure she'd catch cold, get laryngitis and not have to
make the damn collection speech.

It was one thing to write a collection speech—Katie
had volunteered eagerly—but it was another to deliver
it. She hadn't faced an audience this size since the
disastrously sunny day of the Peace Rally at college a
few years back: the embarrassment of that memory
had kept her off the platform until now. Obviously,
this audience was more sympathetic—they'd paid to
get in—but she twisted and coiled and wound the
beads around her index finger, then four fingers, then
her whole hand as she tried not to breathe her fear
into the microphone. It wasn't until she said, "It's a
lot easier to find a good folk singer than a good collection speaker—which is how come you're stuck with
me," and many of them laughed, that she freed the
beads and relaxed.

2

It hadn't occurred to Katie—as it had to Stash and the Benefit Committee—that she looked even younger and more vulnerable in front of the huge blowups of Roosevelt and Stalin. Her face with its long, oval eyes was too original to be beautiful or pretty, even, to her Liberal beholders; it was too young as well, but that they found attractive. (Time, of course, would catch up, but fortunately, so would fashion.) The clothes which concealed her body helped her appeal. Except for the junk jewelry, they would have been perfect for a tall blonde who lunched at "21." Katie usually had toasted bagel and soup du jour in the CBS drugstore.

"We *do* have Soviet-American friendship," she said fervently, aware of eyes turning up to the banner over the proscenium. "That's why the tide has finally begun to turn in this terrible war." Applause as expected. "What we don't have is food and clothing and shelter for the thousands of anti-Fascist refugees who ever since the Spanish Civil War . . ."

The beads dangled and swayed; the pink patches on her white cheeks reddened with pleasure; her fierce eyes glittered, and most of the men visualized her passion elsewhere. In the wings Stash and Vivian uncrossed their fingers and stacked blank checks, pledge cards and leaflets on a bridge table. Stash signed a false name to a check with a grand flourish.

"This can be the five dollars from A Policeman."

"Katie knows all your signatures," Vivian warned. "Why don't you give her cash?"

"Why don't you give me your body?" Stash giggled.

The difference, to Katie, between political necessity and lying involved her in endless cafeteria arguments.

But she considered it very unkosher to say anything she didn't believe, and wouldn't.

"We've got to help free the hundreds of thousands trapped in Hitler's concentration camps." Never mind the State Department: she *knew* the camps existed. "We've got to fight home-front apathy and prejudice. Overseas, they're asking for their lives. I'm only asking for money. And here, tonight, to help collect it are men just back from offering *their* lives!" She pointed up to the balcony. "Up there is a Seabee."

"Yo!"

The shout from high up in the now lighted hall caught her by surprise, echoing an unplaceable memory. Her hand tugged again at the orange and yellow beads.

"Down here is a paratrooper." She leaned out over the edge and peered to her left. "Is that a Bronze Star?"

"Yo!"

During the applause she tried to focus the memory. Shading her eyes, she searched all the way up the long aisle to her right.

"Back there is a Navy—" she began to twist the neck-lace—"ensign?"

"Yo!"

The memory clicked into place and her heart jumped: the soft green of the Arts campus and the pantherlike walk of a tall, broad-backed boy named Hubbell Gardiner: a towhead like this ensign; the same full, wide mouth that showed very white uneven teeth when he grinned, as this ensign was doing. The necklace broke, the beads clattering to the stage and rolling off into the laughing audience.

It didn't matter that she looked like a gawking idiot. Her eyes clung to the ensign as he gracefully dashed down the long aisle to scoop up a handful of the rattling orange and yellow stones. With a dazzling grin, he held them out to her, and she looked down into his face and it was only a handsome ensign's face, it wasn't Hubbell Gardiner's. The pink patches came home to her cheeks. She laughed, took the beads and quickly holding them up, shouted into the mike:

"O.K., folks! What am I bid for my beads?"

It was more than saving a situation: she got a puritanical pleasure from giving up something she liked for something she believed in. But she was really sore later about the check from A Policeman.

In the control room of the broadcasting studio Katie handled the rehearsal with addled efficiency. The director was late: he must have missed his plane back from Washington. Like a liberated jack-in-the-box, she hopped in and out of her swivel chair, flicking switches so that the cast could hear her or she them, giving cuts and write-ins, asking for more or less volume from the sound engineer beside her, punching her stopwatch, scrawling on her script and the director's, chewing gum furiously, and switching her long string of red-and-hopefully-amber beads to the back of her neck. The engineer filled her requests without losing his place in a trade publication devoted to the coming of television. The cast, in the hospital-colored studio on the other side of the thick glass window, read from the script in the self-protective mumble of a first rehearsal on mike. Most of the men were middle-aged and had the resentful look of understudies; most of the women were girls who even at that hour of the morning looked as though they were on their way to a party.

Peggy Vanderbilt (no one believed her), the girl at the microphone, was not particularly pretty, but she had beautiful legs (and a matching pair of shoes for every outfit). Her protesting, babyish whine became more irritating as she read on:

"'And don't tell me about D day. It came and it went, and I—'"

Katie hopped up, flipped a switch, bent over the microphone on the control panel. "Hold it, Peggy. Let's take a cut from 'D day,' halfway down the page to 'and don't tell me about the black market.'"

"Katie Morosky, you're making me a complete bitch. If you're so concerned with your old black-market propaganda—"

"Look!" Katie flipped the wrong switch: Peggy's voice droned on into the control room. The engineer leaned over to flip the right switch.

"Look, Peggy!" But in her embarrassed anger, she leaned too close to the microphone: her beads swung into it, sending a reverberating machine-gun effect into the studio.

Peggy took the barrage as a personal attack. As she flounced away from her mike, the heavy door from the outside corridor opened and Bill Verso stalked in: a big man with a big black mustache and a big head of always tousled hair. Verso cultivated looking and moving like a director: he wore a Hemingway trench coat and strode straight to the control room without a good morning or an apology. Nor was anyone surprised at the sleepy, elegant redhead who trailed behind him in a sleek raincoat.

By the time he reached the control room Katie had his bottle of Scotch ready for him and her chair ready for the redhead. Verso slung his overnight bag in a corner and let Katie hang up his trench coat and jacket as he loosened his tie, checked his script and yelled for coffee. The redhead collapsed into the chair and closed her eyes.

"No commission, kiddo," Verso said to Katie. "No overseas for Uncle Willy. I'm too damned important to the lousy OWI. I need coffee."

Below the big glass window, Peggy fluttered her hands like a frantic bat to attract his attention.

"That broad's always got a feather up her ass. Don't cast her again."

"It takes a reactionary to play one," Katie said. "We're seven minutes, ten seconds over. I—"

"The Pentagon thinks that crappy writer is a Red, but he's just crappy." Verso turned pages rapidly. "Where's my goddam coffee?"

"Why were you so late?"

"The brass maniacs grilled me so long, I got bumped from my plane. Now they think we're all Reds and they want to stick a censor right here—what the hell is this?" He pointed at his script.

"Two lines I wrote to cover the cut on 12."

"Where's my damn coffee?" Verso made big, angry red pencil marks. "Can't the goddam chintzy OWI even afford a go-fer?"

Katie picked up her raincoat and her bag. "Anyone else?"

"Black," the sound engineer said, still reading about television.

"Sugar?" Katie asked.

The redhead opened her eyes. "Hi!" she said brightly.

"Oh, shit," said Verso. "Put her out in the studio."

They got through the show as they always did, and the actors were gone in two minutes as they always were after a government broadcast which only paid scale.

"An A-1 stinker," Verso said exhaustedly.

"Did you tell them Ernie wasn't a Communist?" Katie asked. Ernie, the writer, was a T/5 on special assignment to the OWI for the series.

"I said he wasn't to my knowledge." Verso yawned. "Anyway, they shipped him out to Burma, so maybe we've lucked out."

Katie dumped the litter of poor Ernie's lousy script and their coffee containers into a wastebasket. Verso stretched, then plastered his face against the glass window.

"Where's that subversive redhead?"

"She shipped out at 7:23," Katie said.

Verso tousled his hair. "Well, kiddo, you're in luck. To the Stork."

This time, he wasn't catching her unprepared: in her bag she had earrings to match her beads. She sat down, to appear casual. She stood up: it was contemptible to be excited about going to a café society night club. Even though she'd only read about this one. Even though her boss wanted company. Her chewing gum plopped into the wastebasket.

8

"Do I have time to—"

"No." He was putting on his trench coat. "Just come as you are."

In places like the Stork Club, Katie tried to leave her commitment in the checkroom. What if there was a whole disgusting world which enjoyed the war? It still was lovely to be dazzled for one night by these marvelously gleaming men—officers and civilians—who seemed to share the same tailor and the same banker. And if some of their laughing girl friends looked at her as though they'd forgotten to tip her, they all had a style which made every one of them seem a beauty. There was no reason for that monopoly either: a politically progressive person with style could be very effective. She made a mental note not to wear a raincoat at night. Or to buy a new one.

While Bill Verso checked theirs, Katie hugged the foyer wall and added a helping of lipstick. He didn't like to see girls fix their faces, and he didn't like Katie to go to the powder room unless he was on the make. At the red velvet rope, two short, very young enlisted men were being ignored by the tuxedoed trusty. Their even younger dates (who held hands) wore awful bouffant dresses and each had a little corsage of gardenias.

Katie stared at the gardenias and saw herself pinning on that same corsage in the college gym where they had held her Senior Prom, and then pulling it off in the darkness behind the gym where revolving, colored lights and dance music filtered through a small, high window.

Abruptly, she was angry; angry at the timid little

enlisted men waiting to get into the Stork Club, angry at their overdressed little dates, angry at all four for coming from New Jersey which she was sure they had. She had an irrational dislike of people from Jersey: their big dream in life was to die in Scarsdale. When the two soldiers, who would be damn lucky if they died in the U.S.A., stepped back to allow another party of four to waft through the velvet rope into the bar or the main room or the back room or the Cub Room or the cellar—the target of Katie's anger shifted to its mainspring: injustice.

"But, sir," she heard the cherubic corporal say, "we have a reservation."

"Clear the way, please."

"Just a minute!" Katie said sharply to the self-appointed St. Peter. "What's your name? I want to know your name! And why aren't you in uniform!"

"Oh, Jesus and Mary," said Bill Verso, who had come up behind her.

Like an indignant father, Katie thumped the corporal's shoulder. "What do you want on this shoulder? Gold bars? Or a ten-dollar bill, you Fascist snob!"

The two veterans of Anzio slunk back; their dates emphasized a distinct space between Katie and their tiered skirts. Verso stepped into the breach and, with several ha-ha's, reached out a bribing hand to the trusty.

"Hello, Fred!"

"Don't you tip him!" Katie protested.

"Bill Verso? OWI?"

"Sorry, no tables."

"I was in the other night with Colonel—" tried Verso with more ha-ha's, but Katie was louder.

"I want your name; I certainly can't get your rank and serial number!"

She grabbed the velvet rope and fumbled with the hook. The trusty, uncertain whether to push her, hold on to the rope or summon reinforcements, was further confused by Verso waving a ten or possibly twenty dollar bill. The dates dropped hands to protect their corsages, but the two soldiers, released by the familiarity of physical action and confusion, began to punch one another joyfully.

Later Bill Verso claimed he had gotten all of them in. And, in a way, he had. A huge Air Force captain returning from the men's room saw him and remembered a beach party one rainy Sunday afternoon in Verso's Madison Avenue walk-up.

"Hey, Verso!" he bellowed. "Hairy old Billy Verso! O Captain, my Captain, stand back for a real captain and a real prince, if a hairy one!"

He deftly lurched into the rope and Katie unhooked it. He gathered up the two enlisted men and peered down at one of the corsages.

"Hello, daughter," he said, "you're late. You're all late! Forward—hut!"

The four kids became four smiles. Like snake dancers, they wriggled through the bodies crowding the bar and headed for the cover of the dance floor. The Air Force Captain laughed and hugged Katie and Verso under his big wings, Verso busily stuffing his ten-dollar bill back into his pocket. Then, Moses parting a human sea, the Captain opened a path for them to the bar.

On the other side of the velvet rope, the band was playing a tune Katie knew; the voices were no longer a foreign babble; the laughter was contagious and somehow sexual. Hands touched and patted and even groped: she was being welcomed. She smiled as though she had just passed someone she knew, and alternated between turning back gaily to Bill Verso and possessively putting a hand on the Air Force Captain's hulking back.

At a far corner of the bar was the Captain's crew: four or five officers from various branches and their— oh, they were lovely girls. More than merely pretty, they shared that style, a cultivated simplicity that made Katie put her hand over her beads as she smiled small hellos. The officers were so confident and bubbling, they all seemed to be good-looking: maybe it was their tailor-made uniforms.

He was on a high stool at the corner, the last of the officers to be introduced to her and the most beautiful by far in his white summer uniform of naval lieutenant. She had known he was in the Navy; she should have known he would be more than an ensign. No longer a towhead, he was a sun-streaked dirty blond now; and he looked older than she knew he was. Maybe when he stopped smiling, all the new lines—obviously the result of squinting at Japanese planes in the Far Pacific sun—would clear themselves as just white streaks in his deep tan.

His smile was unfocused: she couldn't tell if it was meant for her, and she wasn't close enough to hear if he had said her name or even hello. He had sort of nodded his head, so he must have known he had been introduced to someone. He didn't seem drunk, but he was sitting too erect, and the unfocused smile had an aspect of permanence. Then some officer's big shoulder shifted and Katie saw that the lovely ash-blonde was actually standing between Hubbell's legs and methodically licking his left ear.

The blonde wore the kind of dress Katie did battle for at Klein's and her soft hair fell effortlessly to her shoulders the way Katie continued to hope hers would. She was Bill Verso's type. Katie considered tactics.

"Do me a favor, Morosky," Verso said as he handed her a glass of Dubonnet. "When Uncle Willy takes you into café society—sorry, fella." He took his double Scotch from the bartender and some spilled on one of the laughing officers. "—Leave the soapbox home, will you please?"

"They've been in combat," Katie said, looking at all the ribbons on Hubbell's chest. "I mean these boys. Like that one."

She was sure Verso's black eyes would see the blonde, not Hubbell. He did.

"Oh oh oh to be in uniform."

"This is the good part," Katie said.

"Oh, PR boys get to wear ribbons too."

"They've got combat faces." She meant Hubbell.

"From free booze," Verso said, prodding Katie to move around to the ear-licking blonde and Hubbell. "They're all Bucker Boys. Bucking for promotion, bucking for cushy berths—oh, Jesus, kiddo," he said wearily. "I'm a jealous old OWI fart and a horny one."

Katie was close enough now to reach out and touch Hubbell, but he seemed to have fallen asleep. At least his eyes were closed, and although he still sat upright —one hand on the bar, the other balancing his beer on his knee—his decorated chest rose and fell in the steady rhythm of sleep. The ash-blonde had her eyes closed too, and was licking his ear in the same rhythm. Katie and Verso sipped their drinks, watching intently like new animals at a water hole.

Suddenly the Ear Licker turned to them.

"Is it possible to sprain one's tongue?" she asked.

"No. Let's dance," Verso said.

"It aches like mad." The Ear Licker had an expensive drawl. "And look at him! I suppose they learn that incredible balance on board ship."

"Right," Verso said. "Let's dance."

"My tongue hurts."

"Give it a rest," Katie suggested. "I'll mind the store."

The Ear Licker looked at Katie. It was a familiar look, but this time Katie didn't care. She made a crazy face and giggled.

"Thank you," said the Ear Licker.

Verso stepped back politely to let her out, one hand grazing her thigh, the other squeezing Katie's behind. They headed for the dance floor.

Slowly, carefully Katie moved into the space between Hubbell's legs. She had never been this close to him before. She started to put her glass of Dubonnet on the bar, then made herself hold it tightly in front of her with both hands. She was unaware of anyone else, deaf to any other voice, any music. She was on the verge of happiness.

She remembered a short story she had written in high school about what happened to Sleeping Beauty after the Prince kissed her awake. Since she'd been asleep for a hundred years she knew nothing of the Depression or Franklin D. Roosevelt or the WPA or the Okies. She was a bore, and the Prince quickly packed her off to Reno.

14

One leg was trembling: maybe she had been resting all her weight on it. She wondered whether to hope Hubbell didn't recognize her; that when he awoke he wouldn't hear chimes from the campus bell tower and her growl as she hawked her leaflets under that big sycamore: "Save Spain and Stop Fascism Now!" Oh Jesus, what she'd been like then.

two

"For Peace Now, Write F.D.R. Now!"

Her voice was so familiar on campus that barely anyone listened. Each morning before her first class, she materialized under the big sycamore at the head of the main path to the Arts Quadrangle and handed out her leaflets. Or tried to. A few giggled or booed, a few felt guilty, a few took the doomsday brochures.

Her hair was frizzy, her brown skirts were lumpy, her brown shoes flat and scuffed. Sometimes she sported a red blouse which was no more dashing than her oatmeal beret. But the electricity in her eyes was a magnet, and when she did smile it was surprisingly endearing. Still, she looked like someone to be found picketing N.Y.U., not proselytizing this ivy-green Greek-and-Gothic university sprawled across the highest ridge of a graceful glacial valley.

At one end of the university's domain was a staggering rocky gorge spanned by a suspension bridge leading to Collegetown and the diner where she worked weekday afternoons and the boardinghouse where she had a cell to herself (she shared the bathroom with three other pariahs). The dormitories, fraternities and sororities she had never even set foot in trickled down the wide, steep hill below the Arts campus. At the bottom was the town—supported mainly by a machine works—with the newspaper for which she read proof on alternating nights. The trolley line she used those nights ended at the enormous lake where Hubbell Gardiner stroked the Varsity crew.

"Save Spain and Stop Fascism!"

Her growl was weak. It was at last the beginning of spring, her last spring, the spring of her senior year. The sudden warm, the new green, the announcement of leaves on her sycamore made the campus, breathtaking in any season, so breathtaking now that she found it difficult to hawk her leaflets and wished they at least were in verse.

"If you want Peace Now—"

"Hey, Katie!"

Everyone knew her name was Katie Morosky, just as everyone knew his was Hubbell Gardiner. His appeared often in the college paper, hers had been used twice in the humor column.

He was lolling back in the new white-and-red convertible owned and operated by his lackey, J.J. Something III. One of its sweeping running boards grazed the curb nearest her sycamore; the back seat was empty: there were no cashmere-sweatered coeds in attendance. She was conscious of J.J.'s tweed jacket and his bow tie and his already receding hairline, and of Hubbell's un-crew-cut towhead and his Varsity sweater, but not of the frayed collar of his clean shirt.

"Katie!" Hubbell called again. "What're you selling?"

"The ROTC," she snapped. "You can have it cheap."

He put out his hand for a leaflet. "Come on. I'm convertible."

"I wouldn't try to make a Jew out of Hitler, either."

He laughed. "Well, I guess I'll just have to write my congressman."

"You'll have to learn to read first!"

"No, he will."

"Oh, go eat your goldfish!" she shouted, but J.J. had already driven him away, leaving her blushing and angry and overexcited.

"Fascist," she said automatically.

They both took Dr. Julian Short's class in Creative Writing. "He thinks it's just a crap course," Katie said to Frankie McVeigh as she jammed all the leftover leaflets into her book bag. Frankie was vice-president of the Young Communist League. He was wiry, stronger than he looked (he ran laps every morning), with dark-red hair. He always wore a shirt and tie with his shiny suit and carried a worn briefcase bulging with leaflets and plans.

"Well, he certainly can't be a good writer."

"Oh God, Frankie! How do you know?" she said belligerently.

"A good writer has a social conscience."

"Oh. Well, that's undeniable."

Chimes started to ring; they hurried across the campus. Two books tumbled out of her bag, but Frankie resisted the impulse to pick them up: Katie was also fierce about equality between the sexes.

"Know what?" She crammed the books back in the bag. "I'm going to be a Marxist-oriented Jane Austen." (She was the fourth youngest in their class.)

"I know," said Frankie.

"Jesus, how do you know? I never told you before!"

"If you want to be, you will be," Frankie said, and believed it. She had wanted to be president of the YCL and she was.

Walking to work at the Greasy Spoon in Collegetown, she ran over her speech for the YCL meeting that evening. It was certain to be one of the most important of her presidency and she bubbled with anticipation. On the suspension bridge she paused and looked down into the steep gorge to memorize the size and shape of the jutting rocks and the color and sound of the rushing water for the new short story she was writing for Dr. Short's class. It was easy for her to switch from her speech to her story: she thought of her mind as a seven-layer cake and was surprised when Frankie McVeigh told her his mind had two, at the most three, layers.

Her story was to be about a coed who had upheld the university's tradition of a suicide-a-semester by leaping off the bridge into the gorge the previous fall. Katie's girl had been rushed by all the best sororities, but pledged by none when it was discovered her maternal grandmother was Jewish. The sororities and fraternities on campus took all that crap as seriously as the stupid girl did: the Gentile ones were called "white houses" by everyone except the YCL.

Katie wasn't worried about her lack of sympathy for her heroine. Her concern was with what the gorge water looked like in the fall and with sorority ritual. She didn't know anyone who actually belonged to a Greek letter society except Hubbell Gardiner, and she couldn't and wouldn't ask him. Just a week ago, before class with Dr. Short, she had heard him remark that a Jewish fraternity which had painted its house white was "trying to pass." She had got hot with anger then, but now, gripping the iron railing of the suspension bridge, she blushed: he had been joking. She backed away and hurried across the bridge. She *had* to do something about her sense of humor.

He and J.J. were having hamburgers in the Greasy Spoon. J.J. always ate one more than anybody else; he probably won the goldfish-eating competition in *their* white house. As Katie waited for the saddle shoes and gray flannels and swing skirts and pastel cardigans in the booth behind them to decide what to order, she eavesdropped contemptuously.

J.J.: "If you ask Linda, Joanne will come too. I'll spring for the tickets . . . Jeez, Hubbell, you always laugh!"

Hubbell: "Sorry, old buddy. I won."

"Won what?"

"My bet with myself. On what the deal would be."

Hubbell laughed again, but when Katie sneaked a look, he had stopped and his face was odd, almost sad. Then he quickly flashed that grin.

"Fair's fair," he said, and J.J. punched him like a moronic Cub Scout. He was always punching and pawing and touching Hubbell, as though he hoped something would rub off.

She knew that when they left J.J. would pay the check and overtip. His old man was supposed to be president of half a dozen banks and cartels. He'd probably wangle Hubbell a fat job after graduation. One hand washes the other. They were all disgusting.

In her boardinghouse she shucked off the GREASY SPOON uniform and put on one of her better red blouses. Her room, which was in earshot of the roaring waters of the gorge when they did roar, had the same friendly disorder of her father's candy store in Rochester. She thought it might be a family trait, one of the good ones. Instead of the sliding mounds of newspapers and periodicals (leftist) and the oddments of stationery and school and office supplies which threatened her father's boxes and bottles and jars of candy, she had books and brochures and posters and notebooks and typing paper encroaching on her bed, desk, two chairs and bureau. The clutter was amiable, and she had brightened the vague wallpaper with posters and prints apparently chosen as much for the combination of orange, yellow and red as for political connotations.

Chewing slowly on one of the two chocolate Mallomars she allowed herself per day, she avoided the bureau mirror and pulled tightly on the ends of her hair in an attempt to straighten the frizz. She wanted to look sharp for the YCL.

Their new meeting room had been one of her campaign promises. At the outset of her regime she had stormed the Administration. If the Student Council and the Young Republicans and the American Student Union and the Alliance Française could have a room in Founders' Hall, why couldn't the Young Communist League? To her disappointment, she won rather easily, merely by intimating to the Dean that she might be forced to expose the Deutsche Verein—which had a nice, clean room—as a Nazi Bund. Her little band was given a small but equally clean room in the basement for their posters, their mimeograph machine and the huge ball of tinfoil they were saving for Spain.

Now there was a dusty skin on the tinfoil, and the flag-marked military map of Spain and the old posters —SAVE LOYALIST SPAIN! SAVE YOUR TINFOIL!—were partially obscured by new ones: WORLD PEACE NOW! TOTAL DISARMAMENT NOW! New leaflets had to be stenciled for the hungry mimeograph machine, but the new line had to be cast first.

Katie presided in an armchair behind the leaflet table. Unable to stay seated, she bounced up and down, walked back and forth, chewing gum furiously as she addressed the members. There were more than a dozen folding chairs, ten of which were occupied. The entire membership was present, all white, unfortunately. Once, when Katie and Frankie McVeigh were returning from an unsuccessful Negro recruitment, she reminded Frankie of the joke about the two Communists who decided to throw a party and one said, "O.K., you bring the Negro."

"What's really so awful," Katie said, "is why do we think a Negro would come?"

"Would you join a sorority if they asked you?"

"Of course not!" And added: "I haven't got the money." She laughed, but Frankie didn't get it.

As usual, he was sitting directly in front of her, between the physics genius and the poetess with the bangs and the Mexican silver jewelry. He was a challenge to Katie, but only politically, which disappointed her.

"We have to face it: that bastard Franco has practically won—for the moment," she told the members. "What we've got to do now is fight to get those 'volunteer armies of Schickelgruber and Benito out of Spain before the Loyalists are completely decimated. We've got to fight for World Disarmament *now*—particularly in Germany! They've abrogated every treaty, and don't think Nazi-lovers like Charles A., Colonel Lindbergh are going to get the people on Hitler's side. He may be an all-American hero, but the people don't like Nazis. They'll listen to us!"

The poetess snorted, fluttering her bangs.

"Yes, us: the YCL!" Katie pounded the table. "We have more influence than you think! I have proof positive, which is why I called this meeting. Comrades—" she paused dramatically—"I was called in to see the Dean today."

"Oh, you're always being called in to see the Dean," Frankie said.

"This was special," Katie snapped back. "The Dean said . . ." She paused again, feeling the flush of excitement rise from her chest to her throat to her small face. She fought a crazy impulse to laugh, she was so proud and happy. She went back behind the table and sat in her chair, testing her throat as she did so to be certain her voice would emerge with calm dignity.

"The Dean said—and I quote—this entire university is going to be investigated by the State Legislature—as a Hotbed of Red Activity!" She had to bounce up out of her chair again. "Do you know what that means?

Comrades, do you understand our importance?" She looked directly at the wide-eyed poetess. "Sixteen thousand students are going to be investigated! Because of eleven YCLers with eight dollars and forty-five cents in the treasury!" She turned to the physics genius. "Correct my figures if I'm wrong."

"Oh, boy!" Frankie said.

"Question!" The poetess called out over the babble. "What do we do?"

"What do we do?" Katie didn't bother to give her a withering look. "We protest, that's what we do! What else?"

Frankie applauded; the physics genius applauded; the poetess applauded; they all applauded. Katie laughed triumphantly and, Russian-fashion, applauded them back. They got to their feet and the little room rang and rang with their applause. She loved every one of them, even the poetess.

The applause was fainter but she could still hear it as she dreamed along the main street of the town. The soft night sky was decorated with stars. On one bank of the marble steps rising to the entrance of the elegantly faded Old Dutch Hotel, a crew-cut boy in a Glen plaid jacket and a girl with beige hair in a lilac cashmere sweater sat drinking beer from large steins. Katie barely noticed them; for once, she passed under the hotel's stained-glass canopy like a sleepwalker.

Then from down the dark block: "Shake it up, Morosky!"

Eddie, the composing room foreman, stood in the doorway adjacent to the editorial offices, jangling the slugs in the pocket of his printer's apron.

"You going to dock me?" Katie asked anxiously.

"On a night like this?"

"Listen," she said, following him into the composing room, down the aisle between the chattering machines, "good weather is precisely when I have bad luck."

"I didn't know Commies were allowed to be superstitious," Eddie said, thrusting a sheaf of galleys at her.

She hung the long snakes of paper on their hook and, standing at the high wooden table she used for a desk, began reading proof. She enjoyed it; she felt more at home in the composing room than she did on campus. Even though she was a kid and a girl, she really got along with the linotypers once she quit reminding them they were all proletarians together. The youngest—who had a profile like Hubbell Gardiner's and was unmarried—let her bring him coffee some nights but never asked her for a date. But dating was bourgeois and when she did go out it was usually with Frankie McVeigh to Plan and Discuss, and they went Dutch.

Her pencil stopped abruptly in mid-air, hanging over the galley like a sword. She was reading the story for the second time when Frankie came sprinting down the aisle in his shiny suit, his freckles almost in bas-relief.

"On the radio!" he gasped.

Katie looked at him with false but superior calm and waited for him to stop wheezing. What good were all those morning laps?

"The Legislature—is going—to investigate—the whole university as a Hotbed of Reefer Smoking." He finished in a gallop.

"So what?" she said.

"So what!"

"So you flew down here to gloat!" She tossed her pencil aside in disgust. "Nothing like a disaster to put color in *your* cheeks!"

Frankie took several deep breaths. "Oh, Katie. I came right down here to plan and discuss."

"There's nothing to discuss, so there's nothing to plan." As president, she couldn't expose her fear.

"Katie, if the two investigations are linked, ours won't be taken seriously."

"Frankie McVeigh: who, I ask you, is going to take that decadent dope junk seriously? Particularly when they can have Reds? The Republicans merely had to dummy up *their* election issue."

"The Democrats."

"Republicans!"

"We know there's no essential difference between the two parties, but as it happens—"

"As it happens!" She glared at him.

Frankie waited. He was accustomed to her explosions, but they made him uncomfortable because they somehow aroused him sexually. He picked up the pencils she had thrown down.

"You broke the point."

She looked at the pencil, not at him. "Frankie," she said finally in a small, quiet voice, "do you think it's true? I mean, *are* we a Hotbed of Reefer Smoking?"

Frankie looked at her. "Are we a Hotbed of Red Activity?" he asked wistfully.

"Warmongers to Investigate Liberals! Campus under Attack!"

The wind was threatening the new leaves on her sycamore; spring wasn't keeping its promise. The sun danced and sparkled on the lake, shimmering like a huge pan of water at the bottom of the valley, but it had no warmth for Katie. She was thankful that her sister—a high school diploma in one hand, a marriage license in the other, the moron!—had knitted her the long red scarf and the mittens to match.

"Write the Governor Now!"

She stopped and listened. She heard singing, had been hearing it for several minutes: not trained, choir-like singing, but more the tuneful yelling she associated with May Day parades. The melody was familiar —"Maryland, My Maryland"—but the original, wasn't the original "O Tannenbaum"? Wasn't it German? Yells from Nuremberg rallies and cries from Yellow Stars clogged her ears until, rocking gaily around the bend below the sycamore, drawn by two fat, snorting white horses, came a droshky. It was overflowing with boys in Cossack coats and tall Russian fur hats, and girls wearing babushkas; and running alongside were students laughing like Tolstoyan peasants who didn't know the revolution was for them. The words they were singing to that tune came clear and distinct and infuriating:

"Oh, Maryjane, Oh, Maryjane, gimme a drag of Maryjane."

Banners along the sides of the droshky proclaimed a "TEA" PARTY and a MASS MARIJUANA MASS. Posters waved inside and alongside: FREE TOM REEFER, DON'T BE A DRAG—TAKE A DRAG. J.J., singing and yelling, threw handfuls of alleged reefers to the ever-increasing followers. And Hubbell, wearing a black Cossack coat trimmed and fastened and braided with gold, was driving the two white horses.

Katie understood now why the weather had turned cold again. Nature, constantly perverse to *her*, delayed spring for *him*, the bastard. Another bastard, hooting and racing to catch up with the droshky, knocked into her and sent her sprawling against her tree, her leaflets scattering and blowing away on the biased wind. She stayed there, hugging the tree; angry, furious, raging. Even without turning her head, she could see the droshky rollicking up the road. It rounded a curve and suddenly Hubbell was silhouetted against a perfect sky. She watched until he was out of sight, then wiped her eyes with one of the red mittens her stupid sister had knitted.

"Maybe we could hold a mass meeting," Frankie suggested.

"Oh, sure," Katie said bitterly. "I'll get dressed up like La Pasionara and throw fake bombs and you can sing the Internationale to the tune of 'La Cucaracha.'"

They were drinking coffee in the Greasy Spoon, he on a stool in front of the counter, she in uniform behind it. Fuming, she plucked two jelly doughnuts from under their glass bell and plunked them down on a plate.

"On the house," she said. "Food's the best antidote for anger: Psych 108."

The door to the diner banged open for Hubbell, J.J. and two unspectacularly pretty dates. All four were still singing "Oh, Maryjane" to that lousy German tune. The boys still wore their Cossack coats and fur hats and the girls their babushkas, and they all glistened and glowed and sparkled, unmistakably fraternity and sorority and white-and-red convertibles. And they were all laughing as though innocent women and

28

children weren't being blown to pieces in Spain at that very minute.

Although the diner was almost empty, the foursome made a loud, vulgar production of bowing one another in and out of various booths until they selected one no different from any other.

"Nyet, comrades, nyet!" Hubbell's Russian accent wasn't bad. "Here is reserv-ed for Comrade Stalin, here is reserv-ed for Comrade Harry Hopkinski, here—ah, da da! Here is for lovely Comrade Joannova!" He kissed J.J.'s date, who shrieked and flopped back in the booth with her legs apart.

"Oi, nyet!" cried J.J. An ardent but bad actor, his accent emerged a Yiddish stereotype. "Comrade, vy you don't kiss your own blintza?"

Hubbell glanced quickly at Katie's cold white face, yanked J.J.'s fur hat down over his blubbering mouth and pushed him into the booth on top of Joanne, who shrieked louder. He came over to the counter.

"Hi, Katie."

Her back was to him. She was at the coffee urn, re-filling Frankie's cup.

"Hi," Hubbell said to Frankie. Frankie said nothing. Hubbell put out his hand. "Hubbell Gardiner."

"Frankie McVeigh," said Frankie, putting out his hand to take the cup of coffee from Katie.

She looked at Hubbell frostily. "Black coffee?"

He laughed. "No, we're starving!" Then like a spy: "That's what marijuana does, kid."

"Bushwah," she said.

He reached into the pocket of the magnificent Cossack coat, pulled out a hand-rolled cigarette and, like a magician, waved it under her nose. "Try it. Come on. I'll tell you what: you smoke it and if it isn't the real McCoy, I'll join the YCL."

"Who wants you?" Frankie said, though not very loudly.

"Come on, Katie," Hubbell persisted. His smile was a rhetorical question. "Light up! Get in the groove! Three drags and you'll swear you're in the Kremlin."

"You're decadent and disgusting."

He laughed. "Show me a Communist and I'll show you a Puritan."

He waved the cigarette teasingly again. She snatched it angrily and broke it in half over an ash tray. It was just tobacco, which made her even angrier.

"You're still disgusting! And so was your cheap, rotten 'Tea' Party! You were just making fun of us!"

"We were making fun of politicians. What else can you do with them?"

"You think Franco is so funny?"

Hubbell looked as though he had missed a train connection. "Franco?"

"Yes, Franco!"

"What's Franco got to do with it?"

"He's a politician, is he funny? Is Hitler? He even has a funny mustache! Why don't you throw a Nazi party? You think fun's going to make him go away?"

"Hitler's serious, we're not."

"*You're* not!"

"Not about politicians looking for an election issue, no. Nor about a handful of angry college kids who—"

"Not about anything!" Katie cried. "Or anybody."

Why she added that she didn't know. She felt herself blushing and took her cup to the coffee urn.

"I thought you all would be pleased," Hubbell said to Frankie. *"That's* funny."

"Not to us," Frankie said.

Hubbell shrugged. "Well, comes the revolution, maybe we'll all have a sense of humor. Four hamburgers, please. Two rare, two medium rare."

"Onions?" she asked coldly.

"And heavy on the French fries." Hubbell returned to his friends.

Katie shouted the order through the pass-through to the Chinese student in the kitchen, then noisily began grabbing tinware for four place settings from the metal containers. Frankie was staring at her strangely.

"Well, *he* isn't afraid of you," he said.

She looked up in surprise. "Are you?"

Frankie blushed.

"Jesus."

She glanced from Frankie to Hubbell, who was laughing with the girl next to him. The pink patches on her cheeks began to spread and redden; she dropped a spoon so she would have to stoop and pick it up. When she straightened up, Frankie was still looking at her.

"I am not!" she said.

Katie loved them all: she was crammed, jam-packed, bursting, overflowing with the warmest, the purest, the most generous love for all of them; and she felt, she *knew* it was mutual. Sometimes, she was stabbed with the suspicion that Hitler and Roehm and their original little group, planning their first putsches, had shared that same passionate yet dispassionate loving mutuality which must have pulsated among Lenin and Stalin and *their* little group, which throbbed now among Katie and Frankie and *their* group as they jubilantly worked together on their new project: the YCL Strike for Peace.

Every window was opened wide to the usual sexual sunshine of spring, but the little room was still hot. Posters were being lettered, leaflets cranked out on the mimeo machine, brochures stenciled on the old typewriter.

"Nothing good was ever written on a machine," the poetess announced, her Mexican earrings quivering.

Katie was concentrated on wiping paint off her fingers when Hubbell walked in. He was wearing his Varsity sweater and another frayed shirt and a pair of J.J.'s old gray flannels which were too short. In that room his saddle shoes were a caste mark.

He grinned into the silence. "I'm sort of an emissary from the Student Council. About the Peace Rally."

"Strike, not rally," Katie snapped.

"Nationwide," added Frankie.

"Well, whatever." Hubbell tried to be conciliatory. "The council has just voted to get behind it and we're inviting any interested group—"

"*You're* inviting?" Katie's voice jumped the scale. The pale-blue shirt he was wearing must have been deliberately chosen to emphasize the vividness of his dark-blue eyes; his lashes, which should have been light, were dark; and his look implied a secret he would not tell her. She got wildly hostile. "What're you having, another tea party? You gonna dress up like the American Legion? You gonna come rolling up in a baby tank and toss medals to a pack of morons? This is a strike, jocko, and it's *our* strike!"

"If it's legal, it's meaningless!" Frankie shouted, and they all lashed out, all eleven of them.

"Administration stooge!"

"Fink!" (The poetess.)

"Are you having cheer leaders?" Katie jeered.

"Fascist!"

"When is a strike not a strike?" Frankie demanded.

"When they step on it with their lousy white shoes!" Katie yelled.

Hubbell just laughed and left.

He caught up with Katie later as she tacked a YCL STRIKE FOR PEACE poster on a bulletin board in the Student Union, and he kept on asking questions despite her barrage of sarcasm.

"Then explain to a very stupid Fascist fink."

"A Student Council *Rally*," she said like a substitute teacher to a backward child, "means the Administration has stamped it kosher—you know?"

"Gesundheit." Hubbell grinned.

"Terribly funny. And that means the ruling class, the government *wants* it to be kosher."

"Wants peace."

"No," she said impatiently, "wants the kids to shut up. If the government really wants peace, why don't they want disarmament?"

"It's bad for business and disaster for elections," said Hubbell and laughed at her startled face. "I stole one of your leaflets."

All her posters slid slowly to the floor.

Crossing the budding campus in pursuit of him, it was she who now sought explanations. "Don't you agree that if it's legal, then it's simply an hour when all the kids can legally cut classes?"

"And in this weather, they will."

"Then why aren't you for a strike?"

"Even if a million kids struck on every campus in the country, the politicians wouldn't give a hoot in hell. Kids can't vote."

"I don't know why you're mixed up in this at all!"

He laughed. "You started it, the Council picked it up. There's going to be a Rally—"

"Strike!"

"Whatever. Since there *is* going to be one, let's make it a winner."

"A winner?" She bumped into him and began to tremble.

"Let's get as big a turnout as we can. Make them *do* something, make it exciting—hey! How about you being a speaker?"

"I'm *going* to be!"

He looked at her enviously, then at the campus where classmates waved to him and ignored her, then smiled down at her fierce eyes. "I could've sworn you were a virgin."

"You're disgusting!"

"Well, they didn't get up."

"Who didn't?"

She was lost. They were standing at the center of an asphalt path which bisected the Arts Quadrangle. Hubbell pointed to the large seated statues at each end.

"Our Founder. Our First President. When a virgin walks between them, they get up, meet here and shake hands."

She was bewildered, which bewildered him.

"That's the legend," he said. "You know."

"What legend?"

"You've been here four years," Hubbell began. A car screeched as it broke the campus speed rules, and its horn called him. "You never heard that story?"

Katie wondered whether blushing disappeared like acne. She shifted her posters to the other arm. "I've never been inside a dormitory. Which is where I suppose they make up all that dirty stuff."

Hubbell didn't laugh. One hand moved toward her, then scratched his cheek. The horn honked again and J.J.'s summons came across the soft grass: "Hubbell!"

"For a smart kid," Hubbell shook his head, "you're a cockeyed, screwy combination—"

"Hubbell!"

"Yo!" Hubbell shouted back.

"Combination of what?" Katie cried, but he was off, loping across the green like a beautiful panther. Not that she'd ever seen a panther lope. The single time she had been to a zoo the panther had been asleep.

"See you!" Hubbell's voice floated back.

"See you!" she called, determined that she would.

three

MERELY LOOKING at him was becoming impossible. Her hands were trembling and she had a vision of dark-red Dubonnet staining that dazzling white uniform. Katie set her glass on the bar: now there was nothing to do with her hands except clasp them or put them around his neck. The band paused to shuffle their music sheets for the next set. Panic that the Ear Licker and Bill Verso might return from the dance floor provided inspiration. She took Hubbell's beer from his hand, careful not to spill it but equally careful to bump hard against his knee as she set the glass down next to hers. Hubbell opened his eyes.

He looked at her blankly. He didn't recognize her. Or maybe it was like being farsighted and sitting in the first row at the Roxy. She stepped back just as he leaned back and focused. They both laughed, and the band started again.

"What are you doing in this foxhole?" Hubbell asked.

"I'm a B-girl."

"Oh, still selling." He rubbed the ear the blonde had been licking.

"For the troops, it's free. It's B day."

Hubbell looked at his wet fingers, rather puzzled.

"Let's dance," Katie said weakly.

"Oh, I'm dead. I haven't been to sleep since I hit town yesterday. I think it was yesterday." He turned on his stool and surveyed the bar. "Where's J.J.?" He turned back to her and grinned. "Oh, God, I've been living too long where everybody saw everybody else every day. You remember J.J.?"

The stooge. "Sure. J.J. Something the Third."

"Jones."

"Really?" She was delighted.

"Really. The little shit was supposed to meet me here. Oh, sorry." His eyes teased. "Puritan Katie."

"No—Hubbell." A smile poured out.

He downed his beer and pointed to her glass. "What's that?"

"Dubonnet."

"You would drink something red."

They shared that laugh, and she hastily emptied her glass while he signaled the bartender. She was used to nursing one Dubonnet for an entire evening (a cheap date, both Verso and Stash called her), so after two more it was easy to get Hubbell to the dance floor. She had the strength to insist and he, having had four more beers, was too weak to resist.

She didn't exactly have to hold him up, the other couples on the packed floor did that for her. She was free, then, to put her head against his chest and close her eyes. For a moment he was in white tie and tails, it was their Senior Prom: she could correct that memory. Her cheek caressed his chest, her hand pressed his back. Then she remembered she hadn't washed her hair; and then that he was wearing white and she was wearing lipstick; and then, when she opened her eyes to be sure she hadn't marked him, she saw Verso and the Ear Licker dancing toward them. Verso's eyes were closed; she willed them to open; they didn't. Quickly, to lead Hubbell away, she moved in closer and pressed hard on his back. He smiled down and hugged her even closer. Hubbell always responded to need.

They ended up in the same taxi, all four of them laughing as though two of them weren't planning desperately. J.J. had never shown up—one person less to get rid of. Katie was very nervous: now, at the wire, she might be tripped. While she laughed her mind worked madly, testing devices and counterdevices for various booby traps. She was encouraged by the knowledge that Hubbell was at least half loaded, that Verso was determined to make the equally boozed-up Ear Licker and, best of all, that it was still raining.

Verso gave the driver Katie's address. It was downtown, out of his way, a little apartment on a slanted street in Murray Hill. She couldn't remember how messy she had left it. Anyway, the bed was made. Or was that good?

The cab pulled up to the curb. Katie sat. Verso directed her with a sharp turn of his head. She got out. Verso said good night to Hubbell, shaking his hand so that he pulled him out of his seat. Then he gave him a sharp little directional push, and Hubbell dutifully said good night and stumbled out of the cab which drove away, leaving him swaying on the sidewalk in the gentle rain. Katie was already up the steps of the brownstone.

"Dammit," she said loudly, "I always have trouble with this key."

Her apartment was on the top floor; maybe that did it. She quickly switched on a lamp in the pale yellow living room, then stuck her head out the door to call down softly:

"Only one more."

She listened to be certain he was still breathing and climbing, then switched on the radio and made a pass at tidying up the litter of books and magazines and newspapers and scripts. Actually the room—which was long and narrow—seemed to relish the comfort of disorder. The overstuffed furniture, slip-covered in Mondrian-type prints, was roomy and welcoming. The desk, the coffee table, the gate-leg table and chairs were all dark walnut and, like the ashtrays, meant to be used. There were prints and posters on the walls, and a cork bulletin board featuring a map flag-tacked with the progress of the war.

The apartment had no halls. Katie had just checked the yellow-and-orange bathroom when Hubbell appeared in the doorway opposite. He was panting.

"Home sweet—" she began nervously and then saw the color of his face. "In here!"

Like a matador, she stepped aside just as he charged into the bathroom, slamming the door behind him. She turned up the radio and rushed to make coffee. The kitchen was tiny and had no window, but it was craftily manageable and she had painted it red. The coffee under way, she hurried into the little pale-orange bedroom to take off the bedspread, fold it neatly and then dump it on top of the overflowing bookcase. Quickly, she undressed and put on her new negligee. ("You never know," her friend Pony Dunbar had advised, "you just never know.") She hadn't found the right mules and her slippers were too scraggly; she dashed back to the kitchen barefoot.

Mugs, milk, sugar, then the perked coffee on an orange-and-yellow tray and into the living room. Music had given way to news: casualties on Guam, even more in Normandy. Tonight she was more concerned with the minor casualty on home ground. The bathroom door was open, the bathroom was empty: a trail of Hubbell's discarded clothes led to the bedroom.

She put down the tray and picked up the jacket of his white uniform. She ran her fingers over the stiff ribbons pinned to the chest; then picked up his white T-shirt and his cap and his trousers, and holding them very close to her, walked slowly to the bedroom.

In the doorway she stopped, rigid, staring straight ahead. Then she took a deep breath and looked down at the three-quarter bed. Hubbell was sprawled across the thin summer coverlet. He was naked, he was asleep, and he was snoring. But he was in her house.

She hung up his uniform, put his underwear on the little cane-bottomed chair and went to the bathroom. She brushed her teeth, washed carefully and, not very deftly, inserted her diaphragm. She took off the new negligee and hung it carefully in the bedroom closet next to his uniform. Then, very gingerly, she sat on the edge of the bed. Her heart was banging so loudly, she was glad she'd left the radio on and there was music again.

Gently she traced a welted shrapnel scar on his broad, suntanned back. She bent down, touched it with her lips; the snoring stopped; she stood up.

"Hubbell?"

The snoring resumed, much louder now than her whisper. She looked down at him, spread-eagled on the coverlet, and speculated how to get space for herself in the bed and how to get both of them under the cover. Even on the hottest night, with all doors locked, all shades drawn, she could no more conceive of sleeping uncovered than of having sex with the lights on. She attacked the coverlet first.

Like a burglar, she tried to steal it out from under him. He was dead, snoring weight. She tugged harder, then attempted a quick yank. Instantly, like a released spring, he was in mid-air, shouting firing orders. She screamed, fell to the floor, but recovered just in time to snake out a good hunk of the coverlet before he subsided and flopped back, snoring again.

It was a good half hour before she managed to get into the bed and pull the coverlet over all of him and most of her. It was almost morning—the radio was silent, the orange walls were beginning to show their true color—when she sensed he had stopped sleeping. She was exhausted: each time she had dropped off to sleep he had started to snore. Her left arm was numb: his head was on it. It didn't matter. She marveled that it didn't, marveled that he was in her bed. She was afraid only that he would awake, get dressed and leave.

He turned to her. She felt his erection on her leg.

His head was on her breast. He kissed it, then took it in his mouth. She kissed his hair, wanted to kiss his ear, but was afraid of confusing him. Then he threw back the coverlet and rolled on top of her, and then he was inside her.

It didn't take long, not long enough for her, and he only kissed her on the neck. For a few moments he was still. She knew he was going to move, didn't want him to, but he did. A leg straddled her; his head rested on her shoulder. Before tears filled her eyes and her throat, she had to find out.

"Hubbell?" she whispered. "It's Katie."

He turned his head: his profile was to her.

"You do know it's Katie?" But he had started to snore gently, and the tears came, spilling down her cheeks into her smile.

The sun slammed into the little bedroom. She found Hubbell in the kitchen in his shorts, drinking hair of the dog. Katie started to make a big breakfast and he went to take a long shower. They hadn't looked at one another.

To her delight her cooking was interrupted three times by the telephone. The first call—she poked the phone into the bathroom to be sure Hubbell heard popularity calling—was from Stash about the next meeting and how about a drink after. The second was from her friend Pony Dunbar about having dinner before the meeting so they could dish. She told Pony she had a man in the shower, she had worn the negligee, she needed mules immediately and could they have lunch and shop. The third call was from Verso, who gave her hell.

"I'll be there!" Katie protested. "Just because that ear-guzzling blonde passed out—" Verso interrupted. "Oh, *you* passed out. Listen, Willy, when you pass out, how much do you remember?" The sound of the shower stopped. She rustled up a gay, lilting laugh. "Fine, darling, I'll try to make it." On the other end, Verso began to shout. Very low, she said, "I'll *be* there," and hung up quickly.

It wasn't difficult getting Hubbell to talk over bacon and eggs, it was just difficult to bring up what she wanted to talk about. They ate at the gate-leg table in front of the window facing a cool north. She wore a thin blouse and skirt, he his T-shirt and trousers; they were both barefoot. They looked at the jam they spread on toast and the coffee they poured while he skimmed the details of how he had suddenly been yanked out of the Pacific, sent Stateside, and was now stationed in Washington where he was going to do something in propaganda.

"J.J. swore he didn't pull any strings for me, but when his old man coughs, admirals get hernia."

"Was the Pacific awful?"

"Yes," he said, surprising both of them.

"I saw the scar on your back."

Their eyes met and parted. Well, did he think he spent the night on his stomach?

"I didn't mean awful that way," he said, spreading jam over another piece of toast. "A lot of that was kind of marvelous while we were all learning together what to do. How not to lose. But once we began to win, well, we were unprepared. There doesn't seem to be any way of learning what to do then. And what not to do." He smiled. "I thought of you."

"Me?"

"Yes. There's a *point* to the war in Europe—beyond just winning. And you were the first Jew I ever knew. As a friend."

Was that good or bad? Good; maybe even exotic. But she didn't know they'd been friends.

"I think most human beings are simple shits," he said suddenly. "Sorry."

"I don't agree, but that's all right."

"Not at breakfast." He wasn't in the room.

"Well, anyway, Washington'll be exciting."

"Why?"

"Because Roosevelt is! Thank God, he wants a fourth term."

"Oh, he's no longer an evil warmonger?"

"Who said he was?"

"I seem to remember a leaflet . . ." She didn't care that he was mocking her, she was too delighted that he remembered. "Or did you leave the Party when you left school?"

"I don't necessarily agree with the Party on every issue," she evaded. "How do you know what the Party said?"

He smiled straight at her. "You still think a Varsity letter stands for moron."

"I never did. Well, maybe, sort of. But after the day Dr. Short—" His eyes had changed, he was staring at her very peculiarly. "What?" she asked.

"*That's* what's different!"

"What's different?"

"Your hair!"

"Oh. Yeah. I had it straightened. I go up to Harlem with a friend."

"Does it hurt?"

She laughed. "No!"

"I like it. It really makes a difference. I couldn't figure last night what *was* so different."

He had opened the door for her. "Last night," she began, but then wasn't sure how to continue on in. "Well—do you remember—"

"I remember I wasn't sure it was you at first. Combination of my beer and your hair." He looked at his watch. "Hey, I've got to get cracking."

He finished dressing with the speed of a sailor. Which, she was surprised to realize, he was. He made noises and she made noises, but nothing was said, not even obliquely. She wrote down all her phone numbers—the apartment, the OWI office, the broadcasting studio—for if and when he got up to New York again.

"It's terribly hard to get in a hotel," she said, standing in the doorway to the hall, wanting to keep him there, wanting to ask her question. "So any time you're in town . . ."

"A mezuzah!" His hand had been tracing the molding around the door. "Your house is bless-ed."

"On rainy nights."

"Your family is a load of superstition."

"Nah. My mother died years ago and my father's an anarchist. My demented sister put it up. She's Jewish."

"Only the hair changes." Hubbell laughed. "Well—thanks for putting me up. And putting up with me."

"Hubbell," she said quickly, "last night—"

"Oh, Katie, I apologize. I've been falling asleep all over the place ever since—"

"I didn't mean that."

"Oh, God, did I snore? I did. Oh, you poor kid. It's only when I'm loaded."

"I'll give you a rain check."

"O.K. I'm sorry. See you, Katie."

"See you, Hubbell."

He kissed her forehead and ran down the stairs.

She listened to him run down all four flights, to the front door open and shut, to the silence. Then she went back into the yellow living room and closed the door.

The book was in the top drawer of her desk, its dust jacket almost as fresh as it had been four years ago: she carefully removed it each time she read the book. It wasn't that she had forgotten to ask Hubbell to inscribe her copy, there simply hadn't been time.

In the class in Creative Writing Hubbell sprawled next to the front window where he could look out at the campus. Katie huddled second row center where she could look directly at Dr. Short. He was very short, not quite five feet, and slightly humpbacked. He had sandy hair, a very pleasant face and he was in his early thirties. She adored him. He was gaining a small reputation as a good, constructive critic and a large one as an excellent teacher. She revered him. He had got his appointment immediately after graduating from the same university with all honors, including the hand of the prettiest girl in his class, a Phi Beta Kappa and Magna Cum Laude. She idolized both of them. They both contributed to causes and both took and read each of her leaflets. She prayed for the day when he would untie the knot in her stomach by reading one of her short stories aloud to the class.

The sun on Dr. Short's neatly combed head was a halo. "If I read comparatively few of your stories aloud in class, it's because I think we learn best from what is good or, at least, talented. Today, happily, I'm going to read—and with a good deal of pleasure—a surprisingly good story from an unexpected source."

She held her breath as Dr. Short reached for the pile of manuscripts on his desk. His head wasn't much higher.

"The story is called 'All-American Smile,'" he announced, "and it's by Hubbell Gardiner."

She wanted to throw up. Either Dr. Short had lost his mind or he'd succumbed to pressure from the totally athletic-minded Administration. Hubbell, of course, was sprawled in his chair as usual, looking out the window where the damn sun was shining on a stupid little bird which was probably going to crap right on the ledge.

Dr. Short read from the typed pages: "'In a way, he was like the country he lived in: everything came too easily to him. But at least, he knew it. And if, more often than not, he took advantage of everything and everybody, at least he knew that too. About once a month, he felt he was a fraud, but since most everyone he knew was more fraudulent . . .'"

Suddenly Katie was wildly dizzy: she really did want to throw up. She felt as though she were going over Niagara Falls in a barrel. Her stomach plunged like a broken elevator. She was *sure* she was going to throw up. Or faint. Or both. She took quick deep breaths. She thought of Stalin, of Roosevelt, of her father, but with her father came all that candy, and she silently, desperately quoted Elizabeth Barrett Browning and Karl Marx. She dabbed at her face with a handkerchief; she threw her head back, then down between her legs. She broke out in a sweat.

47

Across the room, Hubbell had shifted his gaze from the ceiling to the floor. He bent down, as though searching for crib notes. He grabbed one foot and peered at the top of his shoe. Then he examined his cuff, his forearm, his elbow: were the notes *anywhere?* He began to giggle and took quick deep breaths to stop the giggles. He blew his nose, he began to hiccup. He dropped his head between his legs, but his stomach made for his throat. He thought he was going to throw up. He broke out in a sweat.

Very quietly Julian Short finished reading the story: "'We can always go on WPA,' she laughed, and it was an echo of his laugh. 'Well, then,' he said, 'there's really no reason for us to change.' But, of course, even if they had wanted to change, by then they were too lost or too lazy."

The room was quiet. Hubbell pressed his lips to prevent a smile, but there were tears of a kind in his eyes and of another kind in Katie's.

Later, she stood woodenly in Dr. Short's office where the sun was even warmer and gentler, and where a leather-framed photograph of his beautiful wife and their beautiful baby rested on his desk.

"Please sit down."

She clutched her manuscript. "I'd rather stand," she said, then realized she seemed to be insisting on being taller. She sat on the edge of a chair. He was barely visible behind his desk: he was really very short. She slumped back and down in her chair. He had a lovely, deep voice, but no sooner had he begun to discuss her work than her stomach started its voyages and she was back in the barrel over Niagara.

"Unfortunately," she did hear him say, "neither commitment nor a first-class mind necessarily makes a first-class writer. Of fiction, that is."

Her eyes were focused on the framed photograph, the red patches burned in her cheeks. Jane Austen would not have to move over.

"Your wife was Prom Queen, wasn't she?"

"I wanted to be a writer myself," he continued, "but I'm afraid I didn't have any real talent either."

"I'm glad you don't say 'eyether.'"

He chuckled. "My wife does."

"Well, she belongs," Katie offered. "Does she work?"

"She's an editor at the University Press."

Katie looked at the lovely face in the photograph, at the lovely baby. "It isn't fair to say it's unfair. But it is."

"You could be a good editor," Dr. Short said. "Or you could write articles. And not only for *New Masses.*"

"*Partisan Review*," Katie said, and stood up.

"Katie, my wife also makes very good coffee. Why don't you come back to the house with me?"

From the moment he said her name, she had to summon all the control she had practiced ever since she had first been snubbed on this alien campus, which was the day she arrived.

"I'm due at the diner. To work, I mean. But thank you. Very much." She started to back out. "You're right and you're fair and—you're a very nice man."

She couldn't quite produce a smile, but at least she didn't hurtle out of his office. Once outside, she bolted down the long, dark hall to the swinging doors at the end. Blindly she pushed one open just as Hubbell, coming from the outer vestibule, pushed the other. She stopped and he smiled, and then he held the door for the pretty coed with him. Katie just stood there. When she finally did say "Congratulations," or something like it, he was gone and the door came swinging back with a great creak.

Chimes were ringing as she hurried stiffly across the campus, her head up, her eyes stinging. She passed between the statues of the First Founder and the First President, passed her sycamore, crossed the road to a trash barrel where she tore up her story. Her heroine dropped into the barrel instead of the gorge without a whimper.

She was standing on the crest of the steep hill which fell sharply to the women's dormitories she had never entered. Beyond, far beyond, was the shimmering lake where Hubbell stroked his crew. She could barely see it, could barely see anything but a blur of grass and stone and water because she was crying very hard.

She plunged down the hill, her frizzy hair flying, her legs running faster than ever before in her life, so fast, it seemed at least one would break if she fell and went crashing into the Gothic citadel at the bottom. She was out of control and the sun was blinding and she kept running and crying, and when she did trip and fall, she missed a cinder path and rolled over on soft green grass several times until she was finally stopped by a big rhododendron bush. She lay there, just crying and enjoying crying, until she realized she had to pee very badly, and that ruined everything: now she would have to go inside those hated women's dorms and ask some stupid bourgeois bitch where the john was.

The meeting was in Vivian's apartment in an old stone mansion on Riverside Drive. Katie sat on the armless oatmeal-colored sofa between Naomi, who took her to Harlem to have her frizz ironed, and Pony Dunbar, who helped her pick out clothes, but not in Klein's. In college Katie hadn't had any girl friends, a case of mutual terror. Except for Frankie McVeigh, she hadn't had any really good friends at all, and until Senior Prom, even that relationship had been ambiguous.

In New York the Party was a warm foster family. Her closest friends and relations were there in Vivian's convent-modern living room, especially Pony Dunbar and Stash. But Pony knew nothing about the whatever-it-was she had been having with Stash, and Stash knew nothing about her delight in going to places like the Stork Club with Bill Verso, and neither of them knew anything about her ambition to be an editor or about Hubbell's novel in the top drawer of her desk. For Katie the word "close" had a double sound.

She watched Stash yawn as Vivian yammered on about the evils of Chiang Kai-shek and the Kuomintang in Chungking, and the gentle glories of Mao Tse-tung and the Communists in Yenan. Whenever Stash was impatient he yawned. Katie yawned herself as she noted idly that even in China the North was more liberal than the South. Climate? These study sessions were informative, of course, but China wasn't something she could *do* something about, it wasn't a raging injustice she could challenge and change here and now. Even Chennault and Stilwell weren't worth an angry letter to the *Times*.

Stash had begun to argue with Vivian. Cherubic and

funny and very smart, he nevertheless was lazy and was inventing statistics as usual. Genteel Vivian, High Priestess of the Last Decimal Point, was not fooled. She was as full of facts as her peasant blouse was full of breasts. Katie could feel Hubbell kissing hers. She wondered again if they were large enough for him, if he had been in New York and hadn't called, if he was coming to New York and would call, if he was on the train from Washington at that moment, if he was calling at that moment . . .

Now they were debating whether support for Roosevelt's goal of making China the fourth Great Power meant supporting a China ruled by Chiang. Katie felt another yawn coming and began biting her beads. It was so academic: Chiang's army was rebelling against him; he had a fat bank account in Switzerland and a thin snake of a wife lobbying in the U.S.; he was a crook and he was doomed. And, anyway, Roosevelt was smarter than all of them and would get whatever he wanted. Her mind followed her eyes as they wandered to the African masks on Vivian's dead-white walls, to the lithographs by Kathe Kollwitz and Ben Shahn and Siqueiros and Degas—how did Degas get there? Where was Hubbell? Maybe he'd hated Washington and got himself sent overseas again despite J.J.'s Fascist father. Maybe to China. Did the Navy go to China? He wasn't in China, he was coming to New York and she would see him again, she knew it. But when?

Pony patted her hand as though she had been mind-reading. Katie had mentioned Hubbell to Pony: she had to say his name to someone. Besides, Pony was experienced. She had been married to a chicken Colonel named Dunbar. She was a juicy Amazon with a small waist which she and her other proportions emphasized. Six feet of her rolled magnificently on very high heels. She preferred her men short: "ponies," she called them. A bombardier had returned the compliment by jettisoning her first name, which was Eloise. Katie had never met any of the ponies: Pony held that an attractive man made even a progressive woman behave like a bitch, and the only way to keep a girl friend was to be a loner after six o'clock.

She hadn't been too sanguine about Hubbell. Although there wasn't much choice with a war on, she was no longer sanguine about military men, anyway. The little chicken Colonel, while still her husband, had flown over embattled Wake Island en route to Australia and deftly awarded himself the combat ribbon and a Bronze Star. Back in the States, he told Pony combat had made him impotent. She bought that, and waited patiently for a return to active duty until she saw the chicken Colonel's new adjutant: six feet two and a WAC lieutenant. Pony went on combat alert and finally caught them banging in a swivel chair in the Colonel's office on the base. She tipped the chair over, beat the shit out of the Colonel, got a Mexican divorce and moved to New York.

After her basic warning, her advice on Hubbell—given as she led Katie from A. S. Beck to I. Miller to Saks Fifth Avenue in search of mules for the negligee —was much like anybody's: indicative and not very helpful.

"Lay off politics."

"Oh, Pony, people *are* their politics! Did you ever know a really nice reactionary?"

"No, but I knew one who was a helluva lay."

"I'll bet you didn't want to have breakfast with him. Anyway, Hubbell's basically progressive. He just needs—"

"Don't try to convert him while he's in uniform. You'll just get his ass in a federal sling." They were in Saks then. "Put those mules back."

"Oh, Pony."

"They're too Bryn Mawr. And stop looking as though *your* ass was in a sling."

"It is. He's not around to convert or unconvert."

"Sit down and try these on." Pony held out a pair trimmed with ostrich pompons. "I'll tell you something, nitwit: no matter how loaded he was, he wouldn't have gone to your place if you didn't have some hook in him. They look great, how do they feel?"

"Oh, fine."

"The main thing is: do they come off easy? Show momma. That's my girl. O.K., from me to you: Happy Boffing."

The mules were in the closet in the pale-orange bedroom where, like Katie, they waited. She wondered if the deadwhite cell Vivian called a bedroom had mules waiting in the closet. Made of nails, if they were. Vivian had flat feet, and her stockings seemed made of mold. She should've saved her nylons.

> *"If you'd be in style*
> *Wear hose made of lisle.*
> *Don't buy anything that's Japanese."*

Katie had sung that on various picket lines, but now the Japanese-Americans were in internment camps and she had protested that. Hubbell would have teased her, the way he did about Roosevelt. Oh, he was right: they *had* called Roosevelt a warmonger; they'd sung about him too:

> *"I hate war*
> *and so does Eleanor,*
> *but we won't feel safe*
> *'til everybody's dead.*
> *Plow them under,*
> *plow them under,*
> *every fourth American boy."*

They had been wrong and Hubbell right. No, it was really Roosevelt who was right. Hubbell didn't understand—she had to stop thinking about him and concentrate on China or she would miss the whole debate. Oh, she had.

Stash was reporting on membership in a quiet, contained voice. That meant he was angry. That meant he would soon make jokes. That meant Vivian would get angry.

"The moment the war is over in Europe," Stash said, "the defense plants will have an excuse to cut payrolls. The government will try to bust the unions or at least to get repressive legislation. The workers will be ready to listen to us. Only—we don't know any workers." He giggled. "How about some of you devilishly attractive maidens getting out your beaded bags and cruising the factory gates?"

"Really, Stash!" Vivian said.

"Hey, do factories still have gates?" He couldn't quit.

"Come on, be serious!" Others joined Vivian.

"I *am* serious. It says right here on the agenda: 'Membership problem: serious!'"

Pony catcalled, but Katie was slightly confused.

"The Left and the Right," Stash had argued once, "have a common curse: they can't laugh at themselves."

This was after a meeting where there had been a rhubarb over Naomi's announcement that she was Eurasian, and Stash's comment that her mother made the best egg rolls on 125th Street and Lenox Avenue.

"The danger of laughing at something," Katie had argued back, "is that you can destroy it. And lose your commitment."

"Come on, Katie! You laugh at yourself and God knows you're committed."

"You don't laugh, you make jokes. But when you care deeply about something—"

"I keep my sense of humor, I laugh! You have to!"

"Did you ever have three thousand people laugh at you?" she asked, thinking back to the Peace Rally at school.

"No, but something must've been goddam funny. And I'll bet it wasn't politics." He took off his glasses. "How about you and me sharing your trundle tonight? We'll laugh it off."

"I said you make jokes." She laughed.

She couldn't laugh at the Party or her commitment any more than she could laugh at her addiction to Hubbell. Probably because she didn't want to. She did wish, though, that her sense of humor could muster up something to convert the twenty-four-hour ache for Hubbell into a twinge on Saturdays, Sundays and Jewish holidays only.

four

THE CALL CAME when she was in the broadcasting studio and in a rage at the Army Captain who had been appointed their Pentagon liaison. His name was Harvey and he looked like a choir boy with a hangover. Katie and Bill Verso called him The Pencil because he censored wildly with a red pencil and because of his fixation on the penis and its output.

They were broadcasting a new series intended to prepare the country for after the war, which was still dragging on and on. The disputed script lauded the Negroes in the Engineering Corps in the drive through Normandy. It noted their segregated status; it mentioned their lack of easy assignments and regular promotions; it hinted at their bleak postwar job prospects. Harvey had arrived half an hour before rehearsal with his cuts in the thirty-minute script.

"You left us nine lousy minutes!" Verso yelled when

Harvey came back from the men's room. "And they're the only lousy minutes in the whole frigging script! I'll bet you just pissed on it and cut where it was wet!"

He and Katie and Harvey and the sound engineer were in the control room. Through the big glass window they could see the cast sleeping or doing crossword puzzles or making passes.

"Now you show us what a spy could learn from this script!" Katie jabbed Harvey with *her* pencil.

"That was last week," he protested. "This week it's policy."

"What policy?"

"The Brass resents any implication that the Army pisses on its Negroes."

"Bullshit," said Verso.

"It's Pentagon policy not to aggravate any situation that—"

"Oh, now the Negroes are a situation!" Katie shouted.

"The Pentagon feels that after the war—"

"It's going to be as cruddy as before!"

"She always yells," Harvey complained.

"Will you both shut up?" Verso yelled. "I've got twenty-one minutes of dead air facing me!"

"His fault! He and his racist Pentagon!"

"Oh, piss off, Katie. I just do what the pricks tell me and now there's a new head prick. For all, repeat, all Armed Forces Radio. And you know what the miserable little dick was before the war? Sports announcer on some two-inch station in the dingdong South!"

"I quit!" Katie yelled as the phone rang.

"So do I!" yelled Harvey.

"There's a war on!" yelled Verso. "Answer the goddam phone!"

58

"Hello!" she barked angrily.

"O.K.," Hubbell said at the other end, "I'll sign the petition."

She laughed and hugged the telephone.

He had come up from Washington unexpectedly, couldn't get a broom closet any place from the Y to the Shelton, couldn't find J.J. "Could you put me up on your couch?"

"Of course!" But not on the couch, not if she had to rip out the springs.

"When can I come by for the key?"

Rapidly she weighed her lady-or-the-tiger choices. If she told him to come by in a couple of hours, he might decide to wait in a bar and bars were open trenches for Ear Lickers. If she told him to come by now, he might drop his bag at her apartment and disappear on the town. On the other hand, he hopefully was so exhausted from the crowded Washington train and room hunting and the war and the heat that as soon as he got to her place he would sack out. The apartment was clean, ready and waiting; it had been for weeks.

"Hubbell? It's Studio 3, 17th floor. Why don't you trot over now? I'll arrange your visa."

She was docile and diplomatic when she returned to the Battle of the Script. Not that she was surrendering, she was just busy planning the menu for dinner.

Harvey's red, white and blue eyes widened in disbelief as he watched them meet through the control-room window. "How did Little Red Riding Hood get a jock like that?" he asked Verso.

Verso looked up from the script and groaned. At the far door to the corridor Katie was gurgling to Hubbell. She had one knee bent and one hand on her hip like a

Seventh Avenue model. She was still wearing her rain hat.

Unaware, Katie gloated with delight that everyone had seen her give Hubbell her keys. "And, oh, yes, there's beer in the icebox and you can stick the phone in the bottom drawer of the desk if you want to nap and—"

"I slept on the train," Hubbell cut in. "Haven't you been to Harlem?"

"What? Oh, Jesus!" She yanked off the hat and clawed at her hair.

"Let it alone, it's pretty."

"Well, it's hair. Listen, that's the only key, but I'll be home early. Before dinner, anyway."

"Katie!" Verso bellowed over the mike.

"Your master's voice."

"Oh, he'd be lost without me. You wouldn't like to meet the gang, as they say?"

"Not really."

"Morosky!"

"He's lost," Hubbell said.

She turned around, waved gaily to Verso, then turned back to Hubbell. He was so splendid in his white uniform. *Some* God was in heaven. She stood on her toes, kissed him quickly and floated back to the control room.

Her pencil flew as she rewrote and restored minor deletions. She cajoled, she charmed, she invented. Harvey relented a bit, even helped a bit. Verso stopped threatening to confine his talents to commercial radio. The message they were getting through might not be worth sending but dramatically the show would work.

It was during the first read-through of the new script

around the big table in the studio that Katie realized Hubbell was sitting in a corner, observing the whole process. He was reading the old script as the cast read the new one. She was pleased and she was ashamed, and wondered whose purse was on the chair next to him.

He looked at her differently when she came over with all the new pages. "How come they listen to you?"

"I yell on them. That shmuck in uniform is the Pentagon censor."

"I gathered. Where's the author?"

"He had latrine duty today."

"So did you. I hope he does as well."

"But he said a lot of good things—"

"The script's better now," Hubbell said. "Never mind the message, it's more emotional."

She might've ruined everything by crying right then and there, except that Verso yelled for her.

"I'll be right back," she said.

"I'm taking off."

"Oh, stay. Keep out of the rain."

"It stopped," Hubbell said and stood up to go.

She didn't ask, she told Verso she was leaving early (he squeezed her behind for luck) and ran madly from store to store in the steaming, sun-baked streets: steaks (she had ration stamps), potatoes, sour cream, chives, salad (did she have endive home? Yes, but arugula wouldn't hurt), wine, flowers, French bread, pie—beer! She had forgotten beer! She got beer.

At the door to her apartment, she came to a panting halt. If she rang, would she wake him? Was he there? If he wasn't, how did he expect her to get in?

By leaving the door open. And he wasn't asleep, he was in the shower. She dumped everything in the little red kitchen. The potatoes were in the oven, the wine and the beer in the icebox before the shower stopped. He really took awfully long showers: what had he done in the Pacific? And then there he was, in the middle of her pale-yellow living room with a towel wrapped around him. Orange looked magnificent against his beautiful tan.

"It's clean," she said.

"It's had a shower," Hubbell said.

"I meant the towel. How about a cold beer?"

"You having one?"

"I'll have a glass of wine."

"Run out of Dubonnet?"

She wondered what else he remembered, but before she had the nerve to ask he went into the bedroom. As they drank and talked, he dressed in both rooms as casually as he had in the Pacific, and in locker rooms before that. She wasn't sure whether she should follow him back and forth, so she did, trying to look and not look, answering his questions instead of asking the ones she had been rehearsing for weeks.

"Oh, before that I was a reader. Boring."

"Well," Hubbell said, putting on his shoes, "you make a damn good editor."

"Ohhh." She waved her hand airily and knocked over her wine.

As he helped her mop up he said, "I hate to put on this straitjacket."

"Then don't." She dabbed wine behind her ears for luck.

He looked at his watch.

"Have another beer."

"Can't." He picked up his jacket. "Can I use the horn?"

"Sure."

The telephone was in the living room on the gate-leg table where she had served him breakfast, where she served dinner when it was fully open. In the mirror over her dressing table she could see him dialing, but her head was pounding so she couldn't hear. If she stayed deaf, she'd have to get out of radio. She picked up his damp towel, took it into the bathroom and folded it neatly over the shower rail. Then, unfortunately, she could hear.

"Carol Ann? Hubbell . . . Hubba Hubba to you. J.J. there yet? Southampton! What a snafu! . . . He's not *my* old man. I'm not getting on another hot train . . . Well, of course I'm coming!"

Katie crossed to the kitchen: the tender steaks were marinating on the cutting board, the young greens were floating in clear water in the white sink.

"You tell her to keep them off." Hubbell laughed. "She'll be cooler. For the moment . . . Oh, five, ten minutes. I'm in Murray Hill . . . No, an old school friend. Bye." He hung up as Katie came out of the kitchen. "Do you have another key? God knows what hour I'll be—"

"You can't," she heard herself say. "I've got steaks and baked potatoes with sour cream and chives, and salad and fresh baked pie. I can cook. I would have made pot roast, I make a terrific pot roast but I didn't know whether you ever had pot roast, it's not very classy, or even if you like it, and anyway there wasn't time and it really should be made the day before. So I got steaks—with ration stamps—and you must be hungry, you didn't have lunch—what with all the room hunting, you couldn't've—you can't go yet! You've got to stay for supper and that's all there is to it."

The silence was frightening. Hubbell stood by the telephone, looking at her shoulder because she was staring at the sun-speckled carpet and her long, soft, straight hair hid her burning face. The silence was strangling; she tried to think of a joke; and then there was a flash of heat lightning, a low roll of thunder, and Hubbell said:

"What kind of pie?"

She couldn't remember. As she started for the kitchen, there was a walloping cannonade of thunder, jagged lightning cracked open the sky, and the rain came pouring down.

"Oh God," Katie said as they ran to close windows, "it looks like it's going to rain all night!"

He made it easy. He joked and kidded while she cooked, he chatted and then talked while they ate by candlelight on the opened gate-leg table. She tried to stop her mind from running in and out of the bedroom in the negligee and mules. But she poured wine as though she had a vaulted cellar.

He chose college as safe ground in a neutral past: remember this, remember that, but there wasn't that much to remember together. She tried to prolong a return to the campus statues which, like Hubbell, had failed to rise to her virginity, but he, oh, more clever than she, led her swiftly across the green to the Peace Rally. To her surprise, he remembered her speech, the fury of her tirade against Franco, the passion of her concern for Loyalist Spain. She served him a big piece of pie.

And then he said, "But your hero didn't lift a finger for Spain."

"Which hero?"

"F.D.R."

If she had taken Pony Dunbar's advice seriously, a casual shrug and an airy dismissal would have been her riposte. But Katie was shrewd enough to know that even with the straightest, softest hair in the world the core of her attractiveness was inside. Besides, she couldn't keep her mouth shut, particularly about Roosevelt. So she discoursed on how he had had to weigh intervention in Spain against getting that hostile Congress to back AAA and WPA and Social Security and all the other reforms he had instituted to lift the country out of the Depression.

"Well, that was part of it," Hubbell said, surprising her again. She really had to stop giving lectures and start having conversations.

"But I also think," he went on, "that your great man was worried about the voters. They were isolationist and he's a consummate politician. Is that how you explain his failure to do anything for the Jews in Europe?" His grin was triumphant, as though he had pointed out a crack in her idol as deep and dangerous as a geological fault.

"Cordell Hull," she countered, pushing the Secretary of State into the chink.

"Hull's wife is Jewish."

"Maybe that's why." She smiled and Hubbell laughed.

The word "wife" sent her thoughts flying to the bed-

65

room again. But Hubbell began to argue with obvious enjoyment and she flashed back. Pony had said she had a hook in him. Was it being Jewish? Did he think that made her smart? But why would he care? He was more impartial about Roosevelt and the Jewish refugees than she was.

Sometimes, listening to Roosevelt's Fireside Chats, she felt the President was speaking directly to her. Now, as they argued, she felt that Hubbell was speaking directly to her, that he had never spoken this way of these things to anyone else. The possibility struck her that he was trying to impress her. She left the negligee in the bedroom closet; pleased, delighted, secure, she stayed at the table.

"Well, he did form the War Refugee Board," she said.

"Late."

"True, but I suspect that all the information got to him very late. I know a lot of it was blocked in the Immigration Section by Breckinridge Long, that anti-Semitic Southern—unfair," she interrupted herself. "There must be good liberal Southerners."

"Paul Robeson. And me."

"You?"

"Well, borderline. I'm from Virginia."

"Ah, patrician!"

"Like Roosevelt?"

"He's a great man, Hubbell!"

"How you do keep your heroes, Miss Katie," he chided in a *Gone With the Wind* accent. "I wonder the Party hasn't taught you better. Or purged you."

"Who said I was in the Party?"

"You did."

"When?"

"Why are you afraid to tell me? Never mind. No, don't. Anyway, you're violently pro-Russian and I don't understand that either."

"Oh, a Red baiter!"

"Katie."

"O.K. Why don't you understand?"

"Because with the possible exception of Poland, Russia is the most anti-Semitic country on earth."

"The Soviet Union is against *all* religion, Hubbell. That's the only way to eliminate prejudice," she said, and they laughed into that debate. Stopping only to open another bottle of wine, they debated the Nazi-Soviet Pact, and the switches of allegiance made by England and the United States.

"And all the powers at the time," Hubbell said. "It's all always politics. And they may start as Don Quixotes but they all become politicians, and you know it, Katie. But Roosevelt, the Soviet Union—" He smiled and shook his head. "You hold on, and I don't know how. And I wish I did."

She put another piece of pie on his plate and refilled both their glasses. Conviction, well, that was something she'd always had and never examined. It could, of course, be communicated in time, but she couldn't ask him to wait until they'd been together in bed for a week or two and had had a lot of discussions over cigarettes after—she'd be smoking, too, by then and could drop ashes in the new ashtray from the Chinese china store, no, not Japanese, don't you see the pattern?

She took a stab at explaining that politics, like any other fact of life, didn't have to be what it was. "Anyway, if we don't try, what's the point in going on?" The point was sitting across the table, interfering with her ideology.

"Maybe you were born committed." Hubbell pushed back his chair. "Well, you're a great cook and no real Southern gentleman would have spoiled your dinner by being so deep-shit serious."

"What's wrong with being serious?" She still couldn't say "shit," not even though she was afraid he was leaving.

"It's the dog chasing his tail." He sat down again. "You'd better quit before you die of frustration."

"Then why are you jealous?"

He laughed.

"You are, though."

"I'll live." He stood up again. "And longer."

"You won't write another novel."

He stopped, halfway to his jacket. She went to her desk and took out the book, still in its glossy sheath.

"How about an autograph? With a personal inscription. Some double entendre like To My Sis-Grad-U-Ate."

He took the book and melted like ice cream into a chair. "You must've gotten one of the two copies sold."

She knew the book, which had got good reviews, had had to compete with Pearl Harbor. "I didn't buy it. It came in a Cracker Jack box."

He laughed and yawned and looked at the ceiling. "Did you get through it?"

"I managed. Three times. It's very good, Hubbell."

He crossed his legs and brushed something off the tip of a spotless white shoe. "Thin. Small."

"Short."

He opened and read or pretended to. "I'm glad you liked it, Katie."

"So was I."

"What didn't you like?"

". . . Do you really want to know?"

"Yes." He looked up at her. "No! Yes! But wait. I need fortification. Any more wine?"

"No. Oh, I'm sorry. Wait! There's a bottle of brandy Bill Verso gave me when I moved in a hundred years ago! You think it's still good?"

"Oh, Katie!" He laughed and put his arms around her.

"What?"

"It's still good."

No, he did *not* want to write a war novel and what's more he couldn't, he said, stretched out on the pale-gold carpet which looked rich and thick in the candle-light. When she came over to refill his brandy glass, she sat down by him, her pleated skirt fanning out around her, touching his shoulder as her fingers would touch it as soon as possible to emphasize some point.

"You can be as negative as you want," she encouraged.

"That's the whole trouble. I can't be negative enough. I can't get angry enough. And I can't be positive enough." He raised himself up to put his head in her lap. "The other day we sat around the most enormous table in the Pentagon—God, that place!—anyway, we were trying to find a positive slogan for the war. Like 'Make the World Safe for Democracy.'"

"At this date?"

"They've been at it since the beginning. Trying to justify themselves. What *will* the war end?"

"Hitler."

"Yeah, that's why I can't be negative enough. And the killing of your people." He rubbed his cheek against her thigh. "The systematic killing, anyway. If there are any left."

"Oh, there will be!" She added emphasis so she could bring her hand down on his shoulder.

"If they're anything like you." He moved her skirt to kiss her knee. "What makes you angriest?"

"Injustice."

"What're you for?"

"Justice."

They both laughed, and he reached around to pinch her behind and then kept his hand there to caress it. "Define justice."

"You coming back from the Pacific in one piece." Her hand slid under his T-shirt.

"Oh, I would."

"You're a winner."

"Maybe that's why I'm short on anger. I'll have to leave the revolution to you." His hand on her knee moved higher.

"O.K.," she said, pulling at his shirt.

"Poor thing, you're doomed. It never has got any happier. Still—" He pulled the shirt out of his trousers. "Still, lousy as it is, it can also be—rather wonderful."

"Well, it could be for every—"

But he pulled her down and kissed her. Then, as he began to undress her, he said, "But you mustn't be too serious."

"All right," she agreed. She would have agreed to anything.

When she was nude in the shaking light of the candles, he looked at her body in awe and pressed his big hands hard against the floor.

"Oh, Katie," he said. "You don't dress right. Don't you know you're beautiful?"

"You are," she said.

He ran his hands lightly over her body, then ran his lips over her, then stood up and quickly shucked off his clothes and as he slowly came down to her, he whispered, "It'll be better this time."

She heard a sound which she was sure was gentle rain, and she was complete.

five

LADIES LIKE Rosa Luxemburg and Emma Goldman, Katie decided, could never have been happy in love.

She didn't ask if Hubbell was in love with her. If he wasn't, he would be: now that she had the hang of it, it wasn't difficult to make a miracle. Besides, she was too delighted with being able to love him, and concerned only that she couldn't see him as often as she wanted. There *was* a war on, he *was* in the Navy, she *did* work for the OWI. She went down to Washington for occasional weekends, but hotels were hard to get and expensive, and he had to salute so much. More often, he came to New York, to her apartment. He began to leave clothes in the closet of the orange bedroom and she gave him a secondhand typewriter for Rosh Hashanah. And all the time she asked questions as though she had to learn him, to memorize him. Unlike a book, however, Hubbell did not open up easily and preferred not to be read very seriously.

"But you didn't just wake up wounded? Where did it happen?"

"In the war. Everybody's wounded in a war."

"Hubbell Gardiner!"

And:

"But your father must do *something!*"

"He's a baseball fan. My mother's a football fan. I went out for crew."

"You just made that up."

"He had greenhouses. But he lost them and had to become a common gardener and now he has Victory gardens. And that's how we got our name."

She tried to slug him, they began to wrestle, and that was another time they made love on the floor.

And:

"How am I for you?"

They were in twin beds pushed together in a hotel in Washington where they had registered as man and wife. The desk clerk had even believed it.

"You surprised me," Hubbell said.

"Good surprise or bad?"

"Spectacular!" He laughed. "It's your secret weapon. Don't give it to the comrades."

"No Puritan, she. A wild woman!" Delight made her coy.

"Uh, uh. Much more."

"How more? What more?"

"I never stopped to think."

"Well, let's do it again, and you stop and think."

"If I stop and think—"

"Oh. Right."

He kissed her. "Let's do it again anyway."

"Oh, yes!"

"Aren't you afraid?"

"Of what?"

"Of being self-conscious."

"With you? I can only be spectacular!"

And:

"Well, who *didn't* get hit by the Depression?" he asked in exasperation.

"My family. There was nothing to hit."

"Then it was a bigger comedown for mine."

"Ah ha!"

"Not as big as you'd like to think, ah ha!"

They were having tea in the Palm Court of the Plaza Hotel. She enjoyed his enjoyment of her enjoyment of the Edens of capitalism. She had spent too much money in Saks for the new dress that outlined her figure. Too much money was being spent at all the little tables, but it was mainly being spent by uniforms and, oh, for God's sake, why not? Nothing could be more romantic than this tall, elegant world of green fronds and pale marble and aquarium light; of velvet voices and tinkling china and sweet stringed music: old show tunes and operettas and Viennese waltzes (*Richard* Strauss was the Nazi). Her new beads-and-earrings-to-match were the brightest color in the room, but they paled next to Hubbell. Even the cucumber sandwiches were beautiful.

"Did you like coming here with your family?" she asked proudly.

"Will you stop making me your class struggle?"

"Oh, endless puns in there!"

"You're an inverted snob. I was here with my family

exactly once. Just after the crash which my crafty father thought was a little fall. They are ordinary middle-middle class, Katie. He reads aloud from the *Reader's Digest* while she knits."

"Then where did you come from?"

"The gypsies were at my cradle."

"Your folks couldn't believe their luck."

"*My* luck. They're Lutheran. They thought it was sinful that things came so easily to me."

"They were only afraid you'd be spoiled."

"You're supposed to make excuses for *me*. Oh, hell. They were always more comfortable with my brother and sister. With me—oh, they behaved as though I were on loan. Come on, it's time to call J.J."

J.J. was beginning to trouble her. He wore glasses now, his vision having receded with his hairline. He chewed peppermints constantly, then blew into his cupped hand and sniffed hard. But his energy was matched only by his enthusiasm, which was manic. Anything was a hopeful excuse for a party, and he always picked up the check. Alone with a girl, he was lost—unless at the end of a very boozy evening with the Gang. Even then he preferred to Old Buddy with Hubbell, his equivalent of the Literary Lion bagged by an insecure hostess. Unfortunately, there was Katie.

She had hoped J.J. wouldn't remember her from college, but he rubbed his cheek at their first reunion: he had even remembered her slapping him at the Peace Rally. He called her Comrade or Mme. Stalin and never introduced her by her last name. She suspected he was embarrassed for Hubbell and wanted to eliminate her. However, when he made dates with

Hubbell, his "you" was always plural, so perhaps she was just being oversensitive, ha ha.

J.J. was stationed in New York now. He had an apartment on Beekman Place which was HQ for his Team, his Gang, his Gung Ho gaggle of young officers and their beige beauties from Bennington or Miss Somebody's or the Something School for Girls. The metallic silvered-green duplex had a terrace overlooking the East River: it belonged to an aunt who was overseas with the USO.

"My God, bird, how old *is* she?" asked Judianne, a regular.

"Nymphos have no age," J.J. snorted, and explained how his aunt had taken six lessons from Mme. LaZonga on the accordion so that his old man—whose bank had some hookup with a movie studio—could infiltrate the aunt into an entertainment unit.

"So that's what banks do," said Carol Ann, the brightest of the beige girls. "I always wondered."

"Did you?" Hubbell grinned.

"Didn't you?" Carol Ann had a cool security Katie despaired of acquiring.

"Well," said the big Air Force Captain who had got Katie and Bill Verso into the Stork Club, "I hope the old girl's under Patton."

"You can bet she's under someone," said J.J., hooting and howling.

Patton was bogged down in France and Katie was mired at J.J.'s, where the war and the world were largely a frame of reference for jokes and quips and funny stories. She was country cousin to the silken-haired girls who used the same number of brush strokes, who shared the same background, who wandered as casually in and out of the bedroom as they wandered in and out of the kitchen (where, to her annoyance, each had a few specialties). Yet, all the young officers had been in combat, and the beige girls were neither unintelligent nor uninformed, and they all had an ease she envied and a laugh that was a knife to her. She took note of the clothes and the hair and the makeup, and of the easy eyes on Hubbell. His were easy in return, but when he looked at her, it should have been clear even to Katie that she was his girl.

Hubbell said that going to J.J.'s was merely like going to a Betty Grable movie. He said J.J. was touching.

"Touching? Where?"

"He yells as loud as he can so he won't hear himself crying for help."

"Ha. From you."

"That usually gets to most people." He moved away from a lump in the mattress (they were in Washington that weekend). "He keeps saying I'm his best friend."

"You are."

"I know, but the poor bastard thinks he's *my* best friend."

"Isn't he?"

"No. You are."

She brought J.J. flowers, but she wasn't going to make a habit of Betty Grable. The next weekend that Hubbell was in New York they passed up Sunday brunch on Beekman Place for an art auction sponsored by the Joint Anti-Fascist Committee. It was returning to church.

Stash was the auctioneer; Vivian, in a tight, bulbous white dress, worked the display easel like a vaudeville magician's accomplice. Most of the faces in the narrow, stark gallery were familiar to Katie. She was pleased they were so intelligent, concerned, aware. She wished, though, that Pony Dunbar had come and that Stash were more serious.

"Forty-five, forty-five. Am I bid fifty? Fifty? Listen, folks, all these works of art have been donated by the artists—and I can see why. No, seriously—ah, fifty! I'm bid fifty!"

The picture, one of the few which wasn't an abstraction, made Katie smile. It had three crazy, lopsided, orange and yellow figures which might have been three sisters hugging in a familial orgy.

"They finally got to Moscow," she whispered to Hubbell.

"They finally got a washing machine."

"Sixty, am I bid sixty?" Stash removed his thick glasses. "This dazzling display of decadence is blinding. No, no! O.K. Seriously now. The war isn't over, but they're talking *now* about deporting refugees for being 'premature anti-Fascists.' That's the beginning, that's—sixty-five! I'm bid sixty-five!"

Hubbell's hand was up.

"Seventy-five! Do I—I do have seventy!"

Katie yanked Hubbell's arm down, but it went right back up.

"Seventy-five! Sold to the Smiling Lieutenant!" Stash cried.

When they collected the picture after the auction, Stash said to Katie, "Long time no chop-chop."

"Oh. Oh, I've been swamped by the new series," she

apologized as the pink patches on her cheeks went
deep red: she had missed two meetings.

"Three," Stash said.

The last Saturday of the month J.J. gave a big party
for Judianne's birthday. Katie and Hubbell didn't go
because he said it would be an R.F.—Hubbell thought
all big parties were Rat Fucks—so they spent a glorious
day alone. Hubbell was trying to start a second novel;
Katie, responsible, was trying to get accustomed to his
work pattern.

He would first stall by reading the newspaper or
talking to her. Then a glaze came over his eyes, he
began to pace, then he sat down at the typewriter. He
went for short walks to think. Once, coming back from
the grocery, she met him in the street and he walked
right past her. Since then she had been frightened he
would get run over. Near the end of his day, he took
a long bath, clambering out of the tub several times
to pencil corrections as he dripped over the carpet.
Finally, it was time for his beer and her Dubonnet,
and for him to read to her. If she hesitated even sub-
consciously, he knew it immediately.

"What? Clumsy or just unclear? You're no good to
me if you hold back!"

He had a good day the Saturday of J.J.'s party. Katie
had made her famous pot roast the day before, so while
he worked she tackled Proust for a bit, then caught up
on back issues of *Masses and Mainstream*. They each
had an extra drink and a bottle of wine with dinner;
there was barely enough pot roast left for sandwiches.
After dinner they were depressed by news reports of
the Battle of the Bulge and debated Allied strategy.

"Of course, our main objective is to defeat Russia at the peace table." She heard her lecture voice.

"How do you know?"

"Well—"

"You don't."

She suspected they were arguing, but he didn't raise his voice or get red in the face or wave his hands. He had a half smile and his manner was altogether casual, and maddening.

"You're like Pavlov's dog, Katie. Whatever bell rings, you jump to the conclusion that the Russians are right and everybody's in a dark conspiracy to gang up on them."

"They are!"

"They may well be. But you don't really know. It's a little tiresome, it's certainly bigoted and, worst of all, it's boring. Why don't you try to see the other side?"

"I do! But you *have* to pick one, and I have! You sit on the fence so much, you won't know it until you have a spike permanently up your behind!"

"Why don't you say up my ass?"

"Because I can't!"

She said it with such earnest despair that he broke up. She felt foolish, but she didn't mind: it was Hubbell, and his laughter was kind.

It was snowing by then, so he rushed her out into the warm, silent streets. Arm in arm they padded through the fat, loving snowflakes to Gramercy Park. By the time they got back home they couldn't get undressed fast enough.

The painting of the Three Sisters was hanging over the bed. They made love with such crazy abandon that it fell down on them. They just shoved it onto the floor.

The next day they went to J.J.'s for brunch: Bloody Marys in silver goblets and bacon and eggs and post-mortems: I didn't really, did I? Oh, yes, you did, bird, don't you remember? My God, you were hilarious! Katie read the papers and drank coffee. Hubbell sat on the floor, leaning against a black sofa struck by silver lamé lightning. Carol Ann was stretched out on the sofa, drinking a Bloody and playing with Hubbell's hair. He ate as though Katie hadn't fed him pot roast the night before.

She got up and pressed her nose against the terrace door. The East River was gray, moving very fast. There was no snow any place, just gray wetness; only the river had any vitality, and that seemed angry. J.J. claimed she was always looking at water because she was a Lorelei Lee. Well-meaning people were usually jerks.

"They're not stupid." Hubbell had come up behind her, his body just touching hers. She could see his worried reflection in the glass door.

"No, but neither am I."

"Flirting is just part of talking."

"Even at breakfast?"

"Brunch."

"I always feel as though I'm invited for drinks and everyone else is staying to supper."

"Dinner." Hubbell grinned.

"Dinner!" She yanked off her earrings.

"Put them back."

"They're gauche, bird!"

"Not on you." He turned her around to him and kissed her gently. "They're fine on you."

"Oh, mostly I wish she weren't so pretty."

"You know, she's Jewish."

"I should be so Jewish," Katie said wistfully.

"Yes, I *will* regret it," Pony had said, "but O.K. Just for you. We'll meet at Billy's on First Avenue. *Only* for drinks."

She still hadn't shown. The windows of the restaurant were steaming from the cold outside and the warm, noisily happy crowd inside. In both front and back rooms, the red-checked tables were taken. The big mahogany bar was jammed. But Hubbell loved it all: the old, frosted gas globes, the sawdust, the dark-wood meat lockers, the waiters in black with long white aprons and, best of all, Mrs. Billy in her long black tent and starched white apron, much wider than the telephone booth at the back of the room and almost as tall. A fraction of Mrs. Billy sat with dignity on the little seat inside the booth while the rest of her overflowed outside and seemed to be standing up.

"Is she watching the register?" Hubbell said.

"She's even bigger than Pony," Katie said. "Maybe that's why Pony likes to come here. You think I should call her?"

"How're you going to get in the booth?"

A waiter tapped Katie on the back: Bill Verso was at a large round table in the far corner with a pair of identical twins who were equally bad actresses. They had been acrobatic dancers, which fascinated Hubbell, but Verso was too intent on talking about himself to an All-American ear.

"It's my own fault they won't let me go overseas. I should never have got all those awards for them. The Brass is creaming, but it's crap! Crap! Right, Katie?"

"Well," she equivocated, hoping he was drunk, trying not to listen, not to look at Hubbell, watching the door for Pony.

"What are we going to have for dessert?" one twin asked the other.

"My own damn fault!" Verso leaned across to Hubbell, his elbow squashing his salad. "I've got to get over there to feel the war, to smell the war! How can I make the home front feel it and smell it if I can't?"

It couldn't have been worse. Then Pony arrived and it was.

She loomed twice as big as Mrs. Billy. Her normally dead-white skin was deader and whiter with powder or pancake or calcimine, or maybe she had dipped herself in the flour barrel and painted her mouth with blood. Everything else was black. Her eyes were heavily mascaraed with black. Her filmy dress was black with floppy black ruffles at her wrists and outlining the heart-shaped bodice. She wore a black lace mantilla and carried a long black handkerchief drenched in a perfume that smelled black. She looked like a madam in mourning for one of her girls. Katie gobbled two pieces of bread.

With Pony was a little brick shithouse of a man with the weather beaten face of a very old child. He was in the Merchant Marine, a veteran of the Murmansk convoys. "We were detained," Pony said in a throaty coo Katie had never heard.

"My zipper busted," the man said.

"Oh, Skipper!" Pony giggled, and waved her handkerchief, tear-gassing the table.

Chairs were brought and Pony squeezed herself between one of the twins and Skipper. "So this is Hubbell," she said, the little gargle in her voice making her seem like a big praying mantis.

"Hubba Hubba!" the twins cried in unison, clapping their four hands.

Hubbell laughed and took charge, ordering for everyone. The drinks kept coming; Mrs. Billy sent a round; the waiter switched allegiance to Hubbell. And suddenly they were all old comrades, having a good time at Hubbell's party for his friends. Katie beamed at him.

"What?" he asked.

She shook her head, unable to explain that she was once again in the minority, but this time the minority was superior. Bill Verso didn't once call her kiddo, he didn't even ask her to move her chair or pass the salt. He knocked down his double drinks and laughed and brayed and directed his philosophies at Hubbell until he saw the twins twinkling at Hubbell and listening to *him*. Verso tousled his hair: *he* was the director.

"I've got to get overseas, boy," he said to Skipper, who had been totally busy drinking boilermakers and eating an enormous slab of roast beef. "Hell, if I can't get over there to feel the war and smell the war myself, how can I make 'em feel and smell it back here?"

Skipper wiped his mouth with his napkin. "You've smelled shit, that's what war smells like."

The twins screeched and everyone laughed except Verso and Katie, who empathized with him.

84

"How you get it to smell over the radio you know better than I," Skipper said.

"Are you saying my shows are shit?"

"I've never heard them, but they probably are. All you people tell a few little truths and a lot of big lies."

"Such as?"

"Such as why we didn't open the Second Front until just this year."

"Why didn't we?" Hubbell asked.

"Because we hoped the Nazis would finish off the Soviet Union for us."

"I don't believe that," Hubbell said.

"I wouldn't expect you to, Annapolis." Skipper was as casual as Hubbell, but he spoke with the assurance of a pope. "It's true just the same. The day the Allies double-crossed Stalin by postponing the Second Front was the day they started the next war."

"Against Communism."

"Against the Socialist Democracies."

"Where's the ladies' room?" Katie asked.

"No politics, Skipper," Pony cautioned.

"No politics?" Skipper smiled at the others. "She'd like you to think she's only a big, gorgeous hunk of flesh." Pony flicked her handkerchief seductively. "Come off it, Pony. Don't hide the brains. 'No politics.' What's his radio show if it isn't politics? What's that swell Navy uniform if it isn't politics? What're all these people drinking and eating their butts off while five or six geezers with varicose veins scurry to serve 'em?"

"Dialectics," Pony answered.

"How do you know they have varicose veins?" Hubbell asked.

"I'm serious," Skipper said, "but that's the No. 1 Crime. Every single thing in our lives is basically political, but we don't want to face it. You know why the Communist Party can't get any place in this country? One: the working class won't face that it *is* working class, it says it's middle class. Two: we believe we really have a democracy because we believe we really elect our government and thus control it. Three: . . ."

The party wilted like a corsage. Katie lost track of Dubonnets, but they couldn't blur or deafen or make her numb anyway. At least Hubbell, unlike Verso, refused to be pushed into right-wing positions he didn't hold. But when he smothered a yawn, Katie finally interrupted Skipper and suggested someone get the check. The party was over, but it was early and she knew they were still laughing at J.J.'s.

They waited for the check in silence.

"It must be twenty after," one of the twins said.

Another pause, and then Pony said in her normal voice: "Katie, you're not wearing beads any more."

"No, they made me feel like a nun." She smiled.

Pony smiled back and wiggled her fingers in a little wave, and Katie waved back as though one of them was going away.

The stars were frozen in a stiff sky as they hurried through the cold wind to Beekman Place.

"My mother's almost as big as Pony," Hubbell said. "But my father's bigger."

"Why does the man have to be bigger than the woman?"

86

"Otherwise, everyone'll know he's henpecked! Hey, you're shivering! Let's run!"

There was no R.F. at J.J.'s, just the regular team and one or two extra cheerleaders. Katie hugged the fireplace but she couldn't get warm: traitor's blood. Progressives were the best people: if they bored, it wasn't with superficial trivia like this roomful of surface riders. Pony was not only a Progressive, she was a friend who helped with negligee and mules. What did it matter if she dressed like a Gargantuan black widow spider and talked like a vampire? To care was bourgeois—was that the root of "bushwah"? Said in that Bennington drawl, it could be. Well, Katie was dressing as a reasonable facsimile of these drawlers; she was assimilating.

Anger worked on the Dubonnet like gin on vermouth: she spoiled for a fight. And when J.J. called F.D.R. the "Yaltese Falcon," she hit. The Gang thought it all very funny and laughed. She let them have it and then stalked into the bedroom for her coat, tearing a stocking on one of the angular beds.

"It's a party," Hubbell said, closing the door.

"You don't have to take me home."

"Everybody laughs at parties."

"Not like they do! They're so damn superior!"

"*They're* superior? You didn't hear yourself. Katie, J.J. knows about Yalta, they've all read about Yalta, no one needs a lecture, particularly me, and particularly not tonight!"

"If what is going on in the world bores you—"

"It bored you just as much! You're being a superior pain in the ass because you feel guilty about it. And worse about Pony Dunbar."

Still surprised that he understood her, she fell in love for the hundredth time.

"Why does she matter?" he asked.

She gripped the seesaw as it came slamming down. "No matter what she looked like, she's worth all those empty bitches in there put together."

"What are you doing down there?"

"Looking for a goddam glove I never should've bought!"

"Did you look in your coat?"

"Of course I did!" But when she shoved her hands in the pockets, she found the glove. He didn't smile as she stomped to the window and stared down at the icy black river; he just lit a cigarette and waited. At last she sat in a chair, her fingers groping for a necklace she no longer wore.

"If you want to wear beads, wear them."

"Pearls or nothing." She pulled her coat around her. "From the time I was Bar Mitzvahed, I've been closest to people like Pony, like Stash, like Skipper—"

"The Party."

"No, they haven't all been in it. Close to it; left wing, anyway. Not long-haired revolutionaries, I mean they're not bomb throwers, they're not out to overthrow the government. Just progressive people who—"

"Katie, I *know.*"

"Well, they care the most, do the most, know the most! They're always the smartest!"

"Oh, I don't think they're that smart."

"Smarter than anyone you know!"

"Possibly. But I don't think anyone who follows any dogma can be very smart. Because that means a closed mind. Which may be one reason you're not a very good little Communist any more."

"I'm still opinionated!" She laughed after a beat, freeing him to laugh. "But they are smart, Hubbell. And nine tenths of the time they turn out to be right."

"Like about the Second Front?"

"Yes! Listen, right after the Revolution, Herbert Hoover went to Russia, supposedly for the Red Cross but really to get arms and money to the White Russians— oh, for God's sake, I don't care all that much about Russia, I'd rather go to Paris! I care about the United States, and the Party is doing more to set us straight than anybody! But all they get for their pains is a rotten, lousy deal. They're either hounded or laughed at!"

"Well, they *are* pretty humorless."

"There are certain things you can't laugh—"

"All right!" He held up his hands in surrender and she wanted to go over so he could put them around her. "Yes, there *are* certain things, if politics is your way of life. But, Katie, it isn't your way of life."

"It used to be," she said sadly. "I'm a rat. They're good, good people."

He laughed. "You know what's really bothering you? Guilt—because you enjoy being with me and you have a good time here."

"I don't have a good time here, you do!"

"You do when you don't stop yourself. And when you're sure of me."

"Sure of you, ha ha!"

"You take Carol Ann, you take all those girls too seriously. You take everybody too seriously."

"Including you?"

He grinned. "Nobody could take *me* too seriously!"

"I'm never sure when you're joking."

"I'm never sure when you are. About yourself."

"Neither am I." They both laughed at that, and he stood up as she came to him, and they kissed. "Laugh more," he said. "Please."

"At me?"

"At you, at me, a lot at me. And most at J.J. and the Gang. Particularly when they laugh."

Suddenly she had frizzy hair and was holding a stein of beer and he was saying much the same thing.

"But certain things I have to take seriously. I just do," she said. "And their kind of laughing hurts."

It was the kind she had heard at the Peace Rally, the kind she never heard from Pony or Stash.

"Because they laugh at what you care about? Or at you?"

"Oh, Hubbell." She kissed his chin. "They're the same thing!"

"Not really." He smiled.

But three thousand people had never laughed at him.

six

THE FIRST LAUGHTER came when she was introduced by the crew-cut prig who was president of the Student Council and chairman of the Peace Rally.

It was the kind of day that made laughing easy. Katie had been torn between praying for gray skies (a good omen for her) or blue skies (good attendance for the Rally-Strike). Concentrating on her frizzy hair, she left the weather in the lap of the gods who endowed the campus with golden sun.

She sat with the other speakers on a row of folding chairs halfway down the cascade of stone steps flowing from under the Greek Revival portico of Founder's Hall (home of Dr. Short's Creative Writing class). She was farther toward the right than she would have preferred, a red beret covering the fruitless result of her struggle the night before, a red imitation-silk blouse tucked into a comparatively unlumpy skirt. Chewing gum nervously, she clutched her file cards and stared grimly at the large turnout of saddle shoes and expensive sweaters.

Most of the crowd sprawled on the warm grass, some merely sunbathing, listening drowsily to the platitudes floating over the microphone. The faculty who came stood on the perimeter like wallflowers. Down front, where they could see and hear everything, Dr. Short and his lovely wife held hands. A few feet away Hubbell, in a grass-stained Varsity sweater and old cords, lay with his head in the lap of a girl even blonder. Next to him J.J. gabbled a running "March of Time" commentary for a few fraternity brothers and their dates. They *were* dates: perhaps because of the glee of legal class-cutting, the Rally Against War had the festive air of a picnic.

The bow-tied president of the Student Council had taken Public Speaking. "We feel that a true Peace Movement covers the entire spectrum from extreme right to extreme left. Therefore, we feel that a truly democratic Peace Rally encompasses all groups—as our next speaker proves. She needs no introduction: Miss Katie Morosky."

They laughed before she reached the lectern. She didn't understand why they laughed when she hawked her leaflets either. The scattered booing (which brought more laughter) she did understand, as well as the vehement applause from a group of ten led by Frankie McVeigh. She couldn't see Dr. Short and his wife applaud or Hubbell, was was sitting up now.

"I guess I do need an introduction," she said too loudly into the microphone.

Someone shouted: "Back up, Katie!"

Someone else: "Yeah—to Moscow!"

Her eyes glittered. "You can still take Communion and like the Soviet Union!"

That got a pretty fair laugh—and too much applause from Frankie and the YCL. She made a mental note as she palmed her chewing gum and wadded it into the lectern.

"Back to Russia, Katie!"

There always had to be a little kid seconding a big kid. This pisher, though, was a girl. Katie grinned cheerfully at the anonymous cashmere cardigan. "Well, I can see why our chairman was afraid to say I'm president of the YCL. That's the Young Communist League for those who don't know—" a few boos "—I guess you all do. Scary? Not compared to what's going on in the Capitalist World!"

"What's cooking in the Kremlin, Katie?"

If she didn't shut them up she could never face Frankie or the YCL again, or hawk leaflets under the sycamore again, or sit in Dr. Short's class across from Hubbell Gardiner again.

"The Kremlin's worried about the Civil War in Spain —*are you?*" She accused like Zola. "The legal, the loyal, the Republican—" she cupped her mouth "—*Republican* government is being murdered while we sit here thinking about lunch! Thousands of Spanish citizens are being bombed and machine-gunned and slaughtered by Franco! But not Franco alone, he isn't strong enough! He's got the help of Nazi dive bombers and Fascist tanks, and the so-called 'volunteer' armies of Adolf Hitler and Benito Mussolini!"

She was so excited, she had to stop and breathe. God,

of all times! But they were quiet, they were listening. She gulped and roared on.

"What does the West do? Nothing! What does the U.S.A. do? Nothing! Only one country sends help— not men, *supplies*. One country: the U.S.S.R., the Soviet Union!"

Applause: it had to be from that idiot, Frankie McVeigh. So, of course, some joker (J.J.) was on his haunches, yelling through the megaphone of his hands: "K-K-K-Katie, be my K-K-K-comrade!" Hubbell pushed him over.

"O.K-K-K-K.!" she said quickly, making the laugh hers. "What are you so scared of, K-K-K-comrade? The Russians don't want anybody in Spain but the Spanish. Is that scary? They're K-K-K-Communists, but they want and we of the YCL want total disarmament *now*. Is that scary? Hitler and Mussolini are using the Spanish earth as testing ground for what they want. World War Two. *Is that scary?*" She waited for idiot Frankie to pick up his cue and then jumped in herself. "You're darn right it is! There is only one thing to be scared of: not me, not the YCL, not the Communist bogeymen. Be scared of anybody any place who will *not* stand up for World Peace Now!"

They applauded. Whether Frankie started it or not, they applauded and kept applauding, and she kept smiling and nodding and beaming. They were kids too; they were her age, she was their age, she was a student at this college with them. The ferocity and anger she carried like a daily burden melted in the sunshine. They were so young and eager and bright and beautiful. They *were* concerned, even if they did belong to fraternities and rode around in convertibles

94

and ate goldfish. They *did* know something was very wrong, and the only reason they didn't know it was the whole lousy system was that nobody ever told them. Well, she would and she could and they would understand her because she understood them. She forgot about her file cards of notes.

"You know, you're beautiful!" she said, blinking in the sunlight.

Someone laughed a warm, familiar laugh, a nice laugh. She found the face: Hubbell Gardiner, a few feet in front of her.

"No, really! Beautiful!" she repeated, and blushed because she was still looking at him. She forced her eyes to focus on the blur of faces farther back. "You're the best, the brightest, the most committed generation this country has ever had!" Applause allowed her to sneak another look at Hubbell. He was applauding, but he caught her look and she lost her point. "You are here today . . ." Oh, God. Oh, yes! "You are here to strike for peace—it *is* a strike, not a rally. And they are striking on almost every campus in the nation at this very minute. Listen! D'you hear them? Do you hear them taking that pledge? Listen!"

She held up her hand and turned her head, listening so hard herself that she thought she heard echoes of the pledge she wanted them to hear. It had been printed in the campus paper that morning, in all the campus papers all over the country.

"Show your solidarity by taking that pledge with them now! Come on! On your feet!"

To her relief, they did get to their feet, and without any of the usual horsing around.

"I refuse to support," she began, and the young voices

joined with her: "I refuse to support—the government of the United States—in any war it might conduct."

They stood motionless as a photograph. Now that they had actually said the pledge out loud they understood its meaning. They were scared—but they meant what they had pledged, and that surprised them. It surprised Katie: she had helped make peace a possibility. And on a bright, sunny day! Suddenly everybody was terribly proud. Applause swept through the crowd like a fire. They applauded themselves and their resolution, and Katie applauded them back. It was a triumph, it was like the day she told her YCL the university was going to be investigated (two congressmen had finally shown up for a one-day tour).

Raising her hands for quiet, she began a loving lecture on war and peace and peaceful militancy. But behind her a long thin American flag began to snake across the topmost step, just in front of the columned portico. It was carried by five students spaced at regular intervals behind the flag, only their feet and grinning faces visible. When the flag was stretched to its full length, the student carrying the front end circled back, the others following in a tight oval. They were facing the flag, their backs to the crowd now. On each back, a large placard was hung; on each placard, a word was printed. The first two to become visible read: ANY—PEACE.

"Now the Student Council calls this a Peace Rally," Katie said, aware only that she was somehow losing her audience. "I call it a Peace *Strike*—and I'm an English Major." Laughter began to bubble in the crowd. "Did you think I was a Russian Major?" Guffaws and hoots and howls erupted and spread. "Hey, it isn't *that* funny!"

But they roared with laughter. They doubled over, they poked one another, they rolled on the grass like sheep gone mad. They pointed crazily at her, or at something behind her. She turned around. She was so close, it took a few seconds to read the slogan spelled in five words on the backs of the five students holding the long American flag:

ANY—PEACE—BUT—KATIE'S—PIECE!

Tears flooded her eyes as all the rage and resentment boiled up in her all over again. Her face burned, her throat made little choking sounds, but she grabbed the microphone and yelled: "PIGS! DIRTY PIGS!"

She drowned in their laughter. She didn't see Frankie run up the steps, his rage greater because it was for her, not himself. He lunged for the nearest placard—KATIE'S—and ripped it off the jock's back. The jock dropped the flag and swung. Frankie swung back. One of the speakers horned in, slamming out at Frankie, and Katie shouted "Unfair!" over the microphone. But they kept swinging and she kept shouting until a horde of buck-shoed peasants stormed the steps, knocking over the microphone and the lectern and sending Katie down with them.

Her beret flew off and her hair exploded. She crouched on the rough stone, crying because her new stockings were ripped, searching for her lost beret. Then she saw Hubbell Gardiner pushing his way to her through the fighting, lunatic mass. Ashamed, she scrambled to her feet and ran; ran up the steps smack into the placard marked PIECE! She grabbed the bitch wearing it by her blonde pony tail, yanked the placard

97

off and brought it crashing down over the head of a
boy rushing at her.

It was J.J. He stared at her stupidly, in shock. Then,
trying to be Hubbell, he grinned, and then he laughed,
and then she slapped him across his popeyed face—
hard.

She was no longer crying, she no longer had the
energy. Everyone else seemed to have lots of it. Everyone else seemed to be having a stupid good time,
punching and yelling and laughing. She heard a police
whistle—the idiot campus cop—and then a siren. Up
and down the broad steps, across the sunny grass, they
were running and fighting and laughing. Her lovely
Peace Strike had turned into a silly free-for-all.

Hiding behind the protective shield of the PIECE!
placard, Katie edged her way into Founder's Hall. The
corridor was dim and cold and empty. There wasn't
even a garbage can for the placard. She trudged past
the locked door to Dr. Short's office, past the locked
door to his classroom, past a poster for the Spring Day
Dance, and then she began to weep. She would have
gone home to Rochester, except that it would be a
waste of money if she didn't graduate.

It was almost Commencement, an odd word for
The End. Katie relinquished the presidency of the
YCL to the physics genius, and Hubbell stroked the
crew to victory on the shimmering lake they had seen
every day for four years.

She hadn't seen the race; she had never seen any
race, any game, any college event except the Peace
Rally—if that counted. She'd never been to a big dance,
but now that it was almost too late she wanted to go

to one, wanted to go to the Senior Prom even if it was bourgeois, as Frankie said. She kept the Rally inside her like a memory of rape. It was discussed only once: at a YCL meeting Frankie praised her speech, but claimed that the melee proved the impossibility of collaborating with the ruling class. Katie accepted his praise modestly and disputed his claim, quietly for once.

"Taking that pledge was a perfect collaboration. They need us to tell them what to do, and we need them to do it. If we haven't learned that we haven't learned anything. It's kid stuff, running around just shaking your fist. That pledge wasn't just a gesture, it was—almost wonderful. What happened afterwards— I should have done something. There must've been something I could've done."

What? they all protested. What *could* she have done?

Dialectical materialism said there was an answer for everything: she wished she'd had it in time for the Rally. Not for herself, for her YCL. Their loyalty, like their affection, was stronger than ever, proof that the most progressive heads had the warmest hearts. After the meeting she embraced Frankie *and* the be-Mexican-silvered poetess.

The one other place she felt at home those last days was the composing room. Except for sporting news, the typesetters only read words, not sentences. The linotyper who had set up the Rally story had misspelled the shameful slogan so that it read: ANY PEACE BUT KATIE'S PEACE. She had let it stand: it wasn't the *New York Times*.

"Coffee, fellas?"

It was one in the morning. She was usually ahead of

the boys at that hour and went out for coffee. They began to collect money, but she insisted it was her treat. She hoped she wouldn't blubber when she said good-bye at the end of the week.

Outside the composing room the night air hung gently, misting the street lamps. A lonely trolley clanged by on its forlorn way to the lake. It was almost summer, the empty street was nostalgic already. Like a kid, she ran her hand along the store fronts as she walked toward the Old Dutch Hotel. Its stained-glass canopy made a mosaic pattern on the sidewalk and darkened the shadows before the entrance. Katie clung to the shadows, grateful for them, as Hubbell came down the far bank of marble steps with Dr. Short and the beautiful Mrs. Short.

They'd evidently had a celebration dinner. It couldn't have been over the crew victory, there was no J.J. Something III. Hubbell, of course, was laughing; too much; he was tight. All three were tight, and laughing and so friendly, and going on and on the way boring drunks do about the Shorts wanting to drive Hubbell home and Hubbell wanting to stay and wanting them to stay for just one more. Jesus, why didn't they all go? Or the Shorts go.

The shadows cast by the canopy seemed to be getting lighter and lighter. No matter how tanked they were they would know she'd been eavesdropping if she didn't move and pass by them as though she were a perfectly normal girl with straight hair and a Republican father and poor marks who was coming not from a composing room but from a date. What date could a normal girl have on Main Street at this hour? Oh, God.

"Hey, Katie!" Hubbell was facing her as she tried to walk by with an invisible dog. "What're you selling at this hour?"

"I'm buying."

Much laughter, much blushing, but the Shorts rescued her and offered to drive her home. She explained about the composing room, and Mrs. Dr. said they'd lose the baby sitter permanently unless they went home this minute, Julian; and then they were disappearing down the misty street, gone, and here she was, sitting on the worn, cool marble steps of the elegant Old Dutch Hotel with a tub of fragrant flowers supporting her back and Hubbell Gardiner next to her in a jacket and tie and gray flannels, and each of them somehow holding a big stein of the best beer ever. And it was a soft, gentle, tender, perfect almost-summer night.

"You're celebrating," she said.

He nodded; then nodded again; then spoke. "I sold a short story."

Out of her grabbag of emotions she picked one. "Not to the *New Masses*." Then another. "I'm envious but I'm not jealous." Then just: "Oh, boy, Hubbell!" She raised her beer stein. "To your first novel." They clinked steins and drank.

He leaned back against the tub of flowers, impossibly handsome, impossibly invulnerable, impossible. She should go: he was probably being polite, waiting for her to finish her beer. She took a sip: she was drinking too fast.

"You know what you should've done?" he said suddenly.

"Huh?"

"You should've laughed."

"When?"

"'Any Peace But Katie's Piece.' You were so good. You had them, you would've kept them. If only you had laughed."

She shook her head. "You don't laugh about a thing like that."

"Why not?"

"You wouldn't understand."

"Try."

"You're not a girl."

"I'm not a Puritan, you mean."

"Neither am I!"

He winked. "No humor."

"I'm very funny sometimes!"

"And so angry."

"*I am not angry!*" she shouted, and he laughed, and then she laughed with him. "You always laugh. Why?"

He grinned: she couldn't tell whether or not he was going to kid her. "Well, ma'am," he said in a singsong, "when I was in third grade, the teachers began sending me back and forth with notes. I got out of a lot of work. Back and forth. One teacher would open the note, look at me, smile or laugh, sometimes kiss me, then send me on to another. Finally it dawned they were sending me back and forth with the same note. So I read it. And it said: 'Did you ever *see* such a smile!'" He smiled the famous smile and took a long swallow of beer. "Why are you always angry?"

"I'm not *always*."

"Because you're Jewish? Or poor? Or first genera-tion—are you?"

"All three."

"I'm only one."

102

"Jewish," she said, and they both laughed.

"Poor," Hubbell said.

"Oh, sure! Why is it when you're poor, people think you'll feel better if they say they're poor too?"

"I've had to work my way through school too." He didn't protest, he merely pointed out the fact.

"How?"

"Waiting table, washing dishes, etc."

"In a fraternity, I'll bet. And I *know* you had a scholarship!"

"Angry, angry," he teased. "I'll bet you had one."

"I still had to work!"

"So did I."

"Well, you shouldn't've," she said, and he burst out laughing.

"What a whacked-up kid!"

"I am not a kid!" She *was* angry. "Just because I'm not a drippy coed . . ." She drank some beer to cool herself. "I don't care. If I had long golden hair like Rapunzel and long American Beauty legs, and if I were a Tri Delt and had a dozen cashmere sweaters in all shades, I'd've sat here probably a hundred times by now. So this'd be just another night." She drank. She was talking too much and drinking too much; the big stein was almost empty. "Mrs. Simpson married the Duke of Windsor. It'll be in the paper tomorrow." With an ad for the Prom.

"Bingo for her," Hubbell said.

"And Bingo for Dr. Short," she said. Fortunately, Hubbell didn't seem to have heard. Maybe she hadn't actually said it.

He peered into his stein. She hoped it was fuller than hers. "Know how the world is divided?"

She tried to figure his associative process. "Commoners and kings?"

"Nope."

"Haves and have-nots."

"Nope."

". . . Adults and virgins."

He laughed. "No. Winners and losers."

"That's awful!"

"True, though."

"You're not a serious person!"

"And I never will be." He grinned. "That's why I'm a winner." He downed his beer.

"I guess I'm a loser then."

He looked at her carefully. "You're very smart, so you don't have to be."

She blushed and felt giddy. "Well, what the hell! Opposites attract. But then I'd be the winner and you'd be the loser." She embarrassed herself. "Jesus, me beer! It must be." She finished the last of it and stood up. "Back to the sweatshop. No, coffee shop first. For the boys in the back room."

Her giggle sounded as if she was ready to be put away. She stepped down hard on one foot with the other and almost fell off the step.

"Katie . . ."

She waited, she prayed. Her hand holding the stein began to shake: she set it down on the ledge. "Unaccustomed as I am to beering . . ."

"You *are* a girl."

"Why doesn't anybody know?"

"They will."

"How?"

"You'll tell 'em." He smiled, but differently: sweeter.

He didn't stand up, though, he didn't even shake her hand, just waved a little good-bye. "See you, Katie."

"See you, Hubbell."

She walked away, conscious that her behind was wiggling for the first time.

The theme of the Senior Prom was Dancing Under the Midnight Sun. The huge gymnasium was stripped of the artifacts of athletics and ROTC: what couldn't be moved had been hidden by the Decorating Committee. Snow-capped paper peaks climbed the walls, changing color under an Aurora Borealis of color wheels. Silver-dusted icicles hung down from the roof; the Midnight Sun, an enormous multifaceted mirror ball, spattered the dancers with glitter as it revolved. Huge papier-mâché igloos housed two bandstands for the alternating Big Bands; smaller igloos were rented by checkroom and setup concessions, and by fraternities.

Katie balanced carefully on new high heels in the entrance to a little igloo. She wore a white satin ribbon through her hair, a white satin blouse with her good navy blue skirt, and her first corsage: two white gardenias. The pink patches in her cheeks literally glowed, her eyes literally sparkled. She clasped her hands like a child at her first circus. The North Pole was gorgeous; the music was gorgeous; the girls in their long formals, the boys in their tuxedos or tails—penguins, yes, but gorgeous.

Frankie McVeigh, in a stiff serge suit, ducked out of the igloo. "Boy, am I glad we're not working on commission!" He peered around. "Come inside."

She was searching the sea of dancers. In a circle nearby J.J. Something III—tails flying, sweat running—

was calling the steps for the Big Apple. With his bulging eyes he looked like a black-and-white frog.

"Come on, Katie!"

She ducked under the frosted icicles and followed Frankie behind the sheet-covered table, behind the cases of soda and ginger ale. He thrust a pint bottle of colorless liquid at her.

"What's that?"

"What do you think it is?"

"Scotch?"

"Oh, Katie. *Gin!* Go on."

"From the bottle?"

"Straight!"

"If that isn't bourgeois!"

"It's obviously what *they're* doing!" Frankie pointed to the unsold setups.

"*They're* bourgeois," she said, and took a swig.

Her eyes stung, her throat burned, she coughed into her gardenias, but all in all felt rather glamorous and toddled on her stilts to where she could see the dance floor. There were two or three Big Apple circles, but the other dancers, the other dreamlike couples dipped and swayed and dance-walked through the Westchester like Fred Astaire and Ginger Rogers. The color wheels spun them from one season of light to another; the mirror ball showered them with a rainfall of silver. Katie held her hand out to catch some, then laughed and dipped and swayed by herself. And then she saw Hubbell.

He was in tails, white tie and tails, dancing with a perfect, honey-haired girl poured like cream into a long, perfect dress. Cheek to beautiful cheek, they dipped and swayed with a romantic elegance beyond practice: they flowed to the music. He danced with another perfect girl in a long, filmy, perfect sea-green dress, a wreath of tiny orchids wound around her wrist. They looked perfect together too.

Katie sniffed her gardenias, made sure the pin was holding them to her shoulder. She brushed her blouse, started to straighten her short skirt and, almost audibly, her fantasy shattered and splintered like a broken icicle. The prom was ridiculous; it was a ridiculous waste of money; they were all ridiculous cretins.

"Boy, I'd like to have the sewing concession when they want to shorten those dresses!" she said to Frankie.

"Why would they want to?"

"To get some wear out of them. Where'd you hide the bottle?"

She took a good swallow. "Let's dance."

"Employees aren't supposed to," Frankie said.

She took another swallow and passed him the bottle. "You weren't suppose to buy me a corsage either. Take another drink." He did. "Let's dance."

He took another swallow. "O.K."

He capped the bottle, hid it behind the cases, and led her out of the igloo onto the dance floor. She looked at him: at his red hair carefully slicked down, at his hard blue suit, at his shiny brown shoes; at his intense, bony, freckled face. "Can you, Frankie?" she asked.

He didn't deign to answer. He merely grabbed her and whirled her out among all the long dresses and vaselined penguins—too elaborately at first, perhaps, but, oh, Frankie had a foot for dancing! He dipped and swayed with the best, and neither his hand nor his cheek was sweaty.

Her anger dissolved into gratitude: she was a coed,

a date, a girl. Affection flowed from her into his wiry body, and he danced better than he ever had with his sister. Katie closed her eyes and let him pilot her around the ice floes of the Arctic, Antarctic, North Pole, South Pole. She was in long chiffon and he was in white tie and tails. She inhaled his gardenias and his gin along with perfume from other flowers and atomizers and after-shave bottles, and tobacco and liquor, and under all the familiar smell of gymnasium: four years.

She loved college, and no longer with the desperation of unrequited love. It was her college, her prom. Dancing under her Midnight Sun was better than fantasy—much better, for she opened her eyes and there was Hubbell Gardiner, walking his panther walk through the dancers, coming toward them, toward her. He winked. She squeezed one eye to make it wink back, and moved her glistening cheek away from Frankie's. Hubbell grinned. Her heart thundered with happiness and she grinned back and kept grinning as he continued past her, not really coming very close at all, and disappeared among the dancers, silver flecks from the mirror ball glancing off his blond head.

She shut her eyes quickly against tears and jammed her cheek against Frankie's just as he was turning to see who she'd been smiling at. She pressed her body against his; there was no other way she could follow him: she had begun to tremble. Frankie moved his head to ask what was wrong; she moved hers to stop him from asking, and their lips met.

She broke away—he thought she was going to slap him—and taking him by the hand dragged him through the dancers, off the floor, out of the gym and around to the back where trees and bushes made the darkness darker. High above, colored light filtered through a small window, separating them from the star-strewn sky. Music from inside muffled any sound; soft, warm air enclosed them.

With a fierceness Frankie associated with YCL debates, Katie grabbed him. She embraced him as he, surely, should have embraced her. She clutched him, she kissed him as though there were something in his mouth, behind his lips, behind his teeth, his tongue maybe, but something that could save her life. He pulled away angrily.

"It's *me!*" he said savagely.

"I know it's you!"

The scent of honeysuckle fought the gardenias on her shoulder. She ripped off the corsage just as a girl's high laugh floated out with the music. She plucked at the petals.

"For God's sake, Frankie, there's just got to be a first time!" She glanced up and saw his eyes. "For both of us."

He kicked at the grass. "Here?"

"At least here we've got a band."

He thought about that, then embraced her and began kissing her clumsily. She put her arms around him and, still kissing, they staggered back and forth in a prizefighter clinch until they half-fell, half-sunk to the grass.

Katie undressed like a millionaire: her skirt, her stockings, even her white blouse and her underwear were scattered heedlessly on the grass. Frankie made a neat pile of his jacket, his tie, his shirt. He went to work on his shoes—and knotted a lace. He yanked at it, pulled at it; he couldn't Do It the first time with his shoes on, not with her. The lace broke and he added his shoes to the little pile. Then he turned his back, wriggled out of his trousers, hesitated, and slipped off his baggy shorts. Cautiously he looked over his shoulder.

Her eyes closed, her lips parted in a slight smile, she was lying on the soft grass like Sleeping Beauty, like Juliet, like Rima the Bird Girl. Frankie crawled closer and started to shake. He gripped the earth to control the tremors that shivered through him. It was not only that her body was unexpectedly beautiful, it was unexpectedly sensual: it had to be touched, it had to be kissed. Even Frankie had to put his lips to each breast, to her belly.

"Oh, hey," he whispered. "Oh, my, Katie. You're beautiful!"

She heard the music and held out her arms to a tall dancing partner in white tie and tails. She caressed his shoulders, kissed his mouth, arched her body to meet his, gave herself with such desire and delight and generosity that Frankie never forgot her. But he knew it wasn't he she meant to give herself to, and he never forgot that either.

seven

YEARS LATER in Southern California Katie was finally forced to recognize the existence of Frankie McVeigh, and at a devastating moment. By then she had almost forgotten him. When she thought of the Prom, she thought of Hubbell; when she danced with Hubbell, even if she didn't close her eyes, she saw him in white tie and tails. Dancing with Hubbell was always sexual.

They danced perfectly together at the Savoy-Plaza, at the Stork (only once or twice: she had no desire to revisit college or Rochester either), and at J.J.'s apartment. Dancing at those Beekman Place shindigs, she felt secure because she was in Hubbell's arms and was deaf to the Gang's laughter. Oddly enough, in Southern California it wasn't their laughter that she remembered, but the laughter at the Peace Rally; and the day she remembered it, she was crying for Hubbell.

Since Beekman Place was not to be avoided—"going

to my mother-in-law's," she called it—she applied herself doggedly to laughing at the Gang's jokes. With her sense of justice she expected them to laugh at her jokes in return. But hers had an edge, were off-center and so unexpected (sometimes even to her) that the Gang was usually a beat late.

"Maybe I ought to preface a joke with 'cat'—the way Judianne uses 'bird,'" she said to Hubbell.

"Miaow, miaow." He pulled her closer under the blankets. "They don't want to eat you."

"No, they want to eat you, bird," she said, and blushed when he laughed.

Inside she was hissing like a steam kettle, fuming at herself as well as at them. J.J. had invented another game—"What would you most like to do after the war?"—and she was horrified to realize she was enjoying the war, was afraid of what might happen to her and to Hubbell afterwards.

She had dropped out of the Party completely. Before Hubbell, most of her week-nights were free for meetings and discussions and Study Groups because most of her weekends were spent in the quiet of the OWI office making her casting list, collating the next week's script, filing last week's, plodding through the bureaucratic mass of tedium in Bill Verso's OUT box. "I know there's a war on," she kept saying, "but do they?"

Since Hubbell, her weekends were all Hubbell; and if she took the long, crowded train ride to Washington, they slopped over into Friday preparing and Monday recovering. So she reasoned that she needed week-nights to catch up on work and thus had no time for meetings. Embarrassed, she avoided Stash and Vivian;

went to Harlem for hair straightening without Naomi; shopped without Pony, hunting by herself for inexpensive copies of what the invulnerable beige girls were wearing.

But she simmered; and then a remark overheard in an elevator, what should have been only an insanely ludicrous remark about the "Jewish war to save Communism," started her boiling. She returned a new dress, sent a donation to American-Soviet Friendship, and helped prepare a pamphlet alerting attention to the dangers of the House Committee on Un-American Activities. The Committee had been given permanent standing and a fat appropriation by Congress to continue Rep. Martin Dies's patriotic crusade to save America from subversion.

"Not by Nazis or Fascists, of course," said the Australian teacher from the New School who was supervising. "By Communists. The aim is to smash the Communist Party and revive the propaganda war against the Soviet bogeyman."

"The people we *should* be trying to reach don't give a damn about the Communist Party *or* the Soviet Union!" Katie snapped angrily. She was angry at everybody everywhere.

"They should," the Australian said dryly. "To achieve its goal, the Committee is going to try to intimidate liberals, repress civil liberties, stifle dissent—"

"O.K., O.K." The same old line. It would probably turn out to be true, but she wasn't going to admit that. "Can't we concentrate on the danger to the liberals? God knows there are more of them!"

"Good idea," said the Australian, making her feel guilty.

That weekend she insisted on meeting Hubbell in Washington (where she bought a string of red beads); the next she refused to go near Beekman Place, substituting a Russian movie and a tour of the Lower East Side. Hubbell extended the tour to Mulberry Street and Chinatown; he liked the movie, he liked her beads, he liked the exotic food. Her feet hurt and she felt as though she had put on ten more pounds of guilt until he took her home to bed.

Then one April day turned out so cruel that the steam kettle blew up.

She was at the broadcasting studio. The calendar said spring, but in that air-conditioned vacuum weather was a sound effect. Bill Verso yawned and complained, bored with the war and the series and not making money. He chewed out Harvey the Pencil, who was starting to analyze the phallic shape of microphones for the tenth time when Peggy Vanderbilt walked into the studio and disrupted the rehearsal.

Katie had not cast Peggy on the program since she had accused them, in her maddening little-girl whine, of cutting her part in favor of propaganda against the black market. The actors were acting away at the microphone, but Verso had cut off his speaker and was only pretending to listen. Through the glass control-room window he and Katie and Harvey the Pencil could see Peggy—little fake pink flowers on her little blue hat, on her little blue suit, on her little blue bag—shout at the cast. One of the actresses started to cry.

"What feather has that broad got up her ass now?" Verso said. He flicked on his microphone. "Peggy, we are having a rehearsal, if you don't mind."

She minced up to the actors' microphone in her little

blue shoes and began talking rapidly, a peculiar smile on her face.

"Sweet Jesus," Verso muttered. He flipped the switch and Peggy's whine boomed into the room.

"—telling you, the sonofabitch is dead! Yessir and ma'am," she giggled, "Roosevelt is dead, you Commie bastards! Now it's our turn!"

She put her hands on her hips, laughed, and strutted out the door, her sharp heels echoing over the microphone. Katie began to cry. Some of the men were crying too.

So many people were crying, and so quietly, as she shivered on the platform in Penn Station that evening and waited for Hubbell's train from Washington. She was cold with fear: who would take care of everybody now? She froze with the first frightening realization that she would die and, more frightening, that Hubbell would die.

She could smell fear on the platform. For once the disembarking passengers didn't push and the people waiting for them didn't shove. They didn't complain about the ride, they didn't shout hello, they barely spoke above a whisper; many couldn't because they were in tears. A strange Hubbell came toward her: she remembered her father walking away from her mother's grave. A wave of white steam rolled from under the train, silently shrouding the gray platform, and Hubbell stopped in it. To hide, she thought, but could see his shoulders straighten as though he were winding himself up like a husband doll to help her. He put on his smile and Katie began to cry, thankful he was alive, and ran to the comfort of his arms.

They walked to Beekman Place, passing a dark funeral parlor they had never noticed before. At the dead end of Fiftieth Street, they leaned on the iron railing and stared at the empty river.

"It isn't fair," Katie said. "He won't see the end."

"He knew he won."

"But he won't see it, he won't see Peace."

"Well," Hubbell said after a while, "could be he's lucky."

It was relatively quiet at J.J.'s. Even he was subdued. His glasses rested on top of his head and he kept changing his chair. The beige girls sat all curled up, hugging their knees. The sharpest sound was ice against glass, but nobody was really drinking. Nobody was really doing anything.

The big Air Force Captain sighed. "That fourth term was too much for the old man."

"The third was too much for my old man," J.J. said.

Someone snickered and someone else breathed in relief. Sunday school had to end; soon they could go out in the sun and play.

Carol Ann said, "At least, it'll end the boring yammer about handing Europe over to the Russians."

"It'll end Creeping Socialism, you mean," J.J. corrected.

"Actually, the Prez saved capitalism."

"Oh, come on, Carol Ann!"

"Really, bird!"

"He did! Mummy had this divine economist to dinner and he said—"

Hoots and howls. Katie, sitting stiffly in her chair, listened to the laughter and cries of "Mummy knows best!"

"All right, chums," Carol Ann said pleasantly. "One fine day—"

"One fine day, my bird," Judianne said, "all the arguments will end, please dear God. Along with those dreary Eleanor jokes."

"Oh, some were pretty funny," J.J. said.

"Mildly, mildly."

"The one about her down in the mine with the hillbillies?"

"Oh, yes." Judianne giggled. "That was a goodie."

"Which was that?" the Captain asked. He had started to pitch pennies into his hat.

"Oh, bird, it's ancient! Her face was covered with grime and—"

"Grime, for Chrissake! You're ruining it, Judi!" J.J. hopped up eagerly. "Eleanor goes down into a mine and her face gets all black with coal dust, and these hillbilly miners see those big buck teeth shining in the dark—"

"HER HUSBAND IS DEAD!" She screamed the way she had wanted to scream at his Yiddish-Russian accent in the Collegetown diner. "Yes, Mrs. Roosevelt went down into the coal mines. When they asked her why, she said, 'I am my husband's legs.' He was a cripple! Did you tell the cripple jokes, too? *Is everything just a goddam joke to every goddam one of you?*"

J.J. was still hunched over like Mrs. Roosevelt in the coal mine. Nobody noticed; nobody looked at anybody else. They were accustomed to physical, not emotional vomiting.

"O.K.," Hubbell said lightly. "Now let's all have a drink. Dubonnet, Katie?"

"I'd rather have a martini, bird."

117

"While you're up, Hubbell." Carol Ann held out her glass and smiled at Katie.

The Captain began to do push-ups. "Say," he asked from the floor, "who makes up jokes, anyway?"

"I have the whole scoop," Judianne drawled. "Mummy had this divine jokemaker to dinner—"

The laughter was too quick and too loud, but J.J. turned on the phonograph and Carol Ann got out the backgammon and banter resumed.

"While you're up, bird." Katie held out her empty martini glass to Hubbell. She sat on a sea-green silver bar stool, her knees crossed jauntily, one leg swinging. "Scads of swell material here for a good novel. If you want to write a really good novel, that is. You know, like one by, oh, say, Michael Arlen; Louis Bromfield; Joseph Hergesheimer. Someone really spiffy. Thanks: cheers!" She gulped half the new martini. "Or John O'Hara. He also wrote a good *first* novel. And he sure appreciates the fancy folk."

"So did Fitzgerald."

"Oh, right-o! Of the *Saturday Evening Post* Fitzgeralds. And then you can go to Hollywood and die of booze."

"I can do that right here." Hubbell smiled, but his dark-blue eyes were almost black.

"Oh, but you are doing that here, though not from booze, I will admit," she trilled gaily. "The reason you can't tell—you do stir a mean martini, bird—is that they're all dead too. See that black thing? You think it's a sofa, but actually that's a coffin J.J. had custom made just for you."

"Knock it off, Katie!"

His voice was sharp. He scared her. She knew precisely how she was behaving, but if she softened, if she relented, she was lost and then he, of course, would be lost too.

She finished the martini and held out the glass. "While you're up," she said charmingly.

The taste wasn't great, but she was mad about the effect, so she had several more. Hubbell didn't have to carry her home. She was dead drunk, but he only had to guide her. She walked by herself, as though she were embalmed, and laid herself neatly on the bed, hands folded on her breast as though she were in a casket.

She woke just before dawn to find he had gone back to Washington.

"I've been doing a lot of thinking," Hubbell said when he came up the following weekend. He didn't take off his uniform, not even the jacket.

"Look!" she cried too gaily, "I didn't wait for New Year's Eve, I have my resolutions all typed up now! I'm joining AA, I'm only going to talk with my hands, I'm going to take a course at the New School in laughing—"

"Katie."

She could imagine him sitting like that at a Pentagon conference.

"Now who's being serious?"

He let himself be kissed. "I am."

"Well, can't you be comfortable and serious? Take your shower and get into your civvies—"

"I'm going up to J.J.'s."

In a white-and-red convertible. She was back under

the sycamore where she belonged, where she'd always known he would leave her. Miracles didn't last either.

"It's not because of your blowup the other night," Hubbell said. "I'm largely to blame for that. And for your leaving the Party. Although there I'll take credit. Not that I'm against the Party. I just think you're too individual to be a good member of any party." His grin was shaky, as though he had rehearsed it, like his speech, in the window of the Washington train, and then lost part of both in the taxicab to Murray Hill. "But you *are* deeply committed to what you *do* care about, and you're unhappy unless you *do* something. Because of me, you've been trying to lay out, but that's wrong, Katie. Wrong for you. I'm wrong for you."

Gentile gentility: meaning she was wrong for him. Any piece but Katie-peace.

"Commitment is part of you, Katie. Part of what makes you attractive, part of what attracted me to you."

Past tense. The past is always present, and waiting to laugh. Like J.J. and the beige girls.

"It still does. Sometimes I wonder if I don't envy it but—you know in college I used to go around saying I wasn't a serious person."

And therefore a winner. Said on the palace steps to a mangy alley cat. Well, hair could be straightened, but to him, who knew you when, it was still and always a mangy frizz.

"To you 'not serious' meant frivolous. J.J. thought it meant I was really very serious, philosophically. Dr. Short just thought it was a cover." He shrugged. "Well, I was really educated in the Pacific and got my Master's at the Pentagon; and I am now firmly devoted to the Virtues and Pleasures of Being Unserious. Political activity is literally for the birds, Katie. It's pointless because it's futile. Getting involved is a game for losers."

One in which she was an expert. She had always been losing him; he had always been driving away in that convertible, running away across the campus green, dancing away at the Prom, walking away at J.J.'s to Carol Ann, to someone who belonged to the Gang.

"Remember Pony Dunbar's friend, Skipper? He said we were just waiting to gang up on Russia. Well, he turns out to be right. I don't know how much Roosevelt knew, but the Pentagon didn't wait for him to be buried in Hyde Park, they didn't have to. Oh, the Russians are just as busy with their gang-up. Skipper would say they're doing it in self-defense. But that's what we say we're doing. One system is only comparatively better than any other, Katie. They all lie, they all share the same goal: self-perpetuation. Put a good guy in power any place, he inevitably becomes the bad guy . . ."

He was wrong, but to argue would be to end up behind another gym with another Frankie McVeigh or in the orange bedroom with another Stash. The excuse of Roosevelt and Russia was pushing Hubbell out of that bedroom, leaving her alone with the Three Sisters, who would never fall on her head again.

"I sound as though I'm trying to convert you, and I'm not. That's *really* a losing game." Hubbell smiled. "But, Katie, you do keep trying to convert me. And that's wrong, wrong for me. Your friends are as wrong for me as mine are for you. Oh, alone we're fine—but we can't stay in this room."

Recall all spies, comrades: the secret weapon has become unspectacular from overuse.

"Yes, I'd write, and you'd help. But if I wrote a mystery, you'd want an evil rich son of a decadent capitalist bitch to be the murderer, and I'd want nobody to care. You wouldn't be proud and I'd feel that I failed."

But his typewriter, like her beads, had just gathered dust while they went partying at J.J.'s. Where she, in a new beige dress, if she laughed at funerals and cripples, could go home with him.

"Skipper said everything is politics. I suppose that includes how you live. It's how you want to live, Katie, how you have to live. Not me. That's really why we're wrong for each other. That's why it won't work."

And now a moment of silence. Black widow weeds by P. Dunbar Rejects & Co.

Katie appraised her new pumps: the heels were halfway between the spikes she had worn to the Prom and the little-girl flats for under the sycamore.

"Beekman Place is right for you, I gather," she said coldly. "My commitment is so attractive, you run to that perennial fraternity house party. Jesus, they're as committed as that tin mobile in the vestibule—pardon, foyer!"

"Oh, they're committed to having a good time," he joked.

"Oh, that's the attraction! I'll bet you like that mobile!"

He laughed. "No. But, Katie, nobody's asking me to. That's the attraction. There's no pressure."

They were too secure to press. When she worked in the Collegetown diner she neither joked nor sat down with the customers. She got smaller tips but more respect.

"I was too easy for you."

"No, Katie."

"I was."

"No! Girls these days are easy for anyone. You were easy only for me. I know that."

"I don't mean sexually. I mean like everything always is." Anger was prowling around in her throat. "Including me."

"No," he said again. "You've never been easy, that's the damn trouble! *You* pressure me. You don't ask, you don't demand, but you *look!* Even when we're asleep I feel you looking and I feel I'm falling short. It's no good, Katie; for me, for you. We're wrong for each other—"

"O.K., we're wrong. You've made the point fifty times, don't belabor it." So long as she didn't look at him she could manage her voice. "But please don't blame it on my being politically committed."

"I said what Skipper meant—"

"A real commitment, a personal commitment, *that's* what you don't want."

"No," he said very gently. "I don't. I'm not ready—"

"*Ready!*" She wheeled on him. He had got his hair cut, but she had not touched it. She wanted to kiss his hair, his mouth; she thought wildly of improvements she wanted to try on positions he had taught her. She wanted him so badly she began to yell and shout and scream.

"You'll never be ready for me because I don't fit on

Beekman Place! *That's what's really wrong!* All that crap about politics and commitment and Russia—I am so sick of Russia! *I* don't belong, that's what it is! You've had me, you've had enough of me, and you want to end it like a goddam gentleman and get your ass up to Beekman Place where you don't belong either! You're too good for them! But J.J., that doormat, that pimp dangles Judianne and Carol Ann—who is only half-Jewish, by the way—and every other goddam Ann in front of your nose like carrots in front of a rabbit! Which you are! But what the hell! Laughs, having a good time, that's what you want! Banging them, that's your good time! Well, go ahead, go on, get the hell out!"

She was trembling so violently she had to sit in the hard chair by the desk and hold on to the seat. His stack of manuscript was still no thicker than the story Dr. Short had read aloud in the sunny classroom: "But of course, even if they had wanted to change, by then they were too lost or too lazy."

Hubbell came over and sat on the arm of the sofa. She turned her head away.

"I'm not going like this," he said quietly.

"But you're going. As soon as I calm down you're going."

She went away from him, to the window, where she pulled the shade on the soft weather.

"I don't want any of those girls, Katie. But I can't take what I do to you."

"Or what I do to you."

"No."

"Oh dear oh dear oh dear." She turned and smiled at him. "A kamikaze combination."

"What is?"

"You; me; love and sex. What idiotic things I said. And such language. They'd never know me in Rochester." She pulled the shade up. "O.K., Hubbell. I'm calm now. You can go."

His clothes were there, his typewriter was there, his manuscript was there: he would have to come back.

"Shall I take my things now or would you rather I sent over for them tomorrow?"

Now she wanted him to go quickly.

"Oh, you don't have very much. I'll pack it up and leave it with J.J.'s doorman."

She didn't hear what he said after that. She did hear the clink of his key on the glass-topped coffee table and the click of the door opening and closing. She went into the orange bedroom and opened the closet. He really didn't have much, mainly some shirts and cotton pants she had washed and ironed during the week. There was a uniform, though, which was wrinkled from his body and had the smell of his after-shave lotion. She buried her face in it, then put her arms around it, and then she began to cry as though her heart would break.

There were no sleeping pills in the medicine cabinet because Katie had never needed any. The shuddering wreck wandering around the apartment tried a couple of aspirin, but they didn't help: she still couldn't stop crying. Unable to remember what time Hubbell had left, she didn't even know how long she had been at it. The electric clock in the little red kitchen said it was two in the morning. She *must* be dehydrated; it was physically impossible to have any more tears. But they kept pouring out.

She mixed a martini, dropped the glass in the sink and cut her finger picking out the pieces. Fresh tears and a fresh martini. This one she promptly threw up. She gargled, brushed her teeth, washed her face, looked at it in the bathroom mirror, and the great racking sobs started anew.

"Oh, stop it!" Katie said to the blotched face. "Do something constructive, for God's sake!"

She took out shampoo for her hair. When she was under the shower with the orange-and-yellow curtain neatly drawn to protect the bathroom floor, she realized she had all her clothes on; so she got out and realized she had forgotten to wash her hair, and started crying all over again.

She dried herself thoroughly, combed her nice straight hair, put on a robe, and sat in his chair in the living room. She relived every moment she'd had with him, rearranging her behavior, sometimes making herself better than she had been, more often making herself worse. She wrote and rewrote endless letters in her mind. And kept on crying.

When she could not stand the pain any more, she broke her resolution and called him at Beekman Place. She put a handkerchief over the mouthpiece to disguise her voice for J.J., but there was a flicker of justice in the world: Hubbell answered himself.

"It's me," Katie said, and then couldn't speak for a full thirty seconds, forcing control, forcing the tears to dry up and stay where they goddam belonged so that her voice could form words distinctly.

"Listen, Hubbell . . . this is kind of peculiar. I know I don't have to apologize for what I said because I know you know, and—" She covered the telephone to muffle a shuddering sob. "And you also know that I feel, well, not exactly bright-eyed and bushy-tailed, as J.J. would say. Anyway, the peculiar thing, Hubbell, it's really a request, a favor. I can't sleep, Hubbell"— she was crying openly now, but there was nothing to do but plow on—"I'm just, I don't know where I am, Hubbell, but it would help if I could talk to someone, if I had a best friend to talk about it with. But you're my best friend, Hubbell, isn't that sad? Oh, not sad, dumb. You're the best friend I ever had, and you know him. So it would help so much if you could just come over and see me through tonight. I won't do anything, I won't touch you or beg you or embarrass you. I just want to talk to my best friend, about our best friend—oh God, Hubbell, please could you come over right away, please?"

He did.

When she opened the door she had stopped crying. "Thank you, Hubbell," she said politely.

He only glanced at her swollen, miserable face. She knew that was because he didn't want to embarrass her. But she sensed or hoped she sensed that it might also be because he wanted to hold fast and not take her in his arms.

"Here," he said.

"What are they?"

"Sleeping pills."

"Isn't one enough?"

"No."

"I'm scared."

"Take them both."

"Will you stay till I fall asleep?"

"That's why I brought this." It was a chilled bottle of their favorite white wine.

"Oh, thank you. I'll open it."

"You sit down." He opened the wine, got out the glasses he had given her, poured for both of them. The whole city was quiet. "I'm sorry, Katie."

"So am I. For dragging you into it. Of course, that's what best friends are for, but you're caught in the middle. I mean you're his best friend too."

"Right now, I'm more your friend."

"There's something I want to ask. I assume he told you everything."

"He never tells quite everything." Hubbell grinned. "Even to me."

"That's what I mean. I mean—those pills are making me drunkish instead of sleepy."

"Stop drinking the wine like water."

"O.K." She put her glass down on the coffee table obediently. "He gave me a lot of reasons, but I think he left out the real one." She tried to breathe quietly. "It's because I'm not attractive enough, isn't it?"

"Oh, Katie," he said.

"Oh, I know I'm attractive. Sort of. Well, with my clothes off, anyway—"

"Katie—"

"I'm not fishing. I'm attractive; I am I am; O.K. But I mean, not in the right way. I don't have the right style for him, do I?"

The room was too small for the clutter. She took a gulp of wine. "Be my friend," she asked. "I'm not attractive enough for him, am I?"

"No," he said, so nicely she thought for a moment he had said yes. "You don't have the right style for him.

You see, no one will ever ask: what is he doing with Carol Ann, Judianne, with any of those girls. And the girls will never ask: what is he doing with me? what is he doing with himself? They all eat oysters, Katie, it's all easy. Living has got to be easy."

"I know it does," she agreed quickly. "But I've been changing my style—"

"But he doesn't want that on his back." She didn't really understand that. "He's seen you trying to be like those Brenda Fraziers up at J.J.'s, to turn Katie into Katherine, but you shouldn't. You're your own girl, you have your own style. You're Katie attractive, Katie marvelous—"

"What's the good of being Katie attractive if I can't have him? *Why* can't I have him? . . . Why?"

He filled his own glass and drank. "Because you're a challenge. Every minute. Except in bed."

"Jesus." But she was flattered, she liked it, she felt powerful.

"I'm serious."

"You are?" she teased.

He smiled. "I am and you are. He isn't and doesn't want to be. And he doesn't want to be challenged."

"Doesn't he!" She was getting strong or drunk on the combination of wine and pills. "Well, he's a fool! He'll end up a loser. He cares so much about winning —with me, he could really win! Sure I make waves: you have to, he has to! I'll keep making 'em until he's every wonderful thing he should be! Will be!" She laughed. "I don't care if I am tight. He'll never find anyone as good for him as I am! He'll never find anyone to love him as much as—"

"Katie, he knows that."

"*You* know that!"

"Yes."

"Then stop playing! I'm not a goddam game!"

"And I'm not a goddam cause!" he shouted back. "Sit down before you fall down! You're the damn fool! Your causes always lose. You think if I come back you'll win. You won't. You'll change, you'll lose! For Chrissake, Katie, don't you understand that I'll win and I don't want to?"

"I will," she said very quietly. She knew her eyes had that old, fierce glitter, so she lowered them. "But you will too. Couldn't we both win, Hubbell?"

"No, you love me too much!"

"That's my problem! Take advantage, what've you got to lose? You can't lose, you said so yourself. Please, Hubbell."

It was light outside. He turned off the lamp. She watched as he looked around the dim yellow room, at the patterned sofa they made love on, at the gold carpet they made love on; at his typewriter; at the three copies of his novel she had got from the publisher. He walked to the window and pulled the curtain aside.

"Nobody really takes advantage of anybody," he said at last, sounding very weary. "And I suppose nobody ever really wins."

"You do."

"Somebody's getting up." He let the curtain drop and turned to her. "Aren't you sleepy yet?"

"You are."

"Exhausted. All this emotion is very un-American."

"It's Jewish." Katie grinned at him. He laughed and

kissed her gently on the eyelids. She wanted to hold him, but she knew she shouldn't yet. "Are you staying?"

"I guess so," he said.

"Well, then," she said with a timid smile, "I guess you love me. Sort of."

"Not sort of, and you know it." His voice snapped and crackled. "You knew it when I came back."

She heard the last echoes of anger, but she didn't care. Nothing was impossible, not past, not present, and certainly not future. She put her arms around him and he kissed her.

"Oh God, Katie," Hubbell said. She felt she had been caught cheating, but then he said, "Well, let's go to bed," and the end did justify the means. With her, he had to live happily ever after.

They went to sleep in the orange bedroom, taking turns at holding each other.

By the time they were married and living in Southern California, she really had changed her style.

eight

THE SUN WAS endless. It bleached the wide-open sky, blanched every room it invaded. Katie wore sunglasses even for reading.

She skimmed the last pages, then plopped the book on her desk. There was nothing to say, not even that it would make a rotten movie. She took off the dark glasses, lit a cigarette, decided on Alaskan king crab for lunch. The rapid clacking of typewriters told her it was at least another twenty, twenty-five minutes.

There were about half a dozen other readers pecking away. The battered room took her back ten years to the YCL meeting room at college. Same creaks, same smells, but these windows overlooked the studio commissary and a sound stage whose glaring white wall worked like a sleeping pill. A glance down to the small mortuary encroaching on the commissary revived her: its owner had spurned varying amounts of movie money, claiming his business would last longer. She was positive he was right.

The other typewriters were clicking out reports on bad novels and plays which presumably might make good movies. After her first months as a reader, Katie had been willing to bet Hubbell that the reports were never read. So she switched to résumés of favorite books, and inserted recipes, travel plans, French lessons, carbons of letters to her father in Rochester, obituaries of living studio executives, etc. More recently she had been amusing herself with résumés of idiot stories of her own invention.

"I wrote an absolute doozy!" she had bragged to Hubbell over their martinis the week before.

"Le six heure, c'est seulement pour le martini and le français." Their teacher said Hubbell had a charming South American accent, but Katie's grammar was better.

"Oh, it's too hot to speak French. Anyway, my story takes place in China." Probably because of the forum on China at the Unitarian Church downtown. Stash and the girl he was living with had dragged her along on one of the nights Hubbell had to work at the studio. She hadn't bothered to tell him: she didn't care all that much about the Chinese Revolution either.

"China?" Hubbell squinted at the sun on the ocean in front of their rented house. "Well, the public's fed up with Westerns, so I guess it's time we had an Eastern."

"It's called 'Shivouth'—exclamation point."

"Ah so. Very Eastern."

"It's about this kibbutz of Chinese Jews living in a rice *paddy* and the girl makes Communist rice *patties*.

133

Well, the boy gets the brilliant idea of calling them—"

"Matzohs."

"Oh, you read the book!"

But Hubbell didn't laugh. He took her hand and said, "Why don't you quit being a reader?"

"Because I'm laying a nice little nest egg for our villa in France."

"Italy."

"France!"

"Spain?"

"Never! Jamais, jamais!" She laughed, but whenever they went over their plans for living in Europe she was adamant that she would never set foot in Spain so long as that bastard Franco was in power.

Filing her nails in the cell for readers, she rejected a Spanish sequel to "Shivouth!" in favor of another rave for Jane Austen's *Sense and Sensibility* with a few sexual hijinks thrown in. The other machines were still clacking, so she appended casting suggestions from the studio's animated cartoon figures until it was at long last time for lunch.

She stopped first in the ladies' room for her ritual of not looking in the big mirror, washing her hands, drying her hands, taking her comb from her bag, always slightly fearful that it might be one minute past pumpkin-coach midnight. But when she did face the stranger in the mirror she sighed in relief. She still looked as though she had always driven in convertibles with the top down, as though she swam and sailed (she did: Hubbell had taught her on their honeymoon in St. Thomas), as though she played tennis (lessons were improving her game rapidly). Unlike most of the women she knew, she wore almost no makeup, her clothes were of unusual colors, and her soft wavy hair was gathered loosely with a tortoise shell barrette. She did wear earrings, though: pearl buttons just covering her lobes. In a drawer were some silver hoops she had bought in Mexico. She wore them only once, to a black tie wingding at J.J.'s. For old times, she claimed.

Her dark glasses—protection against more than the sun—were back in place as she walked slowly down the outside flight of wooden stairs leading to the studio street. She was dawdling because Hubbell might still be working, either in his office or on the set. He was rewriting a movie which George Bissinger was already shooting. He and Hubbell had scored with Hubbell's first screenplay (from his second novel): Hubbell was now Bissinger's boy, his protégé, his Midas touch. They were already planning their next film; Katie took lessons on Bissinger's tennis court; they all had dinner a couple of times a week. Well, the food was good and she liked Bissinger's wife Vicki even though she felt sorry for her.

She was halfway down the wooden stairs when the door to the sound stage opposite opened and a tall towhead in white tie and tails came out. Her heart jumped into her face. A moment later Hubbell came out the same door. He saw her almost instantly, and if the sun hadn't been so dazzling, she would have seen that the look on his face mirrored hers.

He waved and she came running to meet him.

"Lunch?" she asked after he kissed her.

"Can't. George wants more changes." They were walking toward Hubbell's office.

"'Too much dialogue, son.'" She did a good imitation of Bissinger.

"No. Now it's: 'too elliptical, son.'"

"He's getting crass. Doesn't he know the more obscure the more chance of someone calling him an artist?"

"He wants a change of pace." Hubbell grinned.

"Ha ha. To what?"

"To what he calls 'pure emotional vomit.' They have to vomit right after lunch."

They entered the Writers Building, conscious of looking like a leading man and a leading lady who should be going into Makeup. Katie kept her dark glasses on.

"I wonder how much he does care about his picture," she said.

"Well, certainly more than he does about Vicki."

"Or the kid?"

"Maybe. What've you got for the board?"

The cork bulletin board was the only personal item in Hubbell's office. Katie thumbtacked a headline STARLET DUCKS FLYING SAUCER next to GEORGE BRENT'S COUSIN HIT BY FALLING ROCK. She knew why Hubbell had changed the subject: she wanted a baby, he wanted a horse. When he had time he rented one from a stable up the coast near Zuma. He would ride carefully down the cliffs, then canter and gallop for miles along the shore, stripped to the waist, wearing blue jeans and sneakers.

"It doesn't cost all that much to feed a horse," he argued.

"We're saving to live in Europe. If you want to get there—no horse."

"If you rode with me just once—"

"No."

"Why not?"

"Because you don't want me to."

He kissed her. "Do you mind?"

"No," she said, and meant it. "You ride the beach, I walk the beach. But no horse."

And no baby until they got to Europe. Well, she was really in no hurry; she was really in no hurry for anything.

"I think I'll see if Paula's free for lunch," she said languidly to Hubbell. She was still stretched out on the cracked leather couch in his office. He had got up and was rolling a sheet of yellow paper into his shiny typewriter.

"Mmm."

"And afterwards I might get her to help me with my French. Or I might help her blow up the post office. We'll toss a coin."

"Mmm. See you."

He had that glazed look and was starting to type away, so she went out into the cool, highly polished corridor which two middle-aged women were washing and polishing. They stared. Probably the dark glasses. Everybody wore dark glasses, anybody might be a star.

"Kate, baby!"

"J.J., good fellow well met."

He protruded his head for a kiss, and she turned hers to avoid the hot blast of pepperminted breath. J.J.'s hairline was above the equator of his sunburned head, but he had lost twenty pounds between sauna and massage, and looked collegiate in his cashmere sport jacket and his gray flannels and his pastel bow tie.

"Lunch?" She figured he couldn't, but she'd get credit. Still, since the day of her wedding, when she discovered J.J. wanted to belong even more than she did, Katie had stopped resenting him and started feeling sorry for him. Occasionally she even liked him.

"Oh, gee, thanks, Kate. But I'm going brown-nosing in the exec dining room. I've just got to get an assignment." J.J.'s first and only production had been Hubbell's novel, directed by and thus produced by George Bissinger. "This morning I cut myself shaving and bled chicken soup."

She stared as though she were waiting for the punch line. But his secretary had laughed.

"Now that isn't anti-Semitic, Kate. Is it?"

"Oh, mildly. But it's such an *old* joke, J.J."

"Gee. I thought I made it up. Honestly! Well, thanks for telling me."

She straightened his bow tie. "Bringing Annette Sunday?"

"No. She went and got herself engaged to department-store money. But I'm going to ask a sensational girl! Jeanne Twitchell. You'll like her, Kate. I hear she's very smart."

A telephone rang and he jerked open the door to his office, which was almost directly opposite Hubbell's on the good side, the young producers' side of the corridor. In the little outer room, his horse-playing (and resembling) secretary shook her head at him; in the large inner room, his furniture stood like a display window awaiting a customer. He pushed his glasses on top of his head and gestured toward Hubbell's door. "Who's going to produce his next?"

"You know he's trying to get it for you."

"Sure. Oh, I don't really give a merry shit. It'll be a Bissinger production anyway."

His phone rang again and he dashed inside hopefully. She walked down the corridor, knocked on a door on the not-good side, and went into Paula Reisner's office.

"Lunch?"

"Oh, Kate darling, I can't! My genius director wants changes by yesterday." Paula spoke five languages fluently with an unplaceable accent in each, including her own. She was in her early sixties, a red-and-gray-haired woman with the big-boned remains of a sexual body.

"Your plants need watering?"

"No, thanks Got. You drown them anyway." She was writing in pencil on a long yellow legal pad; later she would dictate to a stenographer from the bullpen.

"Mind if I have coffee?"

"Bitte."

In size and shape the office was a duplicate of Hubbell's, but Paula was practiced in making a home for herself anywhere. There were homemade curtains and slip covers whose patterns didn't quite match but were cheerful; thriving plants; a hot plate on which coffee was always brewing; and a profusion of autographed photos of every writer and composer who had come to Hollywood in flight from Germany and the occupied countries. And of several Americans who could be counted on for the generosity of their donations, if not always for the distinction of their work.

Similar photographs were scattered around Paula's small, disjointed, Hansel-and-Gretel house in Laurel Canyon, first stop for all refugees. She provided whatever they needed: beds, food, money (if she had it); English lessons (which resulted in some surrealist dialogue in a few films); and, most of all, a center where the intelligentsia, American and European, could share their exile.

Paula herself was an early anti-Fascist refugee. She had once been an actress in Berlin, or maybe it was Warsaw, or Vienna; or she had done operetta in the Ukraine; or she had directed a theatre in Leipzig or Budapest. Anyway, she *had* translated American and English plays into her various languages—which somehow got her to Hollywood as dialogue coach for foreign lady stars. Then she dug up story ideas for the foreign ladies. Now she was a screenwriter for them.

"Without a drop of talent!" She shook when she laughed. "But a marvelous memory for Molnar!"

Hubbell liked her even before she read his first novel and praised it extravagantly.

"A born novelist!"

"And then he grew up." Hubbell laughed.

Katie slumped in the big, overstuffed chair near Paula's desk and yawned over her coffee. Paula put her pencil down on her yellow pad.

"Hubbell also is making changes for genius?"

"Yes. Magnin's is having a sale. I think I'll go." But she put her head back against the chair and closed her eyes as though something hurt. Her tan always had a healthy, reddish tinge, making it seem new. Paula claimed the best tans were on people who were mindless or trying to be.

"My genius is ersatz," Paula said. "So I screw him and go to lunch with you!"

They went to Frascati's on Sunset in Katie's always clean white convertible with shiny red leather upholstery. They chose Frascati's because it was open-air rather than air-conditioned, and because the smog hadn't crept up past Hollywood and Vine.

"And I'll have another martini, but really dry this time, please," Katie said to the waitress, who didn't like to wait on women. And to Paula: "Oh, of course the Loyalty Oath is bad, but Truman is just a political hack. He wears a belt and suspenders."

"Yes! Hiroshima was his belt and Nagasaki his suspenders!" Paula could shift effortlessly from calm to passion. "He uses troops to break strikes—and arranges for his daughter to squeak with symphony orchestras!"

"Now, Paula, let poor Margaret alone."

"If she weren't the President's daughter—"

"It's a free country."

"Freedom of speech, not freedom to sing like a bullfrog! And it is no longer a free country when there is a Loyalty Oath! When Hitler—"

"This is not Germany, Paula."

"Not yet, thanks Got! But in Munich in thirty-seven, just before I came here—or was I in Basle already? Oh, darling Kate. I remember clearly all the days before I started to run. But since? The years are so mixed up! Where in hell was I ten years ago? Do you know where you were?"

"In college." Saving tinfoil for Spain. Or had Spain already been replaced by the Peace Strike? The months were blurred—or was everything blurring?

"Well, it is very chic to dismiss Mr. Truman as a petit bourgeois bore," Paula said, "but mean, petty little men can get very dangerous in a big chair. That other little shit, Mr. J. Parnell Thomas and his goddam Un-American Committee have poor Gerhardt Eisler en route to jail; they're hunting Hans and poor Brecht."

She shook her head. "Well, you will hear all about it for yourself—"

"I wish it weren't Friday night." Katie fished her checkbook from her bag. "We have to go to Bissinger's."

"My ragout is a damn sight better than his lousy barbecue."

"We have to, Paula."

"Hubbell has to. Let him go alone."

"He's much too attractive." She grinned; Paula ate a piece of celery. "Can I make this out to cash?" Paula's look irritated. "No, that's *not* why, Paula! But if I keep insisting we can't spare the money for him to buy a horse—"

"All right, all right. But it would do you good to come to me Friday, Kate. And Hubbell will be perfectly safe at Bissinger's."

Katie waved the check dry and handed it over. She lit another cigarette, held the match for Paula, finished her martini.

"You don't find him attractive, do you?" she asked.

"He's very good-looking."

"But not attractive."

"Darling, I am a European. Come to the meeting."

"I can't." Her voice was icy. For the first time it occurred to her that Hubbell might not be the most desirable man in the world.

She took her tennis lessons on Bissinger's court from a toast-colored California boy named Noel Watson who had the face of a startled bunny. He had never gone beyond the junior championship but was a good, unruffled teacher, and Bissinger insisted everyone take lessons on his court. The year before there had been a young welterweight who gave everybody boxing lessons until Bissinger broke the nose of his neighbor's son, who was sixteen and a half.

He lived in a big old Tudor mansion on an estate which was thickly wooded for Beverly Hills. In the large, polished-mahogany bar–billiard room off his huge manorial drawing room an enormous, authenticated Matisse could be electrically lowered to uncover the screen on which he showed movies. There was more than enough room to raise the Matisse; Bissinger enjoyed the symbolism of lowering it. A winding path through eucalyptus and golden oaks led from the house to his grand tennis court, which was sunk below a pool-and-tennis house that would have brought joy to a family of four. The Olympic-size pool was fed by a gigantic Italian marble fountain.

Bissinger was a long skinny cat with a sudden crest of pure-white hair which he cultivated like a rare plant. In his early fifties, he had a courtly Edwardian manner abetted by Edwardian-rancher clothes. He spoke very, very gently and was considered cynical.

Katie's lesson on Saturday was a short one on serving because she and Hubbell were to play doubles against Bissinger and Noel. Bissinger wore a King Gustaf of Sweden outfit plus a big white Panama hat.

"Ready to get trounced, little Kate?"

"No, George, but I'm ready to play."

"At long last. Good day, gentlemen." Bissinger snaked a long arm around Katie's waist and made a mock start to the tennis house with her. Before releasing her, his hand seemed to slip up to her breast.

That helped her game. She concentrated very hard

and didn't once stop to admire Hubbell. He was very proud of her and swooped her up in his arms when she won set point for them with a line drive right past Bissinger.

Out of the broiling sun, in the shadowy tennis house, Noel bartended before they all showered. Katie purred; Hubbell stretched from a rafter; Bissinger prowled and toweled his soaking hair.

"You're old-fashioned, son," he told Hubbell with soft regret. "It was *my* lost generation that went off to Europe to write novels."

"We're just going to live there, George."

"Oh? I would have thought screenplays would leave a young writer most eager to write something all his own, something he truly liked."

Hubbell did another chin-up before dropping gracefully to the floor. "Well, you know, dad," he said in a matching soft, gentle voice, "there are truly only two reasons for writing: to enjoy yourself or to make money. I'm lucky: I'm doing both."

Bissinger chuckled. "If you won't let me bait you, son, I may turn on you."

Hubbell grinned. "You won't turn on me, George, unless I turn in a bad script."

"Or keep beating me at tennis."

"He's just a winner, George," Katie said lazily. "We all have to live with that."

"I wonder does he take anything seriously except games."

"Oh, one or two things."

"Such as?"

"My wife," Hubbell said.

"And the horse," Katie said, and she and Hubbell laughed.

"Here's Vicki!" Noel announced happily.

She came down the path under the leafy awning of sun and shade, a very young, solemn, madonna-like beauty with her solemn, sturdy two-year-old son.

"You missed your lesson!" Noel ran to meet her. They looked like two beige fauns under the deep-green leaves.

Vicki Bissinger had been a cellist in the studio orchestra before she married George; except for a few chamber music evenings at Paula Reisner's, she rarely played any more. She refused a nurse for her child; she gardened; she played longhair music on the phonograph in her pale-pink bedroom; she isolated herself at Beverly Hills parties, examining paintings as though she were a retoucher. She was considered sweet, mysterious and frigid.

She sat close to Katie and watched Hubbell toss her baby in the air.

"What a crazy birthday party I took him to." Her eyes saddened everything she said. "All the parents were divorced and remarried so many times. One poor little thing had two mothers and three fathers there. The children were awfully confused; they didn't know who to call mummy and who to call daddy."

"Perfectly normal for this village," Bissinger said.

"What'd they do?" Katie asked.

"Oh, just called everyone mummy and daddy. Even each other."

"How many of my wives were there?" Bissinger asked.

"Three. Including me."

"I've only had two."

"You've had five, dad."

"I don't count annulments, son."

The baby high in the air over Hubbell's head laughed joyously. Katie had never heard Vicki laugh.

"He's so beautiful," she said.

Vicki looked at them. "Yes. He is."

Bissinger uncoiled from the bamboo lounge chair and reached for his son. "This is the sole excuse for marriage," he said, lifting the boy higher in the air than Hubbell could.

The child's head knocked against the rafter. He screwed up his face to cry, vetoed tears, and punched his father in the face instead.

Katie held on to Vicki, who turned to Hubbell. But Bissinger chuckled. "Tough little gent. Does what his mother would like to do." Very gently he lowered the boy to the floor.

"How about batting some balls around, Vicki?" Hubbell asked.

"She missed her lesson," Noel murmured.

"Come on, little George," Katie said, taking the child by the hand, "let's watch Mummy and Uncle Hubbell beat the crap out of Daddy and Noel."

Bissinger invited them to dinner and a two-tent party in Encino, but Hubbell said they were busy. They weren't. He had a perverse consistency Katie adored. He would go anywhere any night during the week "because everyone has to get up early to get to the studio, and we get home early. But Saturday, Christ, that's the lumberjack's night out! It's that same R.F., only under tents."

So Saturday nights they stayed home. He barbecued

while she experimented with vegetables, and they got to sleep very late.

They lived in a ramshackle section of the old Malibu colony, a section where movies were only something to go to if it rained. It was the vacation village Katie had yearned for on summer days when there was nothing to do but poke around her father's candy store. There was a shaded, not too lumpy tennis court (Bissinger's was concrete) which surely belonged to someone but which anyone could use; and she had to maneuver at ten miles an hour between bicycles and go-carts when she drove along the dusty lane to their house.

The garage was at the back; the houses on both sides were too close even to cast a shadow; in front was a beach without rocks and the whole blue Pacific ocean. They had a deck outside their big orange bedroom upstairs which they used for their martini ritual at sunset unless they were still on the beach in bathing suits.

The long, clapboard house came to feel like an old bathrobe (often it smelled like one). Three of the rooms were really spacious and well-shaped: their bedroom, the kitchen (six could sit down for dinner), and the two-storied, white-washed living room which had a vaulted ceiling and an oversize fireplace. They used the fireplace more than they anticipated, the living room walls swallowed up their lithographs and her posters too easily, there weren't enough bookcases, and there was always sand. But their unorthodoxy in taking a beach house for an entire year had got them a cheap rent.

Anyway, Hubbell had been determined to live at the beach. September was still wistful to him: in his boyhood, it had signaled the end of summer at Virginia Beach ("I knew you were a rotten rich kid!" "Ever been there?"). When they took out their maps and booklets of Europe, he searched the southern coast-lines; when they were honeymooning on St. Thomas he had suggested living there. She had protested, rather violently, that they would turn into drunks like everyone else in the Islands; that the Negroes were so oppressed they were bound to revolt and Mau Mau the whites—and should; that they would die of heat in summer—

"It's the same temperature all year round, Katie!"

"Worse: boring!"

Then it came out that she couldn't swim.

"Well, I figured we weren't going to be here all that long, and I could dummy up excuses—"

"Oh, Katie. We shouldn't have come."

"No. You wanted to, and it's beautiful."

So he taught her to swim in the Caribbean and the day she managed ten strokes alone and without a life preserver, they galloped back to the hotel to celebrate, only to find J.J. waiting.

"Well, looka who's here!" His beam matched his Harry Truman sport shirt. "Judianne dumped me. She got married. I wanted you to be the second and third to know . . ." His quaver trailed off.

The day before they had been making love in the late afternoon under the mosquito netting when the native maid walked right in and casually sprayed all around them.

The hotel was called the Splendid. It was a hangout for sailors from the submarine base (it was odd, anachronistic to see uniforms six months after the war). There was actually a beaded curtain between the bar and the passageway to the rooms, and the walls were very thin. J.J. was next door, so they had to whisper.

"I don't care how long we've been living together, it's our honeymoon!" Hubbell said, not Katie.

"I feel sorry for the poor schmuck."

He went into the bathroom to shower and came out grinning. "You've certainly changed since that wedding!"

"I'm secure."

"You're gorgeous. Put your clothes on."

"No."

"I've just showered."

"The water isn't rationed. You can shower again."

"But J.J."

"He can wait."

"That's the girl I used to know!"

He laughed and locked the door.

To their surprise, California—Los Angeles, California —wasn't much of a winter resort. Days that were either drizzly or foggy, but always dank, shrouded the house in Malibu a few months after they were settled in. Some weekends that first winter they drove south to Ensenada, which had fishing and a beach Hubbell liked. And no bullfights, which Katie loathed. Once had been enough. That was in Mexico City, where they had flown with George Bissinger and Vicki.

Katie knew Hubbell expected her to unload the usual cargo of prejudices against bullfighting, so she tried hard to restrain herself. And failed.

"Well, we have prizefighting," he replied.

"They don't get killed."

"No? Just slower. And in Alpine countries there's downhill racing. Where they can merely be crippled for life. But it's a free choice and their one chance to get out from under. That's what they've all got in common."

"What bullfighters have in common, Hubbell, is that they're dirt poor in backward Catholic countries which hand out that Hereafter crap. It's awful for them!"

"And for Negroes. And Jews. And—"

"Not this Jew."

"You bet your ass."

But when she moved her lips from his and turned back to the bullring she was revolted by the blood streaming out of gaping holes in the horses; and even more enraged by the crowd.

"They're savages! If the matador doesn't risk his life enough to suit them, they *boo!*"

"Watch how beautifully he moves," Bissinger said gently. "Really a ballet. A pas de deux with a bull."

"You never sat through a ballet, George," Hubbell said.

"No suspense."

"They can fall."

"Ah, but here they die," Katie said. "And, apparently, one of them has to."

"It's classic, little Kate," Bissinger said. "Man against beast, nature, life—"

"Bullshit," Hubbell said just as several thousand aficionados began to roar with laughter.

It was the matador's first appearance in the Mexico City Plaza and it was to be his last. Shaken by the booing of the crowd, he had lost his head and his style and defiantly plunked himself right next to the bull. The bull retained his cool elegance and stared at the matador with obvious contempt, which carried all the way to Katie. Then, disdainfully, he dipped his head at the bulging satin groin. The horn didn't pierce, didn't cut: it merely nicked the shining crimson pants and flicked out one end of the white gauze wrapped around the matador's otherwise unprotected penis.

With the gauze trapped on the tip of his horn, the bull took a few mincing steps away from the matador and cocked his head at the crowd. The crowd laughed and applauded. The matador backed up, the gauze unrolling; he turned and ran, and more and more gauze unrolled across the arena, explaining the origin of that large, lost bulge. By the time he ducked behind the fence the crowd was hysterical.

The bull danced around the ring like Salome with one veil, but Katie watched the ex-matador, hearing with his ears familiar, jeering laughter. She shook her head and groaned.

"But, Kate, it's funny," Hubbell said.

"I know. That's the whole trouble."

She took a deep breath and smiled, and then applauded the dancing bull with everybody else.

Summer came very early and Hubbell got a new pair of bathing trunks.

"Too much gauze in there," Katie said.

"You keep your eye on the ball," he laughed.

They were playing volleyball on the beach in front of their house as they usually did on Sunday afternoons. It was their easy and only way of entertaining:

afterwards, swimming and drinks and Katie's pot roast or spaghetti with clam sauce.

The quality of the game depended on which of them had done most of the inviting. His guests were better players "because they're richer!", she teased. Some, like Brooks Carpenter, a barrel-chested pipe-carrying ex-Marine who was a screenwriter, made over two thousand a week; some, like energetic Eddie and Rhea Edwards, Hubbell's agents, made more. And some, like the film cutter and the junior writers and the man who owned the good book-and-record store and the two lecturers from USC, made less than Hubbell. Their wives and girls—who rarely wanted to be either actresses or housewives—were usually good at games and did sculpture.

Katie took care of the paybacks. The majority of the few friends she invited dunked in the ocean or argued in the two-storied living room with people like George Bissinger and Paula Reisner. Sometimes Stash and Adele—his "lady," he called her—joined the game, but they were no better than Vicki Bissinger and had to be put on the same team with Hubbell and Noel Watson. Adele always brought her eight-year-old son, Lefty, who had a fantastic IQ and was a mild pain in the ass.

Adele was a small girl with a wide, rather plain Slavic face. But she had a great figure; and long blonde hair, a deep tan, and never wore anything but white. Hubbell was sure her morning newspaper was delivered in the Moscow pouch; Katie liked her because Adele obviously adored Stash.

They had started living together shortly after Katie

and Hubbell came West. Stash had come to the Coast six months before that to be a joke writer for Monty Fielding, a writer-director on the way to producing his own pictures. Or so Monty told everyone: he was a great talker. Stash still pumped jokes into the scripts, but he also helped Monty find his story line and twist it. He didn't get screen credit, but he was fairly well paid. They were very old friends.

Monty's wife, Selma, went to a psychoanalyst six days a week and smiled incessantly. ("So no one will suspect her of murder," Hubbell said. "She's as obsessed as J. Parnell Thomas," Katie said, "except that, instead of Marx, smiling Selma sees Freud behind every bush.")

She did. A perfume ad showing a passionate violinist bending a pretty lady back over a piano had made Selma smile triumphantly, as though she had discovered penis envy.

"Don't you see? He's playing his organ!" she gloated, reminding Katie of the Pentagon's Captain Pencil. "Freud has penetrated the advertising industry—my God! Did you hear the verb I unconsciously chose!"

Monty and smiling Selma had first come to the house in Malibu through Stash, then kept coming on their own. They did that every place, and were welcome because Monty's greatest success was on the living-room circuit, where he was regarded as a wit and where he sang his own comic songs to his own guitar. He had just written a parody of "Joe Hill" especially for Katie, and after the volleyball game, when everyone was sprawled around the living room with drinks and had been smiled into silence by Selma, Monty took up his guitar and sang. His Joe Hill died quicker and more surely than the original.

He had diluted blue eyes which blinked and twitched even when he was secure. After his song they were epileptic. Stash leaped into the lull with a true story (he made up as he went along) about the rivalry between a Latin-American star at the studio and the sedated tiger she dragged around for publicity. Everyone found it very funny, and Monty got himself a big drink. At the climax of his act Stash went down on all fours to imitate the resentful, drugged tiger. There were gales of laughter, and Monty slowly poured his drink over Stash's head.

Stash just stayed there: a little tub of a man on his hands and knees in a sweatshirt and oversize plaid boxer trunks, gin-and-tonic dripping from his hair over his thick glasses and his chubby face.

"That wasn't very funny, Monty," he said quietly.

"Come on, everybody! Pot roast!" Katie called.

The pot roast, fortunately, was even better than usual.

"Not the first time it's saved you," Hubbell smirked.

J.J. held his plate out to be served. "Best buy in town!"

"If you say so, boss," Katie said angrily, still upset for Stash. And Monty Fielding was supposed to be so progressive!

J.J., who was pretty drunk, thought they were back on their old angry footing. "Ah, come on, Kate. Peace?"

She smiled and put a thick slice on his plate. "Piece. And where's the one you were going to bring?"

"Huh?"

"Jeanne Twitchell."

154

"Oh. Tell you later."

She brought wine to Paula and Bissinger, who were arguing Palestine and the terrorist bombings. Paula said she had been anti-Zionist until after the war.

"But, George, they are now homeless! Stateless DPs with no passports—"

"They will have their State of Israel."

"Despite the British?"

"And the Arabs. With whom I agree."

"Why?" Katie's eyes glittered.

"Because, little Kate, I think the Final Solution should be total assimilation. And so must you."

"Obviously, I'm in no position to oppose assimilation, but . . ."

"But what?" Paula urged.

"I have to make with the wine." She went off with the bottle.

Her brain was unraveling; she lost the thread of so many arguments these days. Well, next week less tennis and more reading. *Real* reading. God knows she had all the time she needed for it at the studio. But so many things seemed so far away now, so removed; even the Jews. Anyway, the party was zipping along and she could have another martini.

She spotted Hubbell sitting in a corner with Vicki and went over.

"Oh, I know," Vicki was saying, "the troubles of the world are supposed to make your own seem less important. But it's really the other way round." Her gray eyes were brimming with tears.

"Where's your glass?" Katie asked.

Hubbell stood up. "I'll get one, Kate."

"George?" Katie whispered.

"Ready for Number Six."

Paula was the last to leave. She helped wash up, then collected scraps of the pot roast for her retinue of dogs and cats. One of her sons was a chemist in Berkeley; the other was wandering around Mexico; she had read somewhere that her ex-husband was managing a theatre in Prague.

"Perhaps I shall pick up a nice hitchhiker with a mother complex," she said when they took her to her dented old car.

It was then that they saw J.J.'s Alfa Romeo and realized he hadn't left. They found him sitting at the edge of the water, still drinking.

"They all told me how smart Jeanne Twitchell was," he said, "so I took her to a concert. And foreign movies. Twice. Then Eddie Edwards—he's her agent too—told me she was the hottest piece on the lot. I got so mad, first thing the next morning, I sent for her. I had my thing out before she walked in the office. She just looked and said: 'J.J., there's a piece of string on your pants.'"

They put him to bed in the little yellow guest room.

"Who's going to produce your next picture with Bissinger?" he asked Hubbell.

"You are."

J.J. shook his head. "No, I'm not. My old man's son is." He winked and went to sleep.

Katie and Hubbell turned out all the lights and sat on the deck outside their bedroom, watching the burnt-orange moon.

"Was everybody always this lost?" she asked.

"Maybe in the twenties."

"That was after a war too. You don't think it's this town."

"It wasn't that much different back East, Katie. No, the war didn't work, something went." He put his bare feet up on the railing. "Everything's vague and everybody's vaguely uneasy."

"About the bomb."

"Oh, I don't think anyone can really imagine The End. Anyway, the Russians'll eventually make one and it'll be a standoff."

"Thanks Got."

The ocean, their enormous swimming pool, was quiet and still except for a wide, rippling ribbon of golden-orange moonlight. Far out, just where the sky stopped the water, a gambling boat twinkled. Far down their beach tiny sparks flew out of a little bonfire. They could sniff their honeysuckle.

"God, we're lucky," Hubbell said.

"Yes."

Nevertheless, the next morning, when their little television set announced that the House Committee on Un-American Activities was going to investigate Communism in the Motion Picture Industry, she laughed out loud.

"I know: stupid!" Hubbell said.

But he didn't know. It was as though she had found out she was pregnant. She was suddenly eager and energetic and delighted to be living in Southern California.

nine

THE FIRST TIME Katie ever connected Hollywood with reality was when Stash said he was going out there to work for his old pal Monty Fielding. He came by the apartment on Murray Hill to say farewell, and to deliver (finally) their wedding present.

"Who is Monty Fielding?" they asked.

"Oh, chaps, for shame!" Stash looked at them aghast. "Surely you've heard of Jonathan Swift, Mark Twain, Louella Parsons?"

"Oh, *that* Monty Fielding!"

Stash and Monty had gone to N.Y.U. together, written blackouts for college shows together, lost their virginity together.

"To the same broad! Though not, I hasten to assure you, at the same time. Bessie Barricade, a frizzy-haired creep we met on a picket line. We tossed a coin and she won."

"But, Stash," Katie moaned, "a gag writer!"

"Monty's cleaning up, Katie. It's another gold rush and he says to hurry out while it's still loded."

"If that's a sample joke, don't pack," Hubbell said.

"For them, it's a nugget." Stash giggled. "Listen, Katie, *seriously*, the Coast isn't what you think. Monty says they have a good Progressive group and there's a lot to be done with Mexican-Americans—like Dolores Del Rio—no, no, seriously, there are migrant workers in the valley, and the studios trying to bust the unions, and—oh, what the hell. At least, I won't die an accountant."

"And the climate's good," Hubbell said.

They wished him luck and thanked him for the Ben Shahn lithograph; and when Katie kissed him good-bye, they clung to each other for a long moment.

"Maybe he'll learn to swim and marry Myrna Loy," Hubbell said cheerfully.

"But, oh God, Hollywood!" Katie said. And repeated it several months later when Hubbell told her they were going. All because, she thought, she had misjudged his second novel.

She thought it was better than his first, but his publisher rejected it: oh, perhaps it didn't need more plot, Mr. Gardiner, but it certainly needed incident. The second and third publishers rejected it: more plot, more incident. So he rewrote again. The fourth and fifth wanted stronger plot and more action: he rewrote again. The sixth and seventh said it was mechanical, too plotted, too many incidents.

Candles burned on the gate-leg table where they were finishing after-dinner coffee. On the desk the different versions of the novel were in a multicolored stack.

"I *know* the first version is good. It is, Hubbell!"

He laughed lightly. "Well, you're a bit prejudiced."

He yawned, stretched, got up and turned on the radio. She cleared the table, and while she washed up in the little red kitchen he dried. It was hot. The music stopped for a report on the A-bomb test off the Bikini Atoll. It was the same gilt-edged voice that had reported Eisenhower's progress through Normandy on the night Hubbell passed out in the orange bedroom. She saw the same announcer, graying at the temples, sitting there—when did he eat?—reporting the Battle of the Bulge the night they had quarreled before walking through furry snow to Gramercy Park. But it was July now, the evening sun was glowering, and her throat was hot and thick with pain for his failure, and terror for hers. If she couldn't help, what was the point in his marrying her?

"Hey, I think it's worse for you than it is for me," Hubbell said, and kissed her. Behind his back she ripped off her rubber gloves so she could embrace him without getting his shirt wet.

Then came the sweltering day when J.J. called, wildly excited, almost hysterical: no, he wouldn't tell them over the phone, they had to come right over; no, his apartment—a new one in the Sixties, his aunt having returned from the wars—was air-conditioned and he had champagne ready and waiting. And take a taxi.

But Katie was washing her hair. "I'll meet you there."

"What in God's name do you suppose it is?"

"He's getting married."

"J.J.?"

"Maybe he met Bessie Barricade."

By the time she got there they were both gloriously high. Hubbell hugged her and kissed her and danced her around the furniture while J.J. puffed on a cigar and jumped up and down on a big sofa covered with a hunting print. He had sold Hubbell's rejected novel to the movies.

Well, not *sold* exactly, but they had taken an option and Hubbell was to write the screenplay at seven hundred and fifty smackers a week, and if they liked it— which of course they would—J.J. would produce it and George Bissinger, *the* George Bissinger, was interested and would undoubtedly direct!

"Which version?" Katie asked.

"The fourth." Hubbell laughed. "Or the fifth! One with a lot of plot! Who knows? Who cares?"

The champagne did him in, so J.J. took Katie to a celebration dinner at the Brussels.

"O.K., yes, my old man did have a hand in it," J.J. finally admitted. "But you are pleased, aren't you? I wouldn't have done it if I didn't think you'd be pleased."

She smiled like royalty, then fished the olive out of her martini with her long fingers. "So you've finally found yourself a job."

"Thanks."

"Well, haven't you?"

He pushed his glasses to the top of his head, then took them off and cleaned them with his napkin. His frog eyes were bloodshot. "I did it first for Hubbell, second for you, third for me."

"Interesting billing."

"Jesus Christ, I also got you a job in the story department!"

"Jesus Christ," she repeated coolly, "I am not your old goddam college buddy."

"What the hell do you want? And, for once in your life, *think* before you shoot off your mouth!"

She was so surprised by that, she laughed. She liked him for that, so she thought all during the turtle soup.

"O.K., J.J., I've thought. I apologize. I thank you. I like you, even though you can be a schmuck sometimes. But so can I. I wish us all luck in Los Angeles, California, and if you will get me a great, big, double, very dry martini, I will drink to that and get smashed. To celebrate."

But she put off packing. Maybe if Hubbell rewrote just once more—

"I can't. Not again. I'm dead on it, Katie."

"The screenplay is the same material."

"It's a totally different form, though. And that's fascinating."

"How much of it is the money?" she asked coldly.

He had come out of the Navy with $4,700; her apartment was rent-controlled; as script editor for Bill Verso's new radio series—Great Novels on Tuesdays —she had a nice salary.

"According to your friend Karl Marx," Hubbell said, "everything is economics. But, like the rest of us, he was limited."

"I'm sorry. I just had to ask."

"We're going to the Coast, but we're not staying. Not only because *you* don't want to, *I* don't want to. In the Navy I vowed I'd never again work nine to five. Well, I'll have to: in that studio, they make you punch in. Tough. But I am going to write a good screenplay, they're going to pick up the option, and *we* are going to have a lot of nuggets. Which we're going to save so we can live abroad!"

"Do you mean that?"

"Katie, we've never seen Europe! It may all go Communist—"

"Good! Let's be there for it! We can take a villa where they don't speak any English and you can write a novel and I can learn all about wine— Oh, my God, Hubbell! Me in a villa!"

"I think a villa can just be a bungalow," he said.

She laughed. She'd been rather clever, sneaking in that bit about a novel: she wasn't going to nag, but she wasn't going to be defeated either. And the prospect of living in a new country was exciting. Even Southern California.

"What language do they speak there?"

Nevertheless, she wanted to hold on to the apartment, to sublet the sublet. Then she wanted to buy the furniture and take it with them.

"Where to?" Hubbell asked. "Wherever we end up, it's going to be a furnished sublet."

The last night on Murray Hill—the walls stripped, the closets and drawers emptied—he awoke to find her huddled on the faded Mondrian-covered sofa, trying to memorize the pale-yellow living room.

"For a girl who says it's fear that keeps people from changing the system," he said, taking her in his arms.

"Yeah, but they never had it so good."

"You'll have it even better."

The sun was discouragingly bright the day they

moved into the Malibu house. On the other hand, their bedroom was orange. She hung the Three Sisters over the bed and the cork bulletin board in the kitchen; and a few weeks later found a gate-leg table for the white-washed living room. She bought pale-yellow paint but the cans remained stacked in the garage. She was too busy and she had begun to like the house as it was. With the advent of summer and the Un-American Committee, she wouldn't have changed it for the world, not even for a villa in Cannes.

"We're organizing a Thought Control Conference."

"A what?" Hubbell asked.

"That's the real objective of the Un-American Committee," she explained enthusiastically as she checked over a list of names in his office at the studio. "Thought control, censorship, stifling dissent—"

"O.K., O.K., O.K.," he laughed. "Who's 'we'?"

"The Hollywood Council of the Arts, Sciences and Professions of the Progressive Citizens of America," she said in one breath and gasped. "Jesus. A.S.P., for short."

"What the Attorney General would call a Communist Front."

"Well, if he can call Shirley Temple a Communist!" She put her list in her bag and kissed him.

"Hey! Lunch?"

"Can't. I'll see you home. First one there makes the martinis."

Every day now she lunched with Paula, Stash's Adele and Rhea Edwards, the agent-wife of Hubbell's agent, to Plan and Discuss the conference. First on the agenda was drinks; then they dished the latest rumors of the Un-American investigators who were asking questions behind closed doors in the Biltmore Hotel downtown; then they chewed over the progress of the Witch Hunt in Washington and around the country.

Paula was upset over poor Gerhardt Eisler, who had refused to answer the Committee's questions at an earlier hearing.

"He did not come here to overthrow anything! Only to escape the Nazis! But these days, my darlings, it is more patriotic to have been a Nazi than a Communist."

Katie was sure Paula's irony lost a lot in translation—though from what language she still didn't know. Anyway, she agreed that whether Eisler was or wasn't a Communist was his own business: he should not have been indicted for contempt of Congress and he certainly shouldn't be sent to jail.

"It's because he's a foreigner," she said.

"Like Nazi Germany!" Paula ran up her battle flag.

"It will be quite different in Hollywood," Adele enunciated precisely from behind her face. "The studios simply cannot afford to let their employee policies be dictated by a Congressional committee."

She smothered a butterfly shrimp in marinara sauce and inserted it into her mouth without dripping a drop on her white dress. She also took careful notes in pen without staining a finger. Katie marveled, and wondered whether Adele was serene or an iceberg.

Rhea Edwards came to the lunches with the brisk exuberance of a Peck and Peck lady come to the Settlement House. She had a prettiness no one resented, or desired. She always wore a feather-cut cap of graying curls and white gloves and pastel cashmere sweaters one size too small.

"Obviously, I'm determined not to let anyone forget I'm a woman even though I am an agent," she said disarmingly.

"She's brilliantly organized," Katie reported to Hubbell. "Before she whizzes off to close a deal she assigns the rest of us our chores for the day. And we like it!"

"You're crazy," he said as they came out of the ocean after their end-of-the-day swim. "The more work she piles on the more delirious you get."

"Absolutely correct," she beamed. "Going back to the studio tonight?"

"After Bissinger's."

"Oh God, I forgot. Hubbell, they eat so late."

"I told Vicki you probably had a meeting."

"You don't mind?"

"One of us has to make democracy safe for the world."

She crossed her eyes and stuck out her tongue and raced him into the shower. But when they were drinking their martinis on the deck outside their bedroom she said again, "Are you sure you don't mind?"

"Sure."

". . . How are George and Vicki getting on?"

"Vicki is teaching Noel how to play the violin."

Katie thought of Selma Fielding's perfume ad and laughed. "Poor Noel."

"Poor Vicki."

She fished for another topic. "Got anything to show me yet?"

"It's still too early." He had started his screenplay for the next picture. "And George has been after me to help him cut the last one."

He said that casually enough, but the sun was in her

eyes and she couldn't see his expression. Her seven-layered mind rapidly screened vignettes simultaneously. In the first, Hubbell: "All right, George, so long as you really want my opinion and not just my company"; in the second: "I want to learn, George, so I can write *and* direct"; in the third, Hubbell dripped bath water on the gold carpet of the Murray Hill living room as he corrected his novel; in the fourth, he danced around furniture while J.J. trampolined on a sofa covered with a hunting print; in the fifth, an ad clipped from the *Saturday Review* for a villa in St. Tropez; in the sixth, the final list of speakers for the Thought Control Conference which she had to get to the printers . . .

The Conference packed them in at the Beverly Hills Hotel.

"And such a kosher place!" Katie crowed.

She was exhilarated, proud that all the Arts, Sciences and Professions had brought out representatives ranging from Winners—Nobel to Pulitzer to Oscar—to what she supposed Hubbell would call Losers: those who worked hard for their ideals, but rarely had a paying job.

"They're praying for martyrdom," Hubbell said dryly, "so they'll have an excuse for being unemployed."

"Their prayers won't be answered," she said fiercely.

The speakers divvied up the Witch Hunt, covering Washington, the communications industries, the liberal unions, etc. Their tone was Congressional, but the Hunted, unlike the Hunters, documented their words.

Sometimes too much so, even for Katie: she dozed through most of the Legal Panel.

For five well-dressed days the Conference carried the torch, everyone talking and agreeing; everyone— even those who slipped out more and more often to the bar in the Polo Lounge—feeling warm and proud and freshly baptized; everyone going home every night to dream sweetly of Sacco and Vanzetti.

"Who were executed," Hubbell said.

"Didn't you ever belong to anything?" Katie railed.

"A fraternity." He grinned. "And crew—I was on the crew!"

"Smartass. It's your loss," she said, and finally got him to attend the Film Panel because it was on a Saturday and she refused to play tennis.

They sat in the back, Katie delighted that the speaker who introduced Brooks Carpenter emphasized his novels rather than his screenplays. At first she was less delighted with Carpenter. He sucked his pipe like a teething ring; his silk shirt was sticking to his barrel chest; his syrupy Southwestern drawl made him sound soft and apologetic. It was soon clear, though, that he wasn't; clear that while he might doubt his political beliefs, he had absolutely no doubt of his right to hold them and to hold them privately.

To Hubbell it was also clear that Brooks hated public speaking and couldn't wait to sit down. He shifted in his chair in empathy and embarrassment, then turned to Katie. She was so intent, her face was so rapturous that for a moment he was jealous. He looked at Brooks —a large, not unattractive man sweating through a speech—then back at Katie—glowing, hearing what was beneath the words. Her face was equally enraptured for the next man—a lesser writer, a better speaker—and Hubbell had to get up, to get out.

"I'll be in the bar," he whispered.

She stayed there, listening and applauding; then left and went into the shadowy cool of the Polo Lounge. It was almost empty. He wasn't at the bar, he was in a booth, staring at the tall, wet glass in front of him. It might have been the light or the angle of his head that made her remember he was no longer in his twenties. Quietly she sat beside him, kissed him, put her arm through his. He smiled and signaled a waiter to bring another of the same.

In the booth behind them were voices:

"Hell, they were all convinced before they came."

"Oh, they always are at these things."

"And, Christ, how they oversimplify! Every damn thing is a damn government conspiracy to shut them up!"

"Well, why not?" The second man laughed. "They're supposed to be a conspiracy to overthrow the government."

"They couldn't overthrow a shithouse. Come on." The booth creaked as they got up. "One more day."

"Thank God." They were walking out now.

"Did you get all the names?"

"They're printed," Katie said softly to Hubbell.

"Pity those guys came," he said. "Obviously they didn't learn anything."

"Neither did you, I guess."

"Oh, one thing."

"What?"

"How important it all still is to you."

"Not *that* important," she said, moving closer.

"It's important to everyone!" said Stash or one of the Fieldings, someone in that crusading band of angels.

Hubbell juggled the volleyball impatiently. "Are we going to have a game or not?"

"Like it or not, Hubbell, old chap, you too—"

"Come on, team," Katie called.

"Hold it, Kate."

Now even Stash was calling her Kate. She felt cold in her bathing suit but didn't correct him, just followed out to the sunny beach where Hubbell was saying, "I'm involved in what I write. If I have anything to say, that's where I'll say it."

"But if the Committee has its way, you won't be allowed to."

"Then I'll clear out and go to Europe." Hubbell grinned. "Which is where we're going anyway. So knock it off, Stash."

"Knock who off? Where is she?" Stash giggled and pretended to cringe before Adele. "Just a joke, my white goddess. Come on, Lefty. Old Stash wants to win today, so you're going to play on the other team."

Hubbell always played to win, but it was obvious to Katie that he was playing harder than usual. And he drank more and joked more when they all trooped back into the house for cold cuts. She hadn't had time to cook: the Conference was over and gone but there were still meetings. One thing about the Left: they loved meetings. The meetings went on and on. So did volleyball and moviemaking and love affairs, the main topics of discussion in the big living room. In the kitchen the cabal huddled as usual.

"Eight hundred federal employees have been fired by Mr. Truman for disloyalty!" Paula cried with relish.

"Hokey Harry should have stuck to haberdashery," Monty Fielding chortled, winking and blinking like an uncontrollable flirt. "The Republicans have Red-baiting all sewed up as *their* election issue. That's why they're also having a probe of that Negro tobacco union—"

"Probe!" Selma Fielding screamed. "*That's* an interesting word!"

"Break it up: Spy from Switzerland!" Hubbell came in. "Is there any dessert?"

"Fresh strudel from Paula," Katie said eagerly.

"There's a woman! I'll bet you were baking strudel while you were running from Hitler." Hubbell kissed Paula and returned to his group without looking at Katie.

She was alone in the kitchen, stacking dishes—Paula was doing coffee in the living room—when he came back and shut the door.

"I'm sorry about the food," she said.

"Have you been going to any meetings of the Party?"

She giggled. "They haven't asked me in years."

"Well, don't."

"What is it, Hubbell?"

"They complain I don't take it seriously enough. *They're* the ones who don't! They're too damn busy enjoying their heads off! If they're so goddam concerned and involved, why don't they concern themselves with the Mexicans downtown or those poor slob wetbacks picking lettuce—"

"Hubbell, what is it really?" she asked, but the door opened and J.J. said, "Too late for the game?"

"Not if you brought floodlights," Hubbell said.

"Matter of fact, I did bring one." J.J.'s face was all joy as he stood back to let the girl walk in.

Like Vicki Bissinger, she was tall with long cloudy hair. Her eyes were hidden behind big, dark, almost black sunglasses which left her traveling between 25 and 35. She wore a long-sleeved jersey turtleneck and beautifully made sharkskin slacks, and she was barefoot. Everything about her screamed sex, screamed that she knew it, hated it, wanted it. Katie caught the flicker in Hubbell's eyes.

"This is Jeanne Twitchell," J.J. said.

They stayed on after the others. Talk was easy because J.J. was so happy and the girl, when she spoke, was sharp and funny. When Hubbell and J.J. went for a swim, she parked herself on the stone ledge in front of the fireplace and bummed a cigarette from Katie.

"When I was a kid," she said, "I worked in the five-and-dime and broke the light bulbs made in Japan."

Katie looked at the bare feet, at the cloud of hair. "O.K., J.J. told you I was political."

"I'm not any more: too tired." Jeanne shrugged.

"I know another character who wears glasses like yours. She drinks."

"So I'm supposed to be an actress. I can't act my way out of a paper bag, let alone in. Ergo, I've decided to marry J.J. O.K.?"

"It's none of my business."

The girl suddenly barked a laugh. "Holy Mother! You think you landed the big catch and everybody wants him! Too bland for me, baby. I never went for the fair-haired lads. What I did go for—" she shrugged —"each to his own disaster. O.K.?"

"I think I'll join the other gentlemen," Katie said.

As soon as they left, she apologized to Hubbell again for the lousy food.

"Politics isn't the whole banana," he said. "A lot of other life goes on and occasionally there's even progress."

"You think that piece of pornography is progress?"

He laughed. "She's what J.J. wants. If he gets her, that's progress. For him anyway."

It was Stash who told her the subpoenas were starting to appear. Paula wasn't in her office. She found Hubbell in a small projection room with George Bissinger.

"And Brooks Carpenter was served," she finished glumly.

"Assholes," was Bissinger's comment.

"The Committee."

"Both sides, little Kate. The superpatriots who want their names in the paper and the alleged artists who joined the Party with no thought of the risks involved."

"It's a legal party!" she protested despite Hubbell's hand on her arm.

"It soon won't be, and that will be that," Bissinger said with gentle finality.

"I gather you're not pleased with the rough cut of your movie, George," she said.

"I'd have more sympathy with your cronies, little Kate, if they had more talent and a few brains."

"Come on, George," Hubbell said. "Brooks Carpenter?"

"An exception." Bissinger lit a thin cigar. "But he wasn't above feeling he'd made a revolution if he had a shot of two workers shaking hands at a urinal. Or wrote one of those capsule phrases: 'It's a free country as long as you have the money.'"

"Foolish or even stupid," Katie said angrily, "it's his right to—"

"My favorite line," Hubbell interrupted, "is: 'I don't care if she's black, white, pink or green.' Now I would care if she were green. I'd be scared shitless. How about lunch?"

On the way to the commissary he said, "You take George too seriously. He's teasing you. You know he's a liberal."

"I know he's your boss."

He punched a swinging door to open it. "That he is, little Kate. And you might remember that."

She had to walk fast to keep up. "It's just that he's a complete cynic, Hubbell. He doesn't really care!"

"Because he doesn't parade? The total number of people in this town who 'really care' could fit in our kitchen—and usually do!"

But overnight the number grew, the whole town began to care. For not only were there more names on more subpoenas but whispers of other names—names of those who were going to testify *for* the Committee and against their own industry, the industry that gave them jobs, the industry that gave the town *its* name. The studios were like Mafia families and the families got angry. Difficult children—whether they got into the wrong beds or out of the right political line—were to be handled by their parents, not by their siblings.

And certainly not by bloodless outsiders from Washington. It was bad for the family name, the family business, the family box office. The celluloid Mafia took the offensive.

Katie was given a short leave of absence from the studio to assist Bill Verso, who flew out for a nationwide broadcast sponsored by a home-town committee: The Committee for the First Amendment. There was a lot of gray in his still tousled hair, and it was too hot for the trench coat he tossed to the redhead whose expenses were also on the bill. But he and Katie could not let go of one another when they met.

"Remember?"

"Remember?"

"We'll get those bureaucratic bastards just like we got those Pentagon assholes!"

"Oh, Bill, call them something else!"

"Remember?"

"Remember?"

"God, you look sensational, Kate. Who are you?"

Time was short and all hers had to be his. They schemed how to get big stars for the broadcast and were startled to find the stars calling *them*. Writers called, half the town called. George Bissinger could jeer, but the problem became one of turning down people gracefully. Not their donations, of course.

The Saturday before the broadcast she had to call Hubbell. "I know it's Saturday night, but we're overlong, and we're swamped with sulking stars—oh, forget it. I'll be home."

The slightest pause, then his laugh. "No, stay. Rome must not burn. I'll be at Bissinger's."

Verso sent out for sandwiches, but even before they arrived he said, "You're no help. Go home."

"I'm just punchy from not eating."

"Go on. Get a good night's lay and I'll see you in the morning."

She blushed—still—and drove the white convertible through five stop lights on the way to Bissinger's.

There was a quiet handful in the mahogany barroom; not an A group. Swiftly she picked out George and Vicki and Noel and J.J. And the star of George's picture who was a client of Eddie and Rhea Edwards who were obviously taking turns at star-sitting. And an executive and his wife, and a playwright and somebody else's wife. She fixed herself a drink.

"Hungry?" Hubbell had come up behind her with a plate of sandwiches.

"Can't we go home?"

"Not now."

"All right, children," Bissinger called out. "We are now going to have the privilege of viewing one of those subversive films which have been destroying our own, our native land."

As Vicki turned out lights, Katie tried to glance casually around the room.

"It seems poor Jeanne blows up when she has her period," Hubbell said with no expression at all. "So she's home polishing her engagement ring."

"Why don't you marry me?" Katie said.

There was the low hum of the motor as the Matisse slowly slid to the floor, clearing the movie screen, and a slight ripping sound.

"What the devil is that?" Bissinger said sharply. "Hold the lights, Vicki."

He was on his feet, walking quickly to examine the screen. There was a jagged tear down the center.

"Now what did that?"

The whole room watched as one long arm reached around the Matisse and felt the back of the picture. His face didn't change as he straightened up and showed them the small object in his hand.

"Well, children," he said, his voice hard for once, "my home has been bugged. I am going to sue our government for that screen."

"*Alice in Wonderland*," Hubbell said.

"My favorite book in the whole world," said Katie, grinning from ear to ear.

ten

HUAC, THE HOUSE Un-American Activities Committee, had learned something in Hollywood: it opened its public hearings in Washington with the grandeur of a movie premiere at Grauman's Chinese. Katie ran from the radio to the television to the telephone, and drove to the newsstands for each new, screaming headlined betrayal. The first celebrities to step up to the Committee's microphones to greet their fans had never made the front pages before, and never would again.

"The really talented, really creative people are always on the right side," Katie said smugly.

"You mean the Left," Hubbell said, and ducked.

Under the spotlights, however, the lesser talents became surpassingly creative. In the cultivated style of Hearst editorials, they denounced their town as a home for Communists subverting the beloved industry and thus the American people.

"'Share and share alike!'" cried the mother of a star. "That's the kind of filth my daughter was forced to say!"

"At gunpoint," Katie said back home where they laughed and scoffed at these witnesses who were so friendly to the Committee and who were, most of them, members of something called the Motion Picture Alliance for the Preservation of American Ideals.

"What in hell is that?" J.J. asked.

"Just what it sounds like," Katie lectured.

"Oh." Jeanne Twitchell smiled. "Losers."

But the losers were making a big splash which their families didn't appreciate. New committees were formed daily, and George Bissinger chartered a plane to fly a passel of younger and bigger names to Washington for a press conference on the steps of the Capitol. But: no revelations, no headlines.

"Total waste of time," Hubbell complained. "He leaves me to cut that frigging picture when I should be finishing my screenplay."

"He surprised me," Katie said admiringly.

"His work is why he *has* a name!"

"But why have one and not use it?"

"Everybody's just helping that goddam Committee by using anybody's name too damn easily," he snapped. "Well, I'm going to play tennis with Vicki and Noel. I don't suppose you'd care to make a fourth, but there must be somebody in this rabbit hole who wants to enjoy the weather while it lasts!"

Then it changed.

Witnesses presumed to be unfriendly to the Committee turned out to be unfriendly to their friends. In loving, lavish detail they reported what their friends had joined, what their friends had said, what their friends had thought, what they thought their friends had said. They made an old word new: *informer*.

There were tremors, slides and shakes: an earthquake frightened Southern California. The various new committees to defend the Bill of Rights became uncommitteed. Doors shut, mouths closed, citizens stayed in their swimming pools.

Katie and Bill Verso barely managed to get through what was to have been a second broadcast "by popular demand." Phones didn't answer, donations were canceled, and rejected stars who had been hurt the week before were suddenly stricken with laryngitis.

"Give me television and New York any day!" Verso shouted. "I give you pictures and this asshole backwater! It's crumbling, Kate. Get out while you're in one beautiful piece. Where the hell is that moronic redhead?"

"Crumbling," Katie said, pointing to the girl, who was shaking out her hair for a movie agent.

"Remember?"

"Remember?"

But shared failure shortened memory and farewells.

On her way back to the studio and book reports, Katie picked up a newspaper and learned that Brooks Carpenter had been named. She pulled her dark glasses down over her eyes. He had been "identified by Mrs. Rhea Edwards, the literary agent." To save the world, the nation and the movies from Communism, Rhea had name-dropped briskly, and with such charm that the chair had complimented her on being such a friendly witness and on having such a beautiful bosom for a literary lady.

Paula's lopsided house in Laurel Canyon had a little veranda with sagging wooden steps leading to what she called her Garden of Evil. Bigger than the whole house, the garden was thick with trees and vines and bushes except where Paula had cleared a space large enough for a small dinner party. That was the extent of her gardening. She savored the scent of jasmine and honeysuckle, and left the source to nature.

They sat in the garden—Paula, Hubbell and Katie— safe from microphones, having drinks they barely touched before a dinner they didn't want. Candles burned slowly in hurricane globes; assorted cats and dogs slept quietly; it was very still. Once or twice a car labored up the steep road, sprinkling light through the leaves.

"And who besides Brooks?"

"That rude woman who had headed the typing pool forever," Paula said. "And if the name is correct, a very nice little stenographer I have used once or twice."

"And a grip from our last picture," Hubbell said. "Quite a diverse little cell our Rhea was in."

"But why did she do it?" Katie asked again.

"She's an agent." He chuckled.

"Your agent."

"Her husband is my agent."

"My darling Kate, she did it because she must have been told someone had named her in secret testimony. And Rhea is a very practical woman. She knows there are very few producers who will deal with a Red agent."

"Paula made a joke," Hubbell chanted.

"Well, I didn't mean to and it is rude of you to notice."

"I apologize. But who do you suppose did inform on the lovely-bosomed Rhea Edwards?"

"Eddie Edwards." Katie tried a joke.

Hubbell laughed. "Say, did you ever hear the rumor that he's Hearst's illegitimate child by Marion Davies?"

"Who isn't?" Katie said glumly.

"There is also a rumor," Paula said, "of a little man who went to Party meetings with a Minox. And a rumor of a popular psychoanalyst who is employed by the FBI part time. Oh, who knows who informed on who? But in time it will all come out, thanks Got!"

"In the meantime, they may lose jobs or even go to jail," Katie protested.

"In the meantime, in Germany, millions went to the gas chambers."

"Don't be so bloody European, Paula," Hubbell said.

"What does that mean?"

"Superior."

"All right; *I* apologize. But, you know, just the other day, I was with one of the unfriendly witnesses—who shall be nameless—when he was telling a Soviet writer —also nameless—how much he wanted to go to Russia. 'Come any time,' said the Russian. 'But I may have to go to jail,' my friend said. The Russian looked at him bewildered. 'So come when you get out.'"

"O.K.," Katie said. "So you all are used to it. We're not. Not to going to jail in this country for what we think."

"Some of us will if some of us don't keep our mouths shut." Hubbell's tone was light, but there was an odd edge to it.

"Meaning who?" Paula asked.

"Almost anyone." Hubbell laughed. "I name no names."

"Why couldn't Rhea have kept her mouth shut?" Katie said angrily. "Why the hell couldn't she just have answered, Yes, I was until a year ago or whenever it was she said she pulled out, I'm not now, and that's that."

"You know why, Katie."

"I *know* if you answer the $64 question, you're supposed to answer them all. But why couldn't she at least have *tested* that ruling?"

"Because she didn't want to risk going to jail," Paula said impatiently. "Not many would."

"Would you?" Hubbell asked.

Paula gave him a long look. "You don't ask me seriously, I hope."

"No." He laughed; and driving back to Malibu asked Katie, "Is Paula in the Party?"

"I don't know and I never asked."

"Don't. You'd make a lousy liar."

"So would you."

"On the contrary, I'd make a very good liar."

She looked at him, then at the heads turning to look at him from other open cars on the Strip. They stopped for a light, and the tourists in the car alongside looked.

"They think we're a starry couple," Hubbell said.

"Liar." She laughed.

By coincidence—"an anniversary," Katie said grimly —they were again with Paula in her Garden of Evil the night the Un-American Activities Committee ended its hearings on Communism in the movies. Seventy-nine guest appearances had been announced, but after eleven unresponsive turns, the Committee closed its show. One of the eleven, Bertolt Brecht, really couldn't be considered a member of the film family; in any event, he denied all affiliations and was so convincingly bewildered by his interrogators that he bewildered them into dismissing him contemptuously. The other ten stood on the First Amendment, wouldn't talk (although some managed a few speeches) and were canceled out with the threat of being charged with contempt of Congress. The Committee came up with no proof of subversion but much advice that the Industry clean house. Then everyone gave statements to the press and went to work on expense accounts.

Walking into Paula's garden was like coming home after a funeral. "Half the town is in Romanoff's tonight," Katie reported.

"Half the town is idiots!" Paula snatched a cat away from a jealous dog. "Only the *public* hearings are over. The others will continue in secret behind closed doors until everyone has informed on everyone else."

"Not the Ten."

"Not yet," Hubbell said.

"What's that mean?"

"Wait till Congress indicts them for contempt and they face prison."

"Poor Gerhardt Eisler," Paula lamented.

"The Ten will never talk, Hubbell," Katie said.

He shrugged. "Maybe they enjoy being martyrs."

"Standing up for a principle doesn't make you a martyr!"

"They *could* have taken the Fifth."

"No, forgive me, Hubbell," Paula intervened. "If

184

they took the Fifth, everyone would say, Ah, self-incrimination, they must be Reds."

"Aren't they?"

"It's their right to be!" Katie cried. "Under the law—"

"Oh, fuck the law! We don't have free speech either. Ever since the Russian Revolution this country has been screaming 'Better Dead Than Red.' *You* pointed that out at the top of *your* lungs in 1937. They screamed it then, they're screaming it now, and they will continue to scream into the foreseeable future. It's high goddam time you two listened and understood they are frightened enough to mean it."

He had kept his voice so low he might have been whispering Fire! Yet even the animals were motionless and it seemed to Katie that the grass had stopped growing. She could hear Paula rummaging in her grab-bag of Mittel European anecdotes. It was the moment for an earthquake or a gunshot next door. Then Hubbell began to sing softly.

"For he's a serious fellow,
For he's a serious fellow,
A very serious fe-el-low—"

He held the note, and Katie joined in for the last line:

"Which nobody can deny."

"Bravo!" Paula laughed. "Once, when I was doing operetta in the Ukraine—or was it Prague? Anyway . . ."

Selma Fielding came a-soliciting a donation from George Bissinger for the legal defense of the Hollywood Ten, and got more than she expected. The Ten had been indicted by the House of Representatives for contempt of Congress—just in time for everyone to get home for Thanksgiving.

"Fascism can happen here, it has," Selma started, but Bissinger stopped her.

"Selma dear, if you don't take off your smile, I shall have to put on my aluminum jock."

She was dimly aware that she had been eased out in less than ten minutes, but she left in a happy daze. A pearl for her analyst *and* a contribution to her cause: Bissinger donated his house for a fund-raising party.

"A suitable occasion for unveiling my latest acquisition," he said. He had got a new movie screen. The old ripped screen, expensively framed, was hung on the paneled wall opposite his front door with the artist's signature large in one corner: HUAC.

The night of the party Bissinger sat out the speeches in his freshly polished barroom. It was only fair: Lord of the Manor, he had provided space, staff and liquor. He ensconced himself in a cockfight chair at a table with Katie and Hubbell and an edgy Vicki; the silken rabble sat in his stately Adam drawing room and, pleasurably guilty, allowed themselves to be harangued and dunned.

Secretly Katie felt glad to be in the bar. The speeches drifting through the open double doors were as familiar as those she used to write. Causes changed, but not words—well, why should they? Causes, like wars, overlapped. She really should be writing out a check. But if she did, Hubbell might say, What about buying that horse? or, What about Europe? He had only come tonight because it was at Bissinger's: he was drinking more than she. Still, they damn well should be there; they should be sitting in the other room; she should be making a speech, even the collection speech, even without beads to twist, even—

"Boring, masochistic assholes."

"Now, George." She was determined to be gay and charming. "You *did* fly to Washington."

"A foolish attempt to wreak vengeance, out of an inflated sense of my own importance, little Kate. And about as useful as the position taken by these ten conventionally admirable men."

"Just conventionally admirable, George?"

"Virgins and martyrs: considered admirable, actually impractical."

"Can we do without the sophistry?"

"Ah, little Kate is going to be black and white!"

"Yes, very black and white! It's arrogance to claim beliefs and not stand up for them!" She couldn't whisper Fire! "And to sit by and jeer while someone else is fighting for those very beliefs, that is *really* impractical!"

"It's also impractical," Hubbell said, "to board a sinking ship which even the rats are fleeing."

"Like Brecht," Bissinger said.

It was getting impossible to ignore the voice of the collection speaker in the next room. A famous young pianist, he had a painful stutter which he tried desperately to overcome by speaking louder and louder, and by stamping his foot when his palate locked.

"A w-w-witch hunt! A p-p-period of repre-pre-pre-pre—" he sweated and stammered and stamped his foot—"repression!"

"What about Brecht?" Katie challenged.

"He denied everything, didn't he?" Hubbell said. "Which could hardly be the truth. Admirable? Or just practical?"

"But he did *not* inform!"

"A tough opportunist, dear." Bissinger patted her hand. "Always wore silk shirts under those leather jackets."

"Criticize this country and someone is sure to say: 'But what about Russia!'" Katie snapped. "Brecht isn't—"

"They will not s-s-s-stop until they cen-cen-cen—"

"George, please help him." They had almost forgotten Vicki.

"It's my house, not my cast. Or my cause."

"It may have to be your cause," Katie began.

"How do we get another drink?" Hubbell asked.

"And not only the m-m-m-movie industry, but r-r-radio and tel-tel-tel—"

"George, please!" But Vicki looked at Hubbell.

"Rescue him, George," Hubbell said.

"He'd consider that a disservice, son. He wouldn't tickle the ivories tonight unless he could make the collection speech. His analyst told him the best cure for stuttering—" Vicki got up and rushed into the drawing room. "She once accompanied him. Along with the rest of the studio orchestra. Dear little Vicki. Didn't know she was marrying an asshole. Unfortunately, that's all most of us are. Or what we become, at any rate, if we stay in this town."

"*Jesus!*" Her face was blood-red right through her tan. "Is there anything, George, besides your own damn pictures, that you're actually *for?*"

"There must be, little Kate, or I wouldn't have loaned my house."

At least the stuttering had stopped; music came over the elaborate sound system. Hubbell took a drink from a waiter and tossed half of it down. Bissinger never changed his sweet, courtly look or his soft, gentle tone.

"I am for the right of any and all fools to make fools of themselves. Be they heads of studios, fatheaded congressmen, or hotheaded parlor pinks." He kissed Katie's hand. "I also believe if you put your head in the noose, be prepared to hang. And don't expect tears from me." He tongued her palm.

"I'll bet you're not even liberal in the bedroom, little George," she said coldly. "Just selfish. Excuse me, gentlemen."

She got up and walked swiftly across the dark wooden floor, through the French doors, onto the flagstone terrace. The moon—there was always a California moon—showed her the way to the hard dirt path which led from the formal English garden, with its geometric flower beds and its topiary, down through the blue-green eucalyptus to the tennis house. The music pursued her and she broke into a half-run. With her heels and the quickening descent, it was easier. Branches struck across the path and she struck back at them angrily.

"Katie!"

She didn't slow up.

"Katie!" He was close behind her.

"I'll cool off."

"*You'll* cool off?" He grabbed her hand and swung her around. "I work for that man!"

She shot him a murderer's look. "*Why?*"

"Because I enjoy it! He's a marvelous film maker and I'm enjoying while I learn!"

"And getting damn well paid!"

"You're goddam right!"

"How many more screenplays are you going to hack out?!"

"We'll go to Europe when I'm ready to go. And when we do go—"

"I know: we'll go in style!"

He laughed, maddening her. "Right!"

"You might try saving your style for your writing."

"True, but I'd also like it in the plumbing and the heating and the food and the clothes—I am *not* going to grub the way we did in New York—"

Insulting Murray Hill. "It's no crime to live in small rooms!"

"It is when you don't have to."

"We were a damn sight better off there than we are here!" she cried and, turning furiously, tripped like a clumsy idiot and stumbled halfway down the steps to the tennis court. He came quickly to help her but she pulled away and ran down the rest of the stairs.

Her heels clacked loudly across the concrete court. Bougainvillea was trying to get through the wire fencing. There was a racquet at the base line, and a pail of tennis balls. Vicki's racquet: Noel had probably fixed her goddam serve. Katie picked up the racquet and bounced a ball on it angrily. She heard Hubbell coming, kept her back to him. "For he's a serious fellow, for he's a serious fellow."

He walked up to her slowly, taking deep breaths.

"It may gag you," he said, obviously battling his

voice, "but as of this minute you are going to stop being sanctimoniously smartass to George Bissinger. You are also going to stop giving checks made out to cash to Paula Reisner and Stash & Co. or I will buy that damn horse."

She threw the ball into the air for a serve and smashed it into the net.

"You are also going to quit any and every cause that places my job in jeopardy."

She was about to toss another ball for another serve, but she spun around.

"Katie, you are not in college. And, there, you couldn't even get expelled! This is politics for grownups: nobody wins and everybody who gets involved on any side loses! Sooner or later! If I honestly believed in any side I'd be willing to lose." Out of habit, he grinned. "I would. But even though I'm for the principles of the Ten, I'm against their methods. I think they're running to disaster like lemmings, and I'm not going to let sentimental sympathy drown me in the drink." He took the racquet from her hand. "What I'm saying is very simple: as of now you are finished with your causes. Lay out."

She tilted her head like a doll. "Are you telling me?"

"No. I'll never *tell* you. I'm asking you."

The tennis court was like an empty room. They stood face to face, looking just past each other's eyes. He wriggled his neck, seeking to escape his collar: he didn't like clothes or standing still. She wouldn't move, afraid of making the wrong one. He had the tennis ball in one hand, the racquet in the other; very easily, very gracefully, he served to the opposite court. The ball bounced and bounced and rolled into silence.

"Would have been ace," Katie said, and took his arm.

Two nights later she hauled out a long black dress. Hubbell's eyebrows went up.

"J.J.: Beverly Hills: a group," she explained.

"It's an engagement party, not a funeral."

"Be prepared is what I always say." She added the big, glittering Mexican hoop earrings defiantly.

"Very sexy."

Anger, private or political, always gave her a sexual aura. She wiped off most of her lipstick, but left the earrings.

They were greeted by Jeanne Twitchell, barefoot in white.

"Methinks the lady," Katie muttered, fighting a temptation to step on the pedicured toes. Was the future Mrs. J.J. Something III planning to walk down the aisle barefoot? She'd be lucky if she got there.

"I know you want a martini," Jeanne said to Katie, "but I don't know what you want," she said to Hubbell, linking his arm and steering him presumably to a waiter.

She *should* have stepped on her toes; and she didn't get her martini. She peered around the trays of champagne, ducked the Fieldings, and felt someone stroke her behind as she stiffed her way to a couple who had been at Bissinger's: a rubber-tired producer and his futilely girdled Frau. They were discussing contemporary painters with Russell Ryan, Monty Fielding's lay analyst and business manager. Selma had found him.

"I'm not familiar with his work," Frau Producer was

saying. "What price bracket is he in? My heavens, Kate, it's not fair to be so bright and so attractive!"

"Tennis, everyone," Producer chortled. "Listen, Kate, how's about our taking a full page ad in the *Reporter* and *Variety* just quoting Johnston's statement?"

Eric Johnston, president of the Motion Picture Association, had issued a statement on behalf of the studios rejecting J. Parnell's advice to clean house and vowing the studios would never countenance blacklisting.

The ad was a good idea and she said so, proud they knew where she stood, wishing they didn't in case she didn't stand there tomorrow. Although who really cared whether people making two or three thousand a week went to jail, well, yes, to go to jail for what you thought—but was it really and simply for what they thought? And, anyway, what about the secretaries and grips, etc., who only made a hundred-odd bucks a week (if they were lucky) and weren't indicted, just fired—she was grateful to the gleeful J.J., who asked if he could borrow her, and took her over to Hubbell and then out to the terrace which rippled in the lights from under the electric blue water of the swimming pool. The pool looked as though J.J. had lain down on the ground and said to the builder: "Copy me."

J.J. was so happy, she was happy she was in black. "Great news, old buddies! But it's got to be a secret. I've been assigned a picture!"

"Oh, wonderful, J.J.!"

They lifted their glasses and drank his champagne to him.

"What's the picture?"

"I can't tell you."

"Oh, come on," Hubbell said because J.J. wanted him to.

"No, I really can't. Don't ask me. But do me a favor, do yourselves a favor and *don't* say I told you. Stay home tomorrow night."

A rally for the Hollywood Ten was scheduled.

"Why?"

"Just stay home."

"*Why?*"

"Sssh!"

They lowered their voices but kept badgering.

"For Chrissake—all right. You're my best friends, but don't—"

"We won't."

He pushed his glasses over his hairline. "The Ten are going to be fired."

"They can't be," Hubbell said. "They have contracts."

"They're going to be. *And* people like Brooks Carpenter, anyone who won't cooperate with the Committee."

"Won't be a stool pigeon, you mean!"

"Yes, Kate, that's exactly what I mean!"

Well, of course: he now had a picture to produce. Life was really so simple. She couldn't look at J.J. or Hubbell; she stared at the fake blue water and compared floating to swimming, both of which were preferable to drowning.

"I'm advising both of you: don't go to any more meetings, don't give any money—"

"And don't go to the movies," Hubbell said innocently.

"Jeez, Hubbell!"

194

"If the Commies have been subverting the flicks, I don't want to get caught being subverted."

"Christ. You always laugh, she always looks at water." J.J. wheeled to go, then completed the circle and came back to them. "I'm doing you a favor, god-dammit! I got it straight from my old man. It's going to get very rough. If you want to stay here and work here, lay out. I'm not kidding, Hubbell. Lay out! You got it?"

She was damned if she was going to make it any easier for Hubbell, so she turned and looked squarely at him.

"Got it," he said, returning the ball to her.

"Got it," she said.

She raised her glass and, stupidly, they all toasted and drank, and she tossed hers into the swimming pool.

"Hey!" J.J. said. "That's real crystal!"

"Oh, sorry, J.J.," she said and walked across the terrace and into the pool.

So he laid out and she laid out and after the Waldorf Manifesto everybody but the diehards laid out. At the Waldorf upper echelon executives and bankers and chairmen had met and decided it was best, after all, to be patriotic and bow low to the House Committee on Un-American Activities. Eric Johnston issued another statement for the producers. Reprinting was hardly necessary; the whole town got the message.

J.J. had been well informed: the Ten were fired and would stay fired until they purged themselves. ("They've *been* purged!" Katie said, but softly.) In addition, any other Communists, suspected Communists or members of possibly/probably disloyal groups would get the sack. And for a grand, star-spangled finale the executives generously invited the "talent guilds to work with us to eliminate any subversives, to protect the innocent, and to safeguard free speech and a free screen."

"And Free Dishes," Katie said.

"Well, the blacklist, she is here," Hubbell said.

"For how long, do you think?"

"As long as it's box office."

"But, my Got, it will kill the box office!" Paula protested. "You will see. They will drive out every good artist just as they did—"

"—in Nazi Germany."

They were in Paula's office, drinking her coffee. Every morning now she began work with a search behind her autographed pictures for microphones. She was guarded over the phone, which didn't ring very much now anyway: everyone was being too careful too late.

"I'm curious," Hubbell said. "For years the simplest way to write a movie villain was to make him a stool pigeon. Now they've got to convince their public a stool pigeon is a hero."

"First, they must begin in their own nest," Paula said. "There is a meeting tonight—"

"I can't," Katie cut in quickly.

In the small, sad pause she saw herself bringing coffee to the boys in the composing room for the last time.

"Of course you can't," Paula said, not looking at either of them. "It's a meeting of the Screenwriters Guild and I thought Hubbell and I might go together."

"Sure," Hubbell said.

They went in Paula's old battered car. Paula did something she had never done before: she kissed Katie good-bye.

"I'll drop in after the meeting and report, yes?"

"Yes, please. I'll feed you." Katie swallowed and fumbled for her dark glasses.

Driving slowly back to Malibu in the white-and-red convertible she found commuter traffic neither heavier nor lighter. There were the same impatient drivers honking regal horns, the same college kids shouting and singing in jalopies. The red evening sun splintered across her windshield in the same places on Sepulveda. At the turn onto the Coast Highway, she gave a lift to a kid who was a mechanic at Lockheed and didn't go to the movies.

When she heard Paula's car rattle and pop to a stop out back, she closed the book she hadn't really been reading and darted joyfully toward the door. But when she heard the car doors close without any excited voices she walked heavily into the kitchen to take the casserole out of the oven. Daydreaming undercut living. Hubbell did not come home boiling at injustice, burning to battle it; he just came home. Well, one miracle was one more than anyone should expect, and she'd already had hers.

Oh, the meeting, Paula reported, massaging her messy hair, was "very tense. Dramatic speeches, dramatic accusations. Quotes from Tom Paine and Thomas Jefferson."

"And Tom Swift and the Rover Boys," Hubbell added.

It had been technically recessed midway to allow

representatives of the Motion Picture Association to address the writers. One well-liked man, long known for his devotion to liberal causes and to making liberal films, was now head of a major studio. His first personally supervised picture had been a homage to God. Another well-liked, liberal, but more sophisticated man had produced the only Hollywood picture on the Spanish Civil War made during that war. But by the time it was cut and released it was impossible to tell which side the hero was on.

"I suppose they both did a lot of apologizing," Katie said.

"The theme of the evening," Hubbell said wearily. "'You know we feel the same way you guys do'—they actually said 'guys.'"

"To show they have bosses."

"Anyway, the gist was that, as guys, they felt just as lousy as we guys did about the Ten, but those poor guys were sunk and had to be forgotten. The important thing was to hold the line—from now on. They exited to a great round of hissing." He picked up his plate and Paula put hers down.

"Then more dramatic speeches, more dramatic accusations, more dramatic quoting."

Katie served them coffee, suspecting both were wondering how to use the scene in a script someday.

"But what do you think the Guild will do?"

"Nothing, my darling Kate. Perhaps pass a resolution in favor of democracy or some such bullshit. Too much fear, too many jobs in danger."

"And too many up for grabs," Hubbell added, "now that some classy competition has been removed."

"With more to follow." Paula stood up. "In the meantime there is money to be raised for the families as well as for the lawyers." She turned back on her way out. "Don't worry. I will keep you informed." She laughed heartily at her own joke, but Katie was grateful.

She put the unfinished casserole in the icebox and began to collect the dishes. Then she poured herself more wine and lit a cigarette. "Do we just sit it out, Hubbell?"

"What would you like to do that could accomplish something? Something beyond the warm, comfortable feeling that you were doing your bit?"

"Just attending a rally is giving moral support."

"Moral support won't keep anyone out of the clink. And a Communist rally—"

"Ninety percent of the people at those rallies and meetings are liberals, not Communists; it's not as black-and-white as you like to make it!"

"Oh? Since when? Yes, we sit it out! We sit and we do our work until we have the money to clear out!"

She carried the plates into the kitchen, came back with a tray for the cups and saucers and coffee things.

"We're not sitting in Auschwitz," he said. "Nor are we slave labor for Krupp. We're sitting very nicely in Malibu Beach where we have a very enviable life."

She had everything on the tray and was taking it into the kitchen when she heard his wineglass shatter against the fireplace.

"*Goddammit!*"

She stood quietly with the tray, not turning.

"I am not responsible, Katie!"

"I never thought you were," she said with a nasty

dryness, and leaving him to pick up the pieces, took her tray into the kitchen and went up to bed.

Much later, when he came up, she was still awake; and stayed awake, which, she thought, served her right.

Before Run, Sheep, Run, Katie had been quietly collecting donations for the defense of the Unfriendly Ten, as they were now called. She dropped by Stash and Adele's bungalow off Melrose to turn over the money. Stash was working, Lefty was at school. Adele, unlike Adele, fumbled with the latch on the screen door.

(The day before, Katie was leaving one of the cubicles in the ladies' room of the Beverly Brown Derby when she saw Rhea Edwards' reflection in the mirror. In panic, she stepped back into the cubicle, shut the door and quickly slid the latch into place.)

But Adele at last opened the screen door and ushered Katie into the living room. It was cool and pleasant and dim. Everything was white or blue or a combination, except Katie. Adele took the money and asked no questions. She understood. They all understood. It was insulting.

Adele scanned the list of possible donors Katie had approached. "Nothing from Russell Ryan?"

"He kept promising and never being home."

"He's always at the Fieldings'. Stash has the car; could you drive me over?" She saw Katie's hesitation. "You can put the top up and I'll be out in five minutes with a hundred dollars."

She was out in less than five minutes, tucking the hundred in cash in her spotless white purse.

"He must be afraid you'll tell his real name." Katie laughed.

"More afraid I might tell he once worked for the *Daily Worker*, among other things." Adele's enunciation was more precise than ever; either she had just been to the dentist or she was nervous.

"I heard he worked or works for the FBI," Katie said. "Oh, well, it's a rumor a minute these days."

Adele's face didn't change, but it never did anyway. "Mr. Hoover is not as thorough as he would have us believe. It's apparently quite easy to work for both, without either knowing."

"As Hubbell says: *Alice in Wonderland*."

She drove Adele home with the top down, then to Bissinger's to meet Hubbell. He and Vicki were playing a set against George and Noel, so she had a drink, got tired of waiting, went home and had another drink. By the time Hubbell phoned to say they were invited to dinner at Bissinger's, she had the table set, the cutlets breaded and another drink half gone. So he ate with Vicki and George and she stayed home, wishing she had a baby or a dog or something. Not a horse, though.

eleven

THE SUN KEPT shining. "An unusually good December," said natives like the family next door who had lived in Malibu even before the war. They were divided on the Un-American hearings: the plump, freckled wife thought all Reds should be deported; the slow, tanned husband agreed but also thought informers were stool pigeon rats who should be shipped back to New York. Both thought there was too much cleavage in the movies.

The English Colony in Beverly Hills had been busy with a huge garden party celebrating the marriage of Princess Elizabeth to the Duke of Edinburgh. Katie tried to figure how old Elizabeth had been when Mrs. Simpson made off with the Duke of Windsor, and another Katie and another Hubbell sat on the marble steps of the Old Dutch Hotel. But the English were not unaware of the hearings. A great lady of the Lon-

don theatre—it was rumored she was really Australian
—expressed the consensus:

"Anyone who repeats in public what was said in a
private home is not a gentleman, but a cad."

The volleyball games continued as before, although
without the cabal in the kitchen and without players
like Eddie and Rhea Edwards. Eddie had gone on a
two-day bender, only to return home and learn that
the Un-American Activities Committee had informed
on Rhea: Brooks Carpenter she had named publicly;
now, they revealed, she had secretly named two other
Edwards clients. Eddie gave Rhea a black eye.

"I don't know why he got in such a tizzy." Monty
Fielding's blink-blink warned a joke was coming up.
"Those two schmoes only worked for Monogram, not
Metro."

Not a snicker in the whitewashed living room, not
even from Stash.

"Rhea's going to the hospital." Selma Fielding
smiled, stroking her goose neck.

"For a black eye?" Katie asked.

"No, she's got shingles around her throat."

There was also gay, frightened gossip about Selma.
While helping Katie slice the pot roast, Paula reported
that someone else had reported that Selma had been
seen near the FBI office by someone else.

"By Monty," Adele said, tossing the salad.

Katie and Paula gaped. It was the first joke Adele
had ever made. If it was a joke. Adele's face gave no
clue.

"Oh, well," Katie laughed, "Selma is so popular anyone could say anything and everyone'd believe it."

Probably true, but she had defended smiling Selma

because Selma was involved and she herself was detached. Even detached from the volleyball and the pot roast and the party. Conversation, including her own, came over a radio. She felt shorter and thinner and encased in cotton batting. She wondered why everyone was staying so late and then was surprised to find they went home at the usual time, and that they all thought she looked marvelously relaxed. People just didn't see.

Hubbell drove Vicki home. She had come with J.J. and Jeanne Twitchell because George had to work. But Jeanne had a meeting of her 100 Great Books course, so they left early; and, anyway, Hubbell had to go over the first part of his new script with George.

Katie made herself a drink and was contemplating breaking the stack of dishes on the drainboard when Paula came back: she had a flat tire, again. They called the garage, and Paula helped with the dishes, chattering how tired she was from all the meetings but couldn't sleep because she was so excited from all the meetings.

"You thrive on it," Katie said enviously.

"True. In this town I would go mad otherwise. Or drink too much like you."

"It only seems I do." Why was she holding these plates? Oh, yes: to put them in the cupboard. "I wish it would rain. Not drizzle, really rain."

"You are like the goddam palm trees." Paula wiped the glasses very carefully with the special towels she had given Katie. "They do not belong here either. They were brought in, they look it, and I am certain they don't like it."

"Oh, Paula, everybody in this town tells everybody to get out."

"I am an old woman. Thanks Got, they give me a job and let me stay. Soon enough they will catch on and I will go to Switzerland and die."

"You can do that here."

"Ah, but that's *all* you can do *there!* Here—" She stopped: they were at the door neither had wanted to open.

"All right, but I can't ask Hubbell to get involved in something he doesn't believe in."

"But *you* believe, you *need* to be involved. Can't you explain—"

"I won't be a nagging wife."

"What other kind is there?"

"Ohhh—a Jewish mother."

"Yes, but unfortunately you are not Jewish."

Katie looked at Paula, who was wrapping up scraps for her menagerie. "Of course I am. Aren't you?"

Paula looked surprised. "No."

"Jesus, what a town." Katie shook her head and knocked down her drink as the man from the filling station rang the bell.

She had lots of time to walk along the beach; Hubbell rarely was able to go horseback riding. He was working very hard at the studio, often at night. But he usually managed to get home for the end-of-the-day swim and martini. There was a long cord on the telephone in the bedroom so they could drag it out to the deck; but they left it inside now.

"I know it's bad that a lot of people are afraid of the

telephone," he said, "but I can't help being thankful for the peace and quiet."

"In my country it takes all the running you can do to stay in the same place."

"It was the *Red* Queen who said that." He grinned.

She smiled back, rather dizzily. It was a mistake to drink martinis in the sun. "What are you afraid of, Hubbell? Besides writing, that is." The idle voice sounded like hers.

"Oh, a few things."

"Such as?" The white sun was right on the horizon line; she pushed down on it.

"Your sleeping pills."

"I don't take them that often."

"You didn't use to at all."

"Ah, but I'm a classy married lady in Hollywood, U.S.A."

"You never took any before me."

"Oh, well, they're cheaper than buying a horse." She pressed her head hard against the back of her chair and the sun drowned in the sea.

They were struggling to put up the goddam Christmas tree she was determined to have, sun or no sun, when Stash and Adele came by: Stash had been fired. Adele sent Lefty out on the beach to play with the kids next door.

"There aren't secrets at our house," Lefty explained to Katie and Hubbell. "I just don't want to hear it all again."

"Are you sure he's not a midget?" Stash asked Adele.

She sat very erect in her chair, her back straight, knitting a white sweater. "He's more realistic than you are, Stash. He knows the Fieldings informed on you."

"Ah, a psychic midget!" Stash giggled; and explained he had called Monty immediately, only to find that the Fieldings had gone off on a Christmas holiday without telling anyone. Their housekeeper—Progressives never had maids—said they were in Acapulco.

"We called every big hotel, but I guess he used her vanishing cream." Stash laughed. "But, honey, that doesn't necessarily mean he informed. Or even that Smiling Selma did."

"What else can it mean?" Katie asked.

"It could mean Monty is chicken."

"It could *also* mean he's chicken," Adele corrected.

"What reason did they give for firing you?" Hubbell asked.

"Who gives the reason?" Stash said. "The producer. Who's my producer? Monty. Where's Monty? Where's Judge Crater? Where's Amelia Earhart? Say, how about that for a cute meet? Judge Crater is swimming around Acapulco—"

"Stash."

"All right, honey. *Seriously.*"

"Seriously, what can you do?" Hubbell asked.

"Well, I know what I want to do. I want to fight the blacklist."

Katie wanted to say: Stop joking. He was such a roly-poly jester, the idea of his fighting anything was funny. But Adele had stopped knitting, her face very proud. Katie looked at Hubbell.

"How, Stash?" he asked.

"If I could get someone to hire me for a job I'm qualified for, and at my regular salary or even less—well, of course, no studio would allow it, but then they couldn't say it was because of money or because I'm a stumble-bum. They'd have to say Why? and then I could take them to court for being part of an illegal conspiracy."

"But who's going to hire you?" Katie asked.

"Well," Stash diddled with the chess set on the coffee table, "that's where I thought maybe you might help."

Watching Adele's knitting needles, Katie remembered that soldiers wounded in the First World War had been taught to knit. She'd better learn in the Cold War. Except she'd probably get arthritis. Or stab someone.

"Would you want me to approach Bissinger?" Hubbell asked.

"Oh, no. In the first place, you're doing his new picture and, in the second, it's not funny. At least, not intentionally. What am I saying?" Stash's giggle was more of a cough. "No, I'm a comedy writer and, well, J.J.'s producing a comedy . . ."

"How does he stand?" Adele asked.

"Only at a urinal," Katie said.

"That's not fair!" Hubbell said sharply.

"Then ask him!"

"O.K., I will!"

Stash and Adele were immediately very busy, he joking, she packing up her knitting. He pumped hands quickly, gratefully. "Thanks, chaps. Seriously. Come on, my blonde Venus. Let's get your midget and scram. Thanks, Hubbell, really, thanks."

After they left, Katie said, "What guts that little man has!"

"He's dreaming, though. The kid *is* more realistic."

"In that case, I'd better tell him not to bank on it."

"Because of who?" Hubbell challenged.

"Because of J.J., of course," she said with icy innocence.

Waves didn't break on the Malibu beach, they dribbled up and collapsed on the gritty gray sand. She walked the shoreline, kicking at the grains of her discontent, at J.J., at her unfairness to him: he *had* given her her wedding party at the duplex on Beekman Place.

His accordion-playing aunt was still overseas—"As long as there's one GI left," he hooted, "she'll squeeze the old box." There was more food, more booze, more room than they needed, too much really, for it was six months after V-J Day and the Gang was long gone, a diaspora scattered throughout the land. The parties were gone with the Gang, but Hubbell's wedding to Katie was a terrific reason, and J.J. even invited some almost-strangers.

For Katie, it was the best of all parties. In a daze of champagne-colored chiffon (white was impractical, and why risk a bad dye job?), she whirled through the rooms, pollinating the guests with her happiness. Marriage was a bonus on top of a raise; she had never thought of it: her own parents—her Trotskyite mother and her anarchist father—had never been married. Hubbell sleeping in her bed, writing at her desk, crowding her closet—O.K., she somehow achieved the impossible. But marriage? When he suggested it, she said "What for?" and meant it. For a moment. Well, everyone has a Time, this was hers. She was lucky to have him to love and him to love her; to have J.J. as friend and giver of this marvelous party with these wonderful friends, *their* friends, even the almost-strangers.

Good old Judianne was there, and the big Air Force

Captain who, luckily, was passing through town. And Bill Verso and Stash and Naomi (who had to ride up in the service elevator because she was a Negro, for God's sake!) and at the last minute Pony Dunbar. Pony was a globular pile of lemon and orange ices.

"Your favorite colors." She smothered Katie with a kiss and lily of the valley perfume. Katie hugged and hugged.

"Oh, Pony, I'm sorry!"

"For what?" She stepped back, leaving a slab of perfume behind. "The Party'll survive without you, but you wouldn't've without him."

"I meant—"

"You asked me to your wedding. Lunch, we can have anytime."

They'd have lunch tomorrow, no, next week, unless she went on her honeymoon—maybe St. Thomas—and if she did, they'd lunch the first day after she was back. She fought a crazy urge to thank Pony for being such a big, generous, Progressive slob (they really were the best people!); to run and thank Stash for the god-awful jokes that made everything easier; to thank Naomi for long, lovely straight hair; to thank her father for the passion and stubbornness which she had somehow inherited and which had made that incredible tall, blond man from the other side of the classroom ask, *ask* if he could put this ring on her skinny finger.

Her father was as dazed and delirious as his daughter. Swollen with arthritis, shrunken with age—his two daughters had turned up late in life—the old man grabbed a strategic chair and never shut his delighted mouth. In Rochester they'd all heard his theories, his tirades, they'd all heard it all—which didn't stop him.

But here was a new, fresh, untouched audience! And they'd never seen anything like him before, this flame-thrower with a Russian accent and snapping eyes, his gray hair threaded across his bony skull, his over-knuckled fingers jabbing and pointing and continually dropping his black cane. In absolute ecstasy, he ranted and thundered, saying everything that came into his head, repeating himself, unable to stop, hurrying on in fear the party would finish before he did. Some of it even sounded new to him.

"The moon!" he shot at Pony, who came to offer congratulations on his daughter's marriage. "With the moon the Army Signal Corps has made contact by radar! What next? I will tell what next! Millions, billions to fly to the moon while down here the exploited die in poverty or terrible disease! Accident? Deliberate! Here, young man, bring the shrimps here. Thank you. You know why is no accident, miss? I tell why. Soon too many people here. So the rich fly to the moon and drop a bomb down here. When enough killed off, back come the rich. Old story, new style. Well, exaggerated maybe, but you get the point, miss?"

"I get the point, pop," Pony said.

"You wear pretty colors!" The old man spoke in exclamation points. "Katie's colors, like racing horse! You know what is behind horse racing? I will tell . . ."

Hubbell's parents sat quietly side by side like passengers patiently awaiting the announcement of their flight home. They shared their good looks, might have been brother and sister: tall, big, big-boned, with soft, gentle voices. Their constant smiles were more than polite, and Mr. Gardiner always stood up to shake hands. He shook hands with his son, he shook hands with his daughter-in-law. His wife would have done the same, but Katie kissed her and then her husband. Hubbell bantered with them, and they laughed his laugh. They were as kind to her as they were to him. But they behaved as though they didn't know him very well, as though he were a distant nephew and they were filling in for his absent parents.

They were different with J.J. He was exuberant with them, effusively determined to relax them, claim them, make them claim him. They responded as though he were both the bride and the groom. Seeing that, Katie understood what was easy for them and what was not; and was sad for a moment. For them, not for herself: they had no close connection with Hubbell, so they had none with her.

Her father interrupted his own blast against Palestine as a home state for the Jews—he was for total assimilation of everybody everywhere and the annihilation of all states and religions—to lecture the floating, laughing newlyweds.

"Don't let her drop the banner!" he shouted at Hubbell. "Whatever is on it! Her sweet mother carried *her* banner to the grave. Did Katie's sister pick it up? No! Why not? I will tell why not. Marriage, children: vegetable. If you don't have banner, you become vegetable! You hear, Katie?"

"I hear, pop darling."

"He got banner? He laughs too much to have banner."

"Katie's got enough banner for both of us."

"Wrong! Must have own banner. Why? I will tell why . . ."

She left Hubbell to listen to the old man's Niagara roar: one of the almost-strangers came to say good-bye and she had to hunt up J.J. He wasn't with the Gardiners or with Judianne; he wasn't in the den or the kitchen or the bedroom. He was in the foyer powder room, his face against the wall, sobbing hard. He smelled drunk, even over the peppermints.

He tried to gasp out words, couldn't, couldn't stop crying. Don't look, I am ashamed, was scrawled all over him. She took him in her arms, cradled his head on her shoulder, murmured baby words, soothed his balding head—more balding than she had realized because his comb was so clever. But he couldn't stop crying. She stared at the green and silver wallpaper, trying to decipher the pattern; at the silver dolphin faucets, wondering how much they cost; at her face in the silver-framed mirror (she had to shift him a bit to see herself and her long lovely hair).

His tears were dampening her champagne chiffon shoulder. She staggered both of them closer to the sink until she was in reach of an apple-green hand towel. She patted J.J.'s streaming eyes with the towel, then quickly jammed it against her shoulder before his head flopped back into position. She concentrated hard and, Jesus, the door opened and Hubbell came in.

"What is it?"

J.J. broke away from Katie and, holding the towel to his face, sat down on the john, crying and shaking his head.

Hubbell knelt by him. "What is it, buddy? Tell me what it is."

He kept saying that and J.J. kept crying and shaking his head. Katie put her hand under her chiffon shoulder and fluttered the material to dry it. J.J. was only sniffling now, but still shaking his head.

213

"Over," he choked, "over over over."

"What's over, buddy?"

"Oh, Christ." J.J. mopped his face, blew his nose in the towel. "Like college, and I wasn't ready. Like the war, and I wasn't ready. I'm still not ready!" He threw the towel on the floor and got up to bathe his face at the sink. "I'm just a retarded goddam fifth wheel!"

"You're retarded all right." Hubbell laughed. "We'll just beat your ass till you grow up."

"Ma-ma, da-da."

"No," Katie clowned, "him Tarzan, me Jane."

"And that makes me the goddam chump, I mean chimp!"

"You were right the first time," Hubbell said. "It's not over. Katie is not an injustice collector."

Now she couldn't be if she wanted to. But there was no pleasure in whatever small triumph it was either. J.J. was sad, it was all sad, it *was* all over. She put one arm around him, the other around Hubbell.

"We're not very many, J.J.," she said, "but we're a Gang."

He kissed her, touched Hubbell on the arm and then, as the tears welled up again, ducked his head like a shit kicker and darted out.

The groom looked at his bride. Cupping her face in his hands, he kissed her lightly, kissed her again, then put his arms around her and held her gratefully to him.

The oldest of the kids next door was teaching the youngest to swim in the wallpaper-green ocean. The baby was as determined as Katie had been in the royal-blue Caribbean but kept going under. Well, the baby wasn't on a honeymoon, Hubbell wasn't the instructor, and there was no J.J. to applaud and cheer.

Suddenly happy, she ran from the beach into the house, almost out of her clothes before she got upstairs. She dressed quickly, stowed tennis gear for both of them in the trunk of her convertible, and drove like a bride to the studio.

It was Saturday afternoon quiet. Eagerly she threw open the door to his office. His desk was too neat: then he was running the final cut of the picture with Bissinger. Well, she didn't drop a banner for George Bissinger; he could damn well check out the damn picture on company time. He'd probably agree, probably play with them; they'd beat the hell out of him and Vicki or Noel or all three of them. She walked rapidly, elegantly down the gleaming hall to the elevator which silently dropped her to the basement level and the projection rooms.

The projectionist sat reading in the open doorway to his booth, letting the picture screen itself. Bill Verso's sound engineer had buried his face in articles about the coming of television; this technician was reading a comic book and was so absorbed he didn't see or hear her.

She tiptoed along the shining beige linoleum and opened the screening-room door quietly. She needn't have: the sound track was deafening. Movies seemed to be made for the hard of hearing. The dialogue was familiar: she could hear Hubbell reading various versions to her.

She couldn't see him or Bissinger or anyone. She stood close to the wall, peering at the short rows of tufted chairs. The faces on the screen suddenly shut up, turned into a landscape, and she heard an odd moan that hadn't been recorded. She knew then that she should leave, but didn't, couldn't. She waited until some other faces began shouting at each other on the screen; then, clinging to the wall, slowly inched her way down the short, thickly carpeted ramp.

The first row of seats was separated from the screen by about ten feet of warm blue carpet. She knew it was blue because she had seen it before. In the haze below the sharp light beam the carpet was only vaguely blue, the bodies were vaguely suntanned, but the white buttocks were even whiter. She knew Hubbell's body so well, she thought she saw the shrapnel scar on his back. But she couldn't have, any more than she could have seen the girl's face, which was hidden by a misty cloud of hair and by the position they were in—a position Katie had never been in, the girl devouring him and he devouring her.

She was shocked, repelled, fascinated, aroused. For one wild second she thought of tearing off her clothes and joining in; of screaming, of turning on the lights, of walking on them with her high heels and kicking them; of sitting down in the front row and eating popcorn. The sound track went mute and she became afraid they would hear her. She held her breath until there was underscoring; then, suddenly sweating, carefully backed up the ramp and sneaked out of the room as though she were guilty. The projectionist still had his face in his comic book.

Quite calm or quite numb, anyway appearing self-possessed, she went back to Hubbell's office and picked up the phone to call someone. It turned out to be Noel Watson, who was free to give her a tennis lesson. Well, her gear was in the trunk—just part of life in Southern California, like the sun and deftly driving a convertible up to Bissinger's wearing sunglasses and having a husband who showed his versatility on the floor of a projection room in the middle of a sunny afternoon. The bastard. Who was the bitch? Not that it much mattered. *He* was the bastard, no matter how bitchy she herself had been. And he had never done *that* with her, she had never even suspected he wanted to. If she didn't know that, something as basic as that, what else didn't she know about him?

For a second she literally went blind with fear; vision returned just in time to see a red light. Was it because he still thought of her as a Puritan? How surprised he would be tonight—no, too soon—tomorrow night to find her doing that with him! My God, where did you learn to do it so well? he would say jealously. Well, my God, where would she learn? And what else, what more did she have to learn about him?

She hardly spoke during her tennis lesson, hitting the ball as though it were an enemy. She walloped it with all the fierceness she'd ever had, and sometimes it even went in. Bissinger watched for a while. He looked like a long white worm, standing on the porch of the pool house above them, nude except for his white Panama, his long penis dangling over the railing.

"You children look so hot. Come on in the pool."

She slammed, crashed, banged the ball until he had gone. "I'd like to recircumcise him."

Noel blushed. "He's very kind to me."

"Who isn't?" she snapped. "That's your problem."

Instantly she was ashamed and her game got worse, and they quit. Standing under the shower in the pool house, she blushed for herself and for not apologizing. Through the thin wall she could hear Noel's shower in the adjoining bathroom. As she soaped herself she thought of his honey-colored skin, of Hubbell under a shower. They both had that pantherlike walk, both had strong bodies with that dazzling white groin between the suntanned belly and thighs, Noel must have it, must be washing there with white soapsuds as she was.

She watched the water wash the soap away, turned off her shower, walked out of her room and into his. She was still wet: she could say, Wash my back; something. Through the opaque glass she saw his outline, his head tilted back to the stream of water, his mouth half-open. She opened the door.

His rabbit mouth shut; he stepped back in the stall, trying to hide behind the curtain of water; his eyes never left the level of hers and they were the eyes of a pubescent boy looking at his mother in too tight a bathing suit. Katie wanted to drown, wished he would.

"Come for a swim," she said like the hostess in a nudist camp.

"O.K." He scampered after her, tripped on his terror and sprawled on the floor.

She didn't look back. She knew he would follow, and hid herself in the pool as swiftly as possible. When he was in, she thanked him.

"For what?"

"Protection. I was afraid George might come back."

"Oh. That's O.K." The fawn eyes began to relax.

"And I apologize, Noel."

"For what?"

"For being so bitchy before." Ha ha. Fooled you.

"Oh, that's O.K."

"It isn't." She swam nearer. "But I've been very upset lately."

"Oh, I knew that."

"How?" They were treading water, almost close enough to touch.

"Your game was off," he said, diving quickly underwater and not coming up until he reached the other end of the pool.

It was a lousy dinner. J.J. always had bad cooks, but this latest was lousy. Not that any one of them was eating much anyway. Hubbell was silent and nervous because after the lousy dinner they were all going to the first screening of his picture. Jeanne Twitchell was silent and possibly drunk. She sat opposite J.J. at one end of the candelabraed table, a sphinx behind black glasses, not speaking, not eating, just drinking her Crystal Chandeliers: gin and vodka over crushed ice. Katie was silent and watching, watching Hubbell, watching Jeanne, watching his cordovan moccasins, watching her bare feet.

Only J.J. talked, nonstop, marathon. He apologized proficiently for not being able to help Stash, then lost his yardage by giving too many reasons; then tried to regain ground by disclosing, to nobody's surprise, that Monty and Selma Fielding had been the informers; then, realizing no one *had* been surprised, switched to the food, earnestly beseeching that it was much better, wasn't it? Or wasn't it? Katie nodded, Hubbell smoked, Jeanne drank.

J.J. returned to the Fieldings—the only safe ball to run with on this muddy field—saying one of them was a cretin, probably Selma, had to be smiling Selma who had squealed on one of the biggest stars at the studio. He was sworn to secrecy but it would all come out as soon as the studio figured how to get its expensive fish—two films in the can, one shooting—off the hook. That goddam Committee. That goddam dizzy pink-haired diz bomb, *signing* a Party membership card because the creep-musician she'd married had bamboozled her into believing she was an intellectual, the moron. Oh, well, it was late, they could all go to the screening in his car, he'd bring her around.

"She's here," Jeanne talked.

"What'd you say, sweetie?"

"I said she's here, sweetie."

"Who's here?"

"The car, sweetie. Right here. At this table." She sighed. "J.J. sticks his key in the ignition and off he goes. And I'm left with my motor running for the rest of the night."

Katie simply stared at her plate until she heard a door close, a bathroom. She couldn't remember the color of the wallpaper and wasn't going to find out.

"I'll bring our bus around, Katie," Hubbell said.

Jeanne walked Katie to the door with absolutely no difficulty and the faintest aroma of gin. "If he really wanted to give Stash a job," she said thoughtfully, "he could hire him as a chauffeur. You wouldn't believe it, but that chubby little man is a great driver."

Maybe she *was* talking about cars. Maybe she was drunk or drugged or crazy. Or miserable. Maybe she hadn't been on the blue carpet. But poor Adele.

Katie stepped on one of the bare feet and almost fell down the steps to Hubbell's MG.

It was the same projection room. She sat next to Hubbell in a deep, warm-blue chair, listening to the same characters shout the same dialogue. She looked at the screen without seeing it. Her hand drifted off the arm of her chair, over Hubbell's onto his thigh, traveled toward his crotch. In a projection room. Well, what were projection rooms for? She must be getting ready to join the rest of Hollywood on the floor, or on the couch. But he took the hand and enclosed it in both of his. She let it rest there for a reasonable interval, then took it back to light a cigarette.

When the film was over, she stood with Vicki, the other wife, on the blue carpet down front while husband George and husband Hubbell accepted congratulations. Paula waited her turn, her eyes half closed as though she were still entranced. She pumped Hubbell's hand, then Bissinger's.

"So true to life!" she said gaily, her accent thicker than ever.

"She's a bitch," Hubbell said later, driving back to Malibu.

"Well, she thinks you're adorable, much too good to waste your—"

"She's a Marxist bitch. The only movie she hasn't knocked is *Potemkin*." He hairpinned the MG into Santa Monica Canyon, driving with angry despair because he respected Paula.

And because he wanted to talk about what had been up on the screen and she wanted to talk about what had been down on the floor—not about who, about what, about them, Hubbell and Katie. On Murray Hill they would have talked right away—while it snowed, possibly; certainly, rained.

"So true to life!" He mocked, exaggerated Paula. "She's a bitter old dyke."

"She certainly is not! She has two grown sons; you met the one who lives in Berkeley."

"Oh, Katie!" He laughed as he slowed down on the wide Coast Highway where he usually speeded up. "The day you die you'll still be a nice Jewish girl."

She turned her head to the scaly wall of cliffs on her side. "Are you still a nice Gentile boy?"

Silence; the length of it frightened her. She turned to look at him, at his perfect profile against the hanging sky. The moon had a puffy, doughy face. It had risen too early; it spilled yellowish milk across the flat gray sea.

"I never was," Hubbell said finally. "I only looked it to you."

"That's not so!"

"It is, Katie, believe me it is. But when you love someone—from Roosevelt to me—you go deaf, dumb and blind."

She hunched lower in the uncomfortable little seat. "Only at moments, during screenings."

"Like when you put your hand on my leg?"

"Yes."

"Why did you do it just then?"

"Something on the screen reminded me of something someone said. About some girl touching you—there."

"And?"

"And whatever invariably follows in this town. Or so I was told. I suppose you'll say nothing did."

He stopped for oncoming headlights, then guided the MG into the dusty, rutted road to the Malibu colony. "They told you true," he admitted quietly.

The car bumped slowly up and down, in and out of the ruts, a roller coaster in slow motion. Her teeth shook and rattled, but with fear. She never should have mentioned it, she didn't want to be told, to hear any more; she had to stop it; she would talk about the picture.

But "It *was* really nothing," he said. "Everyone out here knocks off a girl now and then."

"I don't!" Her bad joke was as deliberate as his vulgarity. Getting out of the low-slung MG in a tight skirt made her even angrier at herself. "Goddam car!"

She slammed the door, stormed into the house and went to the bar to mix a drink. He got a beer from the icebox, drifted into the living room, sprawled on the sofa.

"Who'd you hear it from?" he asked, as though he were making conversation.

". . . A friend."

"Some friend!"

"Well, it's a friendly town—if you don't mind having your friends inform on you or knock off your husband or wife, as the case may be." Her tone, her manner, her movements—mixing the drink, lighting the cigarette—were annoyingly familiar, reminiscent; then clear. She saw and heard a slew of actresses in a slew of films. Jesus! In this town real life was based on screen life. No wonder the movies were lousy, no wonder the life was lousy.

"The picture's going to be a smash, Hubbell," she said.

"But you didn't like it."

"Let's say I appreciated it."

"Why didn't you like it?"

"Because it's hideously cynical." She knew "hideously" would sting even before she said it, just as she knew that in a moment they would be fighting about the picture, both knowing it wasn't the picture they were fighting about.

She felt good again. The kettle was ready to boil: being burned was better than being cold and numb.

"The picture is meant to be cynical," he said, too patiently.

"I know where it's *meant* to be cynical, Hubbell," she parried with equal patience, almost laughing at her crazy lust for battle. "But not at the end, and that's where it's unintentionally and disgustingly cynical."

"Oh? How?"

"They chase money the whole damn film. They get it by being totally corrupt and vicious. And then, in the nick of time, it literally blows away in a sandstorm—"

"Saying Nature—"

"Saying Hello, box office!"

"Balls!"

"And perpetuating the great American myth that honesty is its own—"

"Oh, bullshit, Kate!"

"My name is Katie!"

"Since when?"

"Since always! But you've even forgotten why we came out here!"

"And you've forgotten *how!*" He was outshouting, maybe even outenjoying her. "Anyone can write a first novel. The second is the test and I flunked! You won't acknowledge that, you never give up! I have to go to Europe and write the great American—"

"When was the last time I even mentioned it? When have I said one word—"

"Oh, you haven't! Any more than you've said a word of blame because I asked you to lay out of politics. But you look, *you look!* Even when we sleep, you still goddam *look!*"

Then he laughed, really laughed, and shook his head. "God, I'm still on that! Do you think I have a problem in that area?" He sat up, came over to ruffle her hair, sat down again across from her. "You're a crazy girl. Does it really matter a hoot in hell whether I write another book?"

"Yes."

"Why?"

"Because you want to."

"No. You want me to. I'm your cause. If I'm not magnificent—" he stretched out his arms, taking in the room, the house, the distance from Malibu to Murray Hill—"what was the point?"

She wanted to say No, but her throat was filling, welling up.

"And despite everything," he smiled, "I like it here. I think part of the creative drive is a drive to belong. But I feel I belong here."

"You've belonged everywhere."

"Maybe that's my problem. But I do like it here. I like driving everyplace. I like living outdoors. I like writing movies." He looked at her, saw her swallowing hard, but had to go on. "Give up, Katie. I told you in New York I'd win and didn't want to. Katie, please give up. Please."

She shook her head, whispered the words. "I can't."

"Not on anything? Not on—"

"You," she said as the tears came, a downpour spilling over the pink patches on her cheeks. She pressed her lips tight to choke off, to strangle and stop the sobs, but her hands shot up and reached out blindly, and he came to her, held her, rocked her, kissed her hair, said over and over, "What is it? Katie, what is it?" until she got control long enough to say:

"I want us to love each other!"

"But we do," he said miserably. "That's the trouble, Katie, we do."

twelve

IT RAINED. Not real rain, just a thin Southern California drizzle but enough to wash the dust off the skinny palm trees which resembled giraffes with a poodle cut. Katie reveled in the omen, hallelujahed the dank drip, went chirping about like a cricket reborn. Her hair began to kink, but she and Hubbell looked at each other much more easily.

Logs burned constantly in the big fireplace. She wore a sweater, inhaled the lovely seaweed smell, and was delighted to find mildew on the floor of the bedroom closet. Hubbell bought both of them duffel coats but refused to put the side curtains on his MG.

"I got an odd letter from Brooks Carpenter today," he said, drying off in front of the fire.

"Why didn't he just phone? Where is he?"

"Didn't say. He asked if we would meet him after dinner at the Driftwood Inn."

The Driftwood Inn was a junky jukebox-restaurant no one ever went to. It advertised fried abalone-in-the-basket.

"That dump? I wonder why."

"He's moved and there was no return address, no phone, nothing. So I guess we have to go."

She laughed. "I guess that was the idea."

The joint was congealed in a dark, beery light which made everyone a failure. About a dozen losers staggered through conversations while the jukebox played "Stardust" as a rhumba. In a damp, neglected, glassed-in extension, Brooks Carpenter sat at a soggy driftwood table in a Bill Verso trench coat. He still had his pipe, but was smoking a cigarette.

"Sorry about the cloak-and-dagger routine," he apologized after the watery drinks arrived.

"Oh, we understand," Katie said eagerly.

"Our protection," Hubbell said.

"Being seen with me won't automatically send you to Leavenworth." He bit down on his pipe. "I should not have said that."

"You certainly should," Hubbell said.

"I should not." He fought in vain against the professorial diction his characters fortunately lacked. "A by-product of the Committee is the oversensitivity to which some of us have become prone. At any rate, the secrecy is for my protection as well. May I bore you with a brief preface?"

"For Chrissake, Brooks!"

"Right." He picked up his drink, put it down. "I'm a novelist. Or was. Thus you might think the blacklist would provide a forced impetus to return me to my real work. Unfortunately, I lived high on the hog. The fat checks were seductive and, arrogantly, I assumed I could allow myself to be seduced for as long as I pleased. Even the house had much too large a mortgage. So we've moved to the valley, rather far out. The schools are not— Well, at any rate, the obscene mail has not caught up with us as yet."

He paused and did drink. And lit another cigarette.

"To the point. I need money rather quickly— Oh, I am not hitting you for a loan." He smiled briefly, put out the cigarette, picked up his pipe. "I've written a screenplay."

"Oh, Brooks, that's wonderful!" Katie could touch his stubby hand now.

"Well, salable, at any rate. A producer at one of the majors is more than interested."

Not J.J., Katie thought, and linked her arm through Hubbell's.

"He's willing to buy it, which is the only real proof we ever have that anyone likes our work. The price— understandably not what I would have gotten before. But not too bad. The hitch, of course, is that for the studio the script needs the name of a politically acceptable author. A member of our Guild. And one whose reputation will deserve the sum my friend is willing to pay." He put the pipe down, lit another cigarette. "And one who can be trusted, of course."

The windows were thick with mist and spray. They might have been sitting in an aquarium; or the waiting room of a hospital; or a madhouse.

"Naturally, the proxy will get his share."

"Oh, Brooks."

"Hubbell. The risk involved is very real. Not for the

producer and not for me." He reached down for a brief-case. "I brought the script."

"I don't have to read it, I know it's good."

"Thank you, but I would rather you did."

"I don't want to." Hubbell grinned. "Say, what do you do when I get the Oscar?"

"Ah. What do *you* do?"

"Wouldn't it be marvelous?" Katie cried. "Then you could—"

"No." Both men said it together. Then Hubbell asked, "How soon must you know?"

Brooks cleared his throat. They could see his large Adam's apple go up and down. "Please don't stall."

"Can I have overnight?"

"Oh, certainly!"

They talked for a few minutes about his children, and his wife, who was typing manuscripts under another name.

Driving back down the wet highway to their beach house, they said nothing. Inside:

"Drink or coffee?"

"Coffee."

He built up the fire while she brewed a big potful in the kitchen. When she came into the living room with everything on a tray, he said:

"I suppose he wanted you there because he was sure where you stood."

"He's not the only one who's oversensitive," she said lightly, setting the tray down on the big, circular wooden coffee table. "I'm sure he figured you'd talk it over with me anyway."

She poured the coffee, held out a plate of the cookies he liked, but he shook his head.

"What would you do?"

"You know what I'd do, Hubbell, but I'm not a writer."

"It'd be so much simpler if he were a bad writer."

He finished his coffee. She poured him another cup. He poked up the fire.

"I'm sure it's a good script," he said. "I'd feel so ashamed, taking the credit. And, God in heaven, how would he feel, seeing my name on his work?" He came back to the coffee table and sat down. "I can't, Katie. All he wants is my name. Such as it is. But the only thing a writer really has is his name."

She reached for his hand and kissed it.

"What's that for?" he asked.

"I'm glad you're still a writer."

"You mean you approve?"

She stroked his palm slowly, then held it to her cheek. "Yes," she said at last. "I'm sure he'll find someone else. Someone who isn't really good."

Paula was having an Evening. Mainly refugees, for it was in honor of the latest arrival at her hostel: Berndt Hoffmann, author of thirty-seven long novels translated into almost as many languages, all of which were being spoken simultaneously in the little canyon house. The drip-drizzle prevented use of the garden, but the door to the porch was kept open to let out the smoke and the heat and the linguistic uproar.

Katie and Hubbell had their raincoats taken from them by a dark, radiant young woman with a marvelous body and wobbly eyes. Her voice bubbled and

she trilled an obscure scale as she skipped through the
dripping trees carrying the coats to the garage. Margo
was a modern dancer who was now ready to be an
actress, Paula said, and she was coaching her. Margo
also studied philosophy at U.S.C. and was teaching
Paula to cook Mexican.

"So it will no more forever be goulash and chicken
Kiev, thanks Got!"

Unlike the sick, the refugees didn't mention their es-
capes from death, or their problems or their politics.
There were outsiders present; complaints, needs, dis-
asters were for whispers in kitchens or in delicatessens
on Fairfax. Here was a party, a gathering, an Evening.
So they talked shop—which that night was literature.
Katie sought a synonym for "kvell" as she watched
Hubbell listening, questioning, participating, debating,
laughing—*included*. He was like the autographed copy
of his first novel, which topped a small pile of books
on Paula's desk next to the large pile autographed by
the tiny old man with the natty bow tie who was the
honored guest. And who sat now in Paula's French
desk chair, his feet crossed jauntily, his long fingers like
flying knives, talking only to Hubbell on the needle-
point footstool before him, honoring Hubbell. Hubbell
had charm and youth and talent and brains—but he
also must have had a press agent. Katie flew to the
kitchen to thank Paula.

A splotched apron over a new silk dress, she was
yanking a pan of what looked like miniature tortillas
out of the oven, and singing merrily in what sounded
like German. The story about operetta in Prague
couldn't have been true.

"You're incredible!"

"*It's* incredible!" Paula laughed, sweating with happiness. "I am sixty-three! What woman of sixty-three thinks it will happen again?"

The blood banged in Katie's ears. "You're not pregnant?" she tried with a grin, but Paula just looked at her.

"Oh," Katie said.

"Oh," Paula said back. "You are some combination: an American Puritan and an Old Testament Jew, and don't tell me I am anti-Semitic." She took salad dressing she had mixed in a Mason jar and poured it over a huge salad in a bowl made of one piece of wood. "You make certain things too difficult for yourself."

"Do I?"

Paula finished tossing the salad. "Would you take this inside?"

The bowl sat there between them, waiting.

"If you are disappointed in people, Kate, the fault might be yours. And I do not speak only of myself."

She picked up the bowl and held it out. Katie took it then, and went into the boxlike dining room. The carved and painted Austrian table, set for a buffet, had been pushed back against the fern-filled bay window. The lamps were turned off and Margo—trilling, humming, burbling—was lighting candle after candle like a gay pyromaniac. Katie set the salad bowl on the table and went quickly into the living room in search of Hubbell.

But he was looking for her, and led her through the animated babble to the porch. His head just cleared the leaking roof.

"What in God's name did Paula say?" he asked.

"About what? What do you mean?" She turned as though something in the dripping garden scared her.

"To Hoffmann, about me. He keeps calling me 'colleague'!"

"Well, you are."

"Katie, one book, one, ein! He keeps saying—" he imitated the old man's accent— " 'so prolific at your age, dear colleague.' "

"Attention! No more talk!" Paula, without her apron, was in the living room behind them. "Dinner is ready, thanks Got! Come, people!"

They turned to her and she smiled, mockingly, Katie thought.

"You two as well. Come on: in you go, in you go."

Katie held back.

"Aren't you having a good time? What's wrong?" Hubbell asked.

"Nothing."

"Come on, what?"

"Nothing. Well, nothing except that you were right about Paula. She is a Lesbian."

He laughed. "Oh, I just said that because I was sore that she didn't like the picture."

"But she is."

"At that age, it sometimes happens. So what?"

So nothing; so clear the floor for an after-dinner orgy; so along with political decay goes sexual decay and the Decline and Fall of the Western U.S.A.; so she was an Old Testament Jew except that she had never read it.

"Mr. Gardiner!" Old Hoffmann plucked at Hubbell's sleeve and smiled astigmatically at Katie. "Excuse me. One further thought. I have run from so many countries

I have run out of countries. Does not matter. Always, I can write. Even in prison. That is my job, our job, we are professionals. Which, dear colleague—" Hubbell pressed Katie's hand—"is our security. Also our pleasure. You are too young, too successful to appreciate." They were standing by Paula's desk: he brought his hand down on Hubbell's novel on top of the small pile of other novels. "Ach, to be so prolific at your age—"

"Berndt, for Got sake!" Paula was back, deftly steering him toward the dining room. "No more talk until you eat!"

"Later!" the old man called back.

Hubbell grinned at Katie. "You're loving it."

"Oh, no!"

"I'm going to be exposed before half of Mittel Europe because he thinks—"

"They eat as much as they talk!" Paula bustled around the room, pushing chairs close to table space, emptying ashtrays. "I hope there is enough!" She cleared all the books off her desk. "Two can eat here," she said, swiftly cramming the books into a drawer.

It was late when they got home from the party, but they both felt they had been whirled in a blender. They changed into jeans and sweat shirts but couldn't just sit in front of the fire.

"It's not raining," Hubbell said.

"It never was."

He took their duffel coats from the hooks in the narrow hall and they tromped out to the beach. The fog hung. She put out her tongue to taste it; there was no taste. No movement, no feeling either: it simply clung to her like confusion. Or fear.

They were walking along the ocean—she could see it lying there under the fog—when he said, "Let's get the hell out of here and go to Europe."

Her heart skipped, stuttered, panicked.

"Oh, yes."

Oh, yes. Oh, Jesus, that was a grand display of enthusiasm after all her nagging looks. What was she afraid of?

"Do you really want to?" she asked.

"Yes."

She trudged through the sand with him, waiting.

"In one of his novels, Brooks Carpenter had a crazy character. A frightened man who always wore a mask. One day he woke up and couldn't get the mask off. It had become his face." He laughed and pretended to tug at his face. "Still comes off—but just!"

"You don't wear a mask!"

"Sure I do. Everyone does."

"You don't. I don't."

"Yes, you do."

"Well, not with you."

"Even with me."

"Well, sometimes maybe. But why do you have to?"

"Katie, I'm as spooked as the next guy! I wouldn't let Brooks Carpenter have my name. What name? Berndt Hoffmann has a name, I don't."

"You will!"

He put his arm around her. "I don't know. I really don't know how much I want one. But the boat's sailing."

"Is that why you want to go?" she said as casually as she could. "Or is it because of me pushing you or because you want to get away from some girl or because—"

"There's no girl I want to get away from," he said, having heard her fear very clearly.

The fog didn't lift, but her heart did. "O.K., then," she said and shouted, "*O.K.!*"

He picked her up, swung her around, then held her high above him as he had held Vicki's little boy in the tennis house.

"Hello, France!" she called.

"Italy!"

"Wherever!" She slid down until her lips met his. Then, her cheek against his, her mouth to his ear, she whispered, "Hubbell, can we have a baby?"

"Yes."

"What?"

"Yes. Why not? Hey, you're choking me!" He put her down. "But we'd better have it here. The hospitals are better and, anyway, we don't want passport problems, not these days."

"You mean it, you do mean it?"

"Well, we can't take a horse on the plane."

"You can buy one there, I promise!"

"But let's get the timing straight. Rewrites, shooting, cutting—Bissinger will want me around but that means more dough—" He was mouthing months, ticking them off on his fingers while she hugged him, singing inside. "Hey! We should be delivering our babies at about the same time!"

"*If!*"

He grinned. "Race you home!"

She was cooking breakfast in one of his sweaters. No

drizzle, no fog, but there was, at least, a distinct chill. The radio on the window ledge told her the time, the weather (unusual), the place to buy the newest used cars, and that Czechoslovakia had fallen to the Communist bloc. Well, in Russia they were undoubtedly saying Czechoslovakia had been saved from the imperialist dogs. Except who had a radio there? Stalin. No, too busy out purging. Paula would be purged there. Well, so would she. And that projection room acrobat should be.

The juice was squeezed, the coffee perking, the French toast in the pan—all just waiting for the master to get out of the bathroom and bounce downstairs for his vittles. She went into the living room and switched on the television. Still shots of J.J.'s pink-haired diz bomb star wiggled and wobbled while a fluctuating voice tried to explain her explanation of why she had joined the Communist Party. It was all for her Old Granddad, a working man, a man of the people, a pioneer who had been duped by the Communists into thinking they were Socialists. On his deathbed Old Granddad had asked Pink Hair to sign the Card to make sure she kept her feet on the ground. She had made a dying man happy—he was still dying at an undisclosed rest home—but she had never gone to a meeting, couldn't tell a Communist from a Fascist, and therefore hadn't named a soul. Except in secret session, Katie muttered as she ran up the stairs and banged on the bathroom door.

"Hubbell! Pink Hair Tells All!" She banged harder. "Come and get it—or we're going to be late!"

The door opened. He looked awful.

238

"I threw up again."

"Oh, Jesus. OH, JESUS!"

The doctor confirmed Hubbell's morning sickness: she was pregnant. He went to work on his screenplay like a madman. She threw out all her sleeping pills, bought baby books, knitting yarn, knitting books, drew up a budget, gave up martinis, opted for domestic wine and beer. And no pot roast on volleyball Sundays: spaghetti or Tuna Fish Delight.

Early one almost really cold morning Vicki Bissinger telephoned, shyer, more tongue-tied than ever. Congratulatory, apologetic, but she had a surprise if Hubbell and Katie could stop by on their way to the studio. Hubbell could handle Vicki's melancholy better than she, but she went along. Vicki was waiting for them in the driveway with her little boy, who grabbed Katie's hand and dragged her through the eucalyptus trees and the oleanders to the orange trees beyond. There was snow on some of the oranges.

Shouting and laughing, Katie and the child ran from tree to tree, scooping up little patches of snow until each had a handful. She rubbed hers on his face and he rubbed his on hers, and then they ran shouting and scooping until each had enough for a little snowball. He threw his at Hubbell but Katie, looking at Hubbell and Vicki smiling fondly like parents, gave her snowball to the little boy for another throw. Paula hadn't thought Hubbell that attractive, but Paula, of course, wasn't that interested in men. Oh, Vicki was too shy; and if Brooks Carpenter was oversensitive, she was oversuspicious and would ruin everything if she wasn't careful.

She hauled out the French lesson records and went at them with the determination of a recruit for the CIA. Hubbell said, "What makes you think they speak French in Italy?"

She wasn't about to buy Italian records. For one thing, she was sure they were going to live in France; for another, she was getting very stingy—Mrs. Silas Marner, Hubbell called her. So she invited J.J. to dinner and blathered so much about neorealism in the Italian cinema and the glorious future of Italian films that J.J. went out and bought a set of records which she promptly borrowed. He had come to dinner alone. Jeanne Twitchell was in New York, scouting the new shows for possible movie material for J.J. At least, so J.J. told everybody. Nobody really believed him and nobody really cared.

Katie used French as a bridge over the gap with Paula. It was easy to avoid the house in Laurel Canyon —there were so many meetings there to raise funds for the Hollywood Ten, etc.—and when she and Paula did have lunch, only French she is spoken here, Katie insisted, effectively limiting the conversation.

One day, returning from Frascati's, Paula said in English, "You're very happy."

"Yes, I am."

"I'm glad." Then Paula said, "I, too, am very happy," and waited.

"I'm glad," Katie did say.

Paula chuckled. "Perhaps I could be a dentist and also pull teeth," she said, and went into the Writers Building.

Morning and evening Katie examined the profile of her body. By the end of March she decided that the doctor was incompetent, it was a false alarm, she was doomed to be barren. Two weeks later she renounced tennis, convinced she was going to have twins. Hubbell said she was knitting and sewing enough for triplets and was making him jealous before even one of them was born.

"That's just a ploy," she laughed. "You want to spend money on horseback riding."

"I'm on my way, Mrs. Marner." But he picked up his tennis racquet and went off to the Bissingers'.

She trailed along that day, but not again. George was irritable—the Un-American Committee was snooping around him—and he nastily recommended Reno as a spa for depressed females. It depressed Katie to see Vicki so depressed; and, more, to see the bewildered little boy.

Adele came to the Malibu house one day, interrupting the language records but knitting now for the center of Katie's universe.

"We won't be here for the shower, let alone the birth," she announced. "We're going back East."

"Why?"

"Stash can't get work anyplace. Not even as an accountant." No protest tinged that flat, overprecise enunciation. "He's perfectly qualified, but then they ask what he's been doing. When they find out why he's not doing it any more, they get very crude. Democracy is in real danger when the citizens accept the word of the bureaucrats as gospel."

"Well, the Russian people aren't exactly up in arms over that ridiculous denunciation of Khatchaturian and those other composers. How can music follow the Party line?"

Adele didn't shrug; she never moved unnecessarily. "Oh, you too?"

"What do you mean?"

"The routine defense of this country is to attack the Soviet Union."

For too many minutes they knitted in silence. Then Katie put down her needles and massaged her face, her long fingers pushing the corners of her eyes upwards.

"What are you doing?" Adele asked.

"Hopefully, getting ready to pass."

"Not a very good joke, Kate. The Chinese undoubtedly will take over one day."

Maybe she was Chinese: there was certainly no clue as to what went on behind that face.

"Stash and I were married last week," she said abruptly.

"Oh, Adele! Why didn't you tell someone?"

"I think marriage is an outmoded institution. I did it because Stash badly needs confidence. Can you lend us money?" She said the sentences as though they followed in perfectly natural sequence. "He makes his customary bad jokes, but he's at the end of his rope. We don't have enough money to go East and he must get back there. I realize the difficulty because of Hubbell's position—"

"Don't say that! You and Stash are his friends just as much as you're mine!"

"I'm not asking for a friend, I'm asking for a political victim."

"Oh, for God's sake, you're asking for your husband!"

"I would never ask for sentimental reasons. I

wouldn't be able to. And neither Stash nor I would accept money given that way."

"O.K.," Katie said wearily.

"If you can help us, Kate, simply put a check in the mail. For cash, of course." She put her knitting away in a big sack. "Whatever you can spare. Anything." She stood up. "Anything at all."

"A thousand! Hubbell, they're not flying East, they're driving. That has to come out of our money for Europe."

"Sure."

Sure. Said so lightly.

"What are you sore about?" he asked, helping himself to more beef stew.

"She'll only accept money for a 'political victim,' not for a friend! She deliberately used that approach to make me feel guilty."

"About what?"

"About—" she caught herself just before she said "laying out." "About not being involved."

He teetered on his kitchen chair (they often had dinner in the kitchen now). "I didn't know you still felt guilty."

"I don't. Oh, maybe a little, sometimes. How about giving them two hundred? Oh, two hundred and fifty."

"Am I bid three?"

"All right, three, but that's it."

"Yes, Mrs. Marner." He cleared the table while she cut him a piece of lemon meringue pie.

"You think I'm being chintzy?"

"No."

"You do want to go to Europe?"

"Sure."

Sure. Said so lightly. Well, they were going and, once there, the sun could shine its head off.

She was so enchanted with her growing belly that she didn't even mind it was hot. Too hot to speak English or French, but Paula pulled her through their weekly lunches in the garden at Frascati's by chattering safely about Current Events. Ben-Gurion proclaimed the State of Israel; the Soviet Union recognized Israel; the Arabs went to war against Israel, and the United States laid out, slapped down an embargo just as it had in the Spanish Civil War.

"Nations are like people," Paula said. "Once the pattern is set, they don't change."

"They change sides."

"For expediency only. Not patterns. My pattern has always been erratic, yours has always been cut straight, rigid." She smiled rather sarcastically. "I speak of you personally, not politically, of course."

Trying to get even, but not succeeding, not with this lovely melon of a belly. Well, succeeding a little: Katie called for the check and paid it.

"My treat."

"Merci. Grazie. Danke Schön. I will contribute the same to the Ten—anonymously, of course."

What a bitch. But Katie wanted to applaud or laugh as they used to; or give the money herself as she used to.

It got hotter. Her belly grew bigger, the palm trees drooped, and twelve leaders of the legal Communist

Party were indicted by a Federal Grand Jury for being Communists, which even their stationery said they were. Shooting started on Hubbell's picture, then stopped: Bissinger was summoned to Washington by the Un-American Activities Committee.

"Well, that proves how insane they are!" Katie said. "I wonder if Vicki knows."

Vicki and George had separated. She had taken her son and gone, not to Reno but to her parents in Altoona or Reading, some place in Pennsylvania where sun meant summer and change.

"She must know," Hubbell said. "It's been in all the papers."

"I hope it doesn't send her rushing back to him."

"Not a chance. Anyway, he doesn't want her back," he added as he packed his suitcase.

The studio adjusted everything for the convenience of the Un-American Committee, including the shooting schedule. The company was shifting to New York for location shots under Hubbell's supervision.

"No, I'm not directing! There's only one half-page scene. The rest is walking along streets, mainly in Brooklyn Heights, on the bridge, past the St. George Hotel—all that stuff. Katie, smile! It's extra dough, and I'll only be gone two weeks."

"You said maybe three."

"At the outside." He tossed a torn sock in the wastebasket. "Leave it there! Now, you're not going to have the baby prematurely, so I'll be back way ahead of time, a month easily."

"O.K. We'll have a coming-out party. I just wish you weren't flying. I wish the Un-American Committee would drop dead. I wish you were back. I also wish I'd just shut up."

"Good idea." He grinned.

When he had finished packing and was dressed, she waddled to the door with him. The studio had sent a limousine to take him to the airport.

"A star at last!" she said.

"Call if there's anything."

"I will. Collect."

"Just say it's Mrs. Marner calling. Be a good girl."

"*You* be a good boy."

"I will."

"Ha. That'll be a novelty."

Out in the dusty lane the studio chauffeur coughed discreetly as though he were auditioning for the part of a studio chauffeur coughing discreetly. Katie and Hubbell laughed.

"See you," he said, going out the door.

She grabbed at the tail of his jacket, caught it. He turned and, seeing her face, dropped the suitcase and tried to put his arms around her. The hall was narrow, the suitcase and her belly got in the way, but he managed to kiss her.

A week after he had left, she was still making too much breakfast coffee, but at least only one glass of orange juice. She had knitted and stitched and sewed more clothes than the baby could wear unless it remained a baby forever, but she had forgotten she was going to be in the hospital too. So she decided to shop for nightgowns and bed jackets during her lunch hour.

It was cool and rich in Magnin's. She dawdled, delighting in all the clothes she could wear afterwards

—but she would buy them in France. Certainly everything was cheaper and better there, she and Hubbell would be better there, the baby would be bilingual—

"Kate!"

It was Rhea Edwards. Feather-cut cap of graying curls, bosom-tight lilac cashmere, piranha smile. She held out a white-gloved claw and Katie had to take it. Rhea, clamping Katie's hand in both of hers, feigned interest in the baby and Hubbell's movie while Katie's eyes darted around, afraid there was someone they knew, darted back, afraid of Rhea. Yet what could Rhea do to Hubbell? They were going to Europe—but passports were being taken away. And Selma Fielding had named people she merely suspected, Selma Fielding who had crossed the street to avoid saying hello to Rhea Edwards.

"You're afraid of me," Rhea accused. "That's unkind and unfair, Kate. You have to let me explain, you must. You were always fair. The least you can do is listen."

Katie couldn't move fast, she lumbered. And since Rhea still gripped her hand, she wasn't escaping, she was sort of dragging Rhea along with her. Christ, it probably looked as though she was going into labor and Rhea was taking her to the hospital! It was ridiculous and hopeless; she was helpless and afraid of Rhea Edwards.

"Well, let's go sit someplace and have something cool," she said. And thought she was being very crafty by insisting they go in two cars.

But Rhea tailed her like a spy, and when they entered the Beverly Brown Derby, paraded her down the aisle like Agent with Hottest Star in town. Lunch was over, there weren't many people, but most knew Rhea:

she was the Star, stuck with her fat, ugly sister. Gratefully Katie crept into the back of the darkest booth. Her belly allowed her to sit sideways and prevented Rhea from sitting next to her.

She didn't dare hide behind dark glasses: Rhea was clever, Rhea would be insulted. So she concentrated on her chicken salad, examining each forkful for a pearl or a deadly bone. She was paranoiac, she laughed. Rhea didn't eat, just explained—so fluidly, so fluently, she must have explained to dozens by now. Maybe she and Selma Fielding had explained fluently to each other.

"Selma had the gall to invite me to dinner!" Rhea said. "The way she crawled to the Committee! And her only motivation was to save Monty's career!"

Rhea, however, had no career to save: Eddie could and did run the agency very well without her. Nor would she pretend she wanted to save the nation. What she did want was to destroy the Hollywood cell of the Communist Party because it was led by intellectual hypocrites who were accessories to murder.

Katie looked up from her chicken salad.

Rhea nodded sagely: oh, yes, all too true. When she was first with the Party, years ago, her work had been to help organize the farm workers. Constructive work, worthy of any party's support. But these overpaid Hollywood slob-intellectuals were only destructive, had no time for workers, only for parroting the Soviet line, for denigrating everything American, particularly for screeching like stuck pigs at the way America treated its writers and artists. But did they ever issue *one word* of protest against Russian treatment of *Soviet* writers and artists? No, never! And, being Americans, their utter silence could be and was taken by the Russians as endorsement of their vile practice of sending writers to Siberian exile, forced labor camps, torture dungeons, the firing squad. In short, by their refusal to protest the Hollywood Communist writers were aiding and abetting the murder of Soviet writers. That was reason enough for Rhea Edwards to destroy the Hollywood cell.

But, Rhea, Katie wanted to ask, lost on the underpass-overpass-cloverleaf freeways of Rhea's logic, but, Rhea, even if everything you say and I can't follow is true, how does it justify informing on others, getting your friends blacklisted, fired, sent to jail? She wanted to ask, but didn't, couldn't.

But Rhea had been giving her course in Mea Culpa for many weeks and had the answers ready for her students. "Oh, I know, Kate. Does that warrant naming these hypocrites? At the time, I thought it did. But, truthfully, I suppose it will be a long, long time before I know whether I did the right thing. And by then it won't matter."

Now Katie was free to look her in the eye and say, "Oh, well, I can tell you now, Rhea: you did the wrong thing. And if it matters, I think you're a shit."

And to her horror she laughed, because she had never used that word before.

She pulled away from the Brown Derby, drove carefully through traffic until she was on some street where sprinklers made lawns into putting greens, and parked at the curb between a hacienda and Monticello. She was trembling, she could hardly light a cigarette. She wanted to call Hubbell, but there was the time differ-

249

ential, telephones were blind, what she really wanted was to look at a face. But the faces she wanted to look at were those she no longer saw.

Paula, Stash, and Adele remained, but like peripheral vision. And they would have been right to say—even though they wouldn't—Where have you been? What else is new?

In the end she drove to J.J.'s.

He was sitting by the pool made in his own image. Jeanne Twitchell was gone, never coming back. The problem, she had told him, was hers, not his: she had the desires of an adventuress with the heart of a slob. Mad as she was for security, she always fell for some intellectual creep who put her through the wringer and made her feel like a moron while she paid the tab.

"I knew that." J.J. sighed. "I knew she was begging to be treated badly, but I could never relax enough to do it. I've never relaxed enough with any woman but you, Kate," he said, biting a large hangnail.

He harked back to Judianne, to girls he had gone with in college, prep school, grade school. She said she had to go to the bathroom and tried telephoning Hubbell in New York. There was no answer at his hotel room; she left Mrs. Marner's name. J.J. picked up his monologue before she got through the terrace door, droned on mournfully, enjoying his misery. She said she didn't want to have to drive back to Malibu after dark and finally got out. Without ever mentioning Rhea Edwards.

She called Hubbell again the moment she got home. His room still didn't answer: probably out to dinner; no, it was too late for that in New York; well, maybe he had gone to the theatre. She left her name, made supper, ate supper, called again. His room still didn't answer; he hadn't picked up her messages. Maybe they were doing night shots in Brooklyn; she tried to remember the script. She left her name again, said it was important, and went to sleep in the big bed hugging his pillow.

She woke up just after midnight and called again. His phone was turned off, he could not be disturbed. Would you please ring through, it's urgent? I am sorry, madame, but I cannot, please don't raise your voice, madame, I cannot ring through, if you want to call, do so in the morning. Click. She got up, made warm milk in the kitchen, came back upstairs, drank the milk, smoked a cigarette, looked at the orange walls, the picture of the Three Sisters, straightened the sheets, got back in bed.

She called again at three. At four. At five. The sleeping pills were gone, so she took aspirin. She called at seven; eight; nine. She called the studio to say she wouldn't be coming in; called later to say she would never be coming in. Called New York all the long afternoon, sat on the deck with a floppy hat to cut off the sun and with the telephone on the long extension cord in her lap.

Thinking of the baby, she tried to make herself eat, make herself sleep. She managed to force food down, not much, mainly milk. The operators at the New York hotel grew irritated, got nasty, were openly contemptuous. She stopped leaving messages, took to a French accent, an Italian accent (worse), put a handkerchief over the mouthpiece, but kept calling. She never left the house, never left the telephone, even dragged it into the bathroom. Her heart crashed when it rang, but she cut short any local conversation before it began: I'm expecting a long-distance call.

And a baby.

Her great belly reminded her that she was not dead. But she felt incredibly dry, numb, third person. In New York, in Murray Hill, she had got under a shower with all her clothes on and cried a shower. Here in Malibu, after two days, she creamed her face, combed her hair carefully, put on a clean tent, cologned, put on her dark glasses, and drove up the coast in the bright white sun. She stopped at a drive-in to give the baby something to eat, then drove back, past Malibu, into Topanga Canyon, over the pass into the Valley.

Heat slapped the face she wore, slammed the body she was in, soaked the back of her dress: she could hear it come unstuck when she moved away from the leather. But she felt dry; her eyes, tongue, throat were dry. Still, the heat was not good for the baby, so she drove back over another pass which turned out to be Laurel Canyon.

It was cooler when she came over the peak, cooler as she dropped down the twisting road in and out of sun and shadow. Lookout Mountain Road was all shadows, a cool leafy road to drive up and up until she was in Paula's driveway. Only the battered, over-age car was there. She parked behind it and went into the lopsided house, into the kitchen where there was a thumping sound. Paula was kneading dough, making strudel. Katie burst into tears and Paula held out her arms.

thirteen

"Good morning. Did I wake you?" Hubbell's voice was cheery.

"Yes, but that's all right. Hold on a second."

She took a sip of coffee from the hot mug on the bedside table, plumped up the pillows, leaned back so that she could see the sun-tipped ocean through the window, put the phone in her lap, and lit a cigarette. All this without hurrying: he could wait; the studio was paying for the call anyway.

"Sorry. How's it going?" she asked.

"Never mind that; how are you?"

"Large."

"What's the doctor say?"

"All's on schedule."

"What's the matter?"

"Nothing, why?"

"You sound as though something's wrong."

"Oh, my voice isn't up yet."

"I'm sorry I woke you, but I was worried. I hadn't heard from you."

Really. "Oh, I called. Twice or so. I left messages."

"At this hotel?" He laughed. "Don't bother. The heat's made everyone irritable and incompetent."

He had once told her he would make a good liar: he was wrong.

"Well, anyway, I'm fine and dandy," she said. "How's the picture going?"

"O.K. Again, except for the heat. You're lucky not to be here. Everything takes twice as long. I'm on the streets at dawn and get back God knows when. I just turn off the phone and flake out in a puddle."

Not bad, almost convincing—if she were still wearing beads and rain hats.

"Bissinger popped up the other day for a few hours. He—was pleased with the work."

She could hear he had meant to say something else. "How's it going for him in Washington?"

"Oh, he says he's playing Edwardian gentleman with a long line of patriotic ancestors. Offended by the vulgarity of the Committee, but too distinguished to allow it to show. He hasn't told them a damn thing and won't."

"He doesn't know a damn thing to tell them." She gave Bissinger a transfusion of her venom. "I suppose if he has to stay on in Washington, you'll be back later than you figured." She was generous with rope; he could have all he wanted.

"No, I'll be coming home pretty much as planned. Around the end of next week. I'll call you. How are things at the studio?"

"I quit."

"Good. Just stay home and admire your beautiful belly."

"I really haven't had time. I've been going to meetings with Paula." She slipped the knife between his ribs, but he only laughed.

"I'm glad you made up with her. Give her my love. I'll be right there!" he shouted to someone.

Probably no one. Or someone in a shower.

"Listen, I have to run, Katie. Please take it very easy. And call. Or I'll call. I'll let you know when I'm coming home . . ."

When she hung up she let her head drop back into the pillows and closed her eyes. Holding back anger was exhausting; she wanted to sleep. But she had volunteered to make arrangements with the Beverly Wilshire Hotel for a dinner honoring Henry Wallace. And Mrs. Roosevelt was going to speak, Mrs. Roosevelt, who no longer went down into the coal mines but still kept her banner flying.

Hubbell had laughed at the idea of a Third Party, and at Henry Wallace:

"How can you have a President who consults rainmakers?"

She wished she knew of a good rainmaker. "Better than a President who drops atom bombs or one who looks like Hitler," she had retorted.

But that was before Hubbell had gone to New York.

Now, she flung the blanket aside and made herself dress. After the Beverly Wilshire, lunch with Paula; then a fund-raising meeting for the Unfriendly Ten. She had only said she might go. Because she might be too tired.

Paula was being funny about Richard Nixon, the California representative on the House Un-American Committee. "The Red-baiting Quacker," she called him.

"Quaker." Katie lowered her voice.

"He also quacks." Paula didn't care who was at the next table. "He is head goose in the new animal act of the Un-American Committee. Attention headline writers! Quack quack! Now presenting, in order to save my country, the one and only FBI-trained white rat: Whittaker Chambers and his Magic Pumpkin!"

"Quack quack," Katie applauded.

"The pumpkin is our national fruit, symbol of Thanksgiving, so let us give thanks to Rat Chambers and *his* pumpkin: In this pumpkin, my fellow geese—quack quack—are secrets so modern, they are on microfilm!"

"Thanks Got!"

"Quack quack quack," Paula said. "A cheap spy novel."

"Alice in Wonderland."

"Malice in Wonderland—that is Nixon."

"No, that's Rhea Edwards. She's an earthquack."

"Earthquake," Paula corrected. "Oh, quack! Yes, oh, mein Got, of course, quack, earthquack!"

They laughed, they giggled, they were silly: they were relieved to be friends again.

Paula had listened to Katie's worried guesses about Hubbell in New York, saying merely, "Accept it or don't. It is really not worth so little sleep and so much crying for a woman in her eighth month. And it is childish to threaten a divorce you don't want." She had gone on making her strudel while Katie cried and cried and used up half a box of Kleenex. But Paula had not said one word about herself and Margo, and Katie hadn't been able to ask. She couldn't; she couldn't understand Paula and any woman, any two women. But then Paula had said that she was happiest when she had a love affair. So if it was love, it was all right. Anyway, Paula was European.

When they left the restaurant they kissed good-bye: an after-lunch-with-hats-kiss where lips might graze a cheek or kiss air, nothing more. Katie touched her hair to see if it was frizzy and needed doing. Her stomach, as she maneuvered to fit herself behind the wheel of her car, was ridiculously gross and unattractive. She put on her dark glasses and looked at the dashboard clock: it was the end of the day in New York. If Hubbell was in his hotel room, he probably wasn't alone. In Westwood, the meeting for the Unfriendly Ten was just about to start. She tried to get over into the fast lane on Sunset and wished she had a chauffeur. It was going to be very nice in the hospital, where she would only have to do as she was told. And it would be cool.

Driving with the top down was driving in a hot tunnel of heavy air. The pale, monotonous haze of sun made the campus coming up on her left shimmer and waver like a green oasis, so she turned off and drove through the university grounds. There were no sycamores, but there were no palm trees. And there was a small rally before a building without white pillars but with stone steps cascading from under a portico. If she had a dollar for every building like that on every campus in the country she would give the money to Stash and Brooks Carpenter, and Hubbell would still be in New York with the girl who was probably the misty-haired vacuum cleaner from the projection room floor. She would put the money in the bank for the baby, for college: to have her hair straightened when she got there.

She stopped the white convertible by the curb. Until that minute she had been certain the baby would be a boy and blond.

Across the green came applause for a speaker at the rally. She eased out of the car: a big fat pregnant lady was not going to get a parking ticket. Slowly she moved both of them across the grass, the woman with the bulky stomach and the girl with the frizzy hair.

Her Peace Rally had had a bigger turnout, and the girl at this microphone wore pigtails, a man's shirt, blue jeans and loafers.

"We must support the Faculty in its determination to resist any Loyalty Oath. Fear must not smother academic freedom. Inroads have already been made: we have our blacklist, our informers in our classrooms, in our laboratories . . ."

Very calm, very straightforward, this girl was. No jokes, no passion, no nerves, but no heckling either. Katie wandered along the fringe of the crowd, leaned against a golden oak and examined them. The same, yet different. Those on the grass didn't sprawl or loll; they sat up and listened as attentively as those standing. More serious, but just as young, as eager, as bright, as beautiful. And more committed.

When the meeting broke up, she was still there, against her tree, tears trickling down her pink cheeks. Two of them came over, helped her back to the white-and-red convertible: a boy and a girl, president and vice-president of the YCL if they had a YCL. They must have thought she was drunk or demented the way she kept wiping her eyes, blowing her nose, smiling at how beautiful they were, how hopeful; silently begging them to keep holding the banner high and not turn into vegetables. Oh, obviously they thought it was all so easy, but that was simply because they were so goddam young.

Hubbell came home on a Crazy Sunday—crazy because of them, not because of the weather, which was perfect—at least, for someone just back from New York or Siberia. On Saturday Katie had telephoned Paula—several times before she reached her—and begged her to come to lunch Sunday, spend the afternoon, help her over the first few hours with Hubbell. And bring Margo, by all means.

"Margo has gone to Mexico City."

"What for?"

"To marry a lawyer."

"Oh, Paula. How are you?"

"Lousy." Paula laughed. "Lousier yesterday, though. I'll bring cold chicken."

They were four anyway: Hubbell called from the airport to say Bissinger had been on the same plane and had invited himself to lunch.

"Sure," she said, suspecting Hubbell was uneasy too. The hope, the possibility that he felt guilty made her light on her feet. She almost danced to the closet for a fresh tent sprinkled with orange and yellow seashells, and planned a picnic lunch on the beach in front of the house.

The ocean was blue, the sun glittered gaily, there was even an airy puff that could be called a breeze.

Katie overflowed her chair like Mrs. Billy. She sat under a pretty umbrella large enough to shade her, the lunch, and Paula, who was chic Earth Mother in a white coolie jacket and pants. Hubbell stretched out on a striped towel, half-drowsing behind sunglasses which also served to deflect the occasional odd barbs thrown at him by Bissinger. The director was buried in sand up to his armpits, a protective towel over his startlingly white skin (even whiter than Pony Dunbar's), his white Panama hat shielding his face.

"This is the last film I make in this asshole town," he said softly. "No loss, however. Hubbell has been trying on my shoes."

"What will you do, George?"

"Leave this pismire of a country."

"Where for?"

"Which of your native lands do you suggest, Paula?"

"Switzerland."

"Dandy," Bissinger said. "Let us all take chalets and ski."

"You and Hubbell can ski," Katie said. Maybe they would, maybe Hubbell and a New York hotel could simply be left on the cutting-room floor. "Paula and I will knit you splints."

"You will have to rent me a room in your chalet," Paula said. "On the cuff."

"Stop giving your money to your refugee leeches," Bissinger said.

"I have," Paula laughed, "too late. The studio has dropped me."

Quack quack. "Oh God, Paula."

Hubbell sat up. "When did it happen?"

"Friday." She shrugged and smiled as she sifted a

handful of sand. "An anonymous friend told the Committee I was a card-carrying member of the Party. The Committee said if I could give them some names—privately, of course—I would be cleared. The studio said if I did not give names I would be fired. Even if I wanted to give names, I do not know any, thanks Got!"

They had all been looking at her. Now she looked up and saw their faces and she laughed. "You don't believe me, either."

"Oh, Paula!" Katie said, reaching for her hand. "They've made us so crazy!"

And Hubbell said, "We all think everybody is either a member of the Party or an agent for the FBI."

And Katie said, "And what if you were a member!"

And Bissinger said, "I'll be goddammed, Paula! You fake!"

She smiled. "Forgive me. I am only a poor, premature anti-Fascist."

They laughed gratefully at that; asked questions, got angry, felt ashamed.

"You know the best?" Paula raised very European hands. "They offered to *give* me some names to name!"

"You're on my picture," Bissinger said quietly.

"Oh, George dear," Paula protested.

"You start tomorrow."

"But George! As what?"

"Oh—technical expert."

"Be sensible. Expert on what?"

"Brooklyn!" Hubbell said triumphantly. *"That's* where you come from!"

Paula laughed loudest of all, then said, "Danke schön, George."

"I loathe the sound of German," he said.

"Oh, George!" Katie beamed. "You're incredible!" She opened her arms, held out her hands. "I'm yours!"

"*After* you drop the melon," Bissinger said, and she laughed. "Then I'll find *us* a projection room."

Her laugh died, but the smile stayed stiff on her face as though she had been embalmed.

Paula drove Bissinger home, and Hubbell brought the umbrella and the chair and the towels back into the house. Katie stood by the gate-leg table, not moving until he returned balancing a tray loaded with all the picnic things. Then she blocked him with her huge bulk.

"And I thought Vicki Bissinger was so shy."

"Katie, I'd like to set this down."

"It is Vicki, isn't it?"

"No."

"Of course it is! I thought it was Jeanne Twitchell. But she doesn't have the right style any more than I do!"

"Katie, will you please let me take this into the kitchen?"

"How long has it been going on? Are you in love with her? Do you want to marry her?"

"I am married," he said sharply, pushing his way past her, "and you're making too much out of very little."

"Did George Bissinger make too much out of too little? Or did he catch you in New York with her pants down? He did, didn't he!"

She was screaming, propelling herself after him to the kitchen, where he set the tray down, holding the walls of the narrow hall to follow him back to the living room, where he fixed himself a drink.

"She wasn't in Pennsylvania, she was in New York, with *you!* I called and called—I didn't leave two messages, I left a hundred! I hope the ringing interrupted you in the middle! I hope the only ones who had a good time were those bitchy operators! Or did you go to Vicki's room to get away from the ringing, away from me? In which bed in what room did you do what you did in that disgusting projection room? YES, I SAW YOU! How would you like to walk in and see me—"

"I'd like it fine!" He slammed down the liquor bottle. "At least you wouldn't be such a Puritan martyr!" He grabbed her by the arm. "Now you shut up and calm down. You're having a baby—"

"Which you don't want!"

"I do! And I don't want you to hurt him or yourself." He relaxed his grip, still held her, but gently. "Come on, Katie. Be a good girl. Sit down and stop beating yourself."

She took a deep breath and smiled. "I thought I was beating you."

"No, always yourself. And you always lose. Because of me."

She always felt a lull, a pause, a silence was her responsibility. "Your arm, sir," she said, and he helped her to a big chair. As she sat heavily she felt a kick in her belly.

"Oh, boy!" she said. "Or girl." She relaxed her hands on the big mound. "It doesn't really matter if it was Vicki or someone else. Jesus, Hubbell, being a nice Jewish girl is a great pain in the ass. But I'm stuck with it."

"So am I." A smile whisked across his face.

"Are you? Oh, wouldn't it be lovely if we were old? We'd have survived all this, and everything'd be uncomplicated and easy again, the way it was when we were young. Oh, Hubbell, where are we?"

"Lost in nostalgia. Except—" even more gently— "nostalgia is for what you wish you'd had."

"O.K. So it wasn't all that uncomplicated, but it was lovely. Well—" she craned her head the way Bissinger did, mimicked his voice—"wherever we are, son, I expect you to see the not-so-little woman through the birth of your heir."

"Oh, Katie." He shook his head several times. "You don't have very great expectations any more."

"I think that title's been used."

"It's still good." He smiled back.

Each night they kissed tenderly and went right to sleep, to dream separately of roller coasters and teeth falling out and chases through tunnels and across deserts. He went to the studio every day, but insisted on driving her to the doctor because it was too uncomfortable now for her to sit behind the wheel.

They didn't need other people so much: there was always her belly or his picture to talk and laugh about. Or they could discuss, but not argue, the new Republic of Korea or the Peacetime Draft or knife-thin Mme. Chiang Kai-shek, who was touring the country, drumming aid for Nationalist China. Katie said Mme. Chiang was so thin because she ate nothing but money. And remembered Stash debating China in Vivian's antiseptic apartment, and wondered how he and Adele and Lefty were doing in New York.

She kept close to the house in Malibu, walking the beach for exercise, dreaming the days away in a golden haze. All seven layers of her mind melted into a single craving for chocolate chip ice cream. There was no volleyball, and he gave up tennis. He took his swim when he came home from the studio, and sometimes his ride along the beach.

One afternoon he came home later than usual to find her playing her French lesson records. She looked up at him with guilty hope, and he came over and kissed her.

"Just so it shouldn't be a total loss," she clowned. "Votre martini est dans le icebox."

"Merci mille fois." He started for the kitchen.

"Aren't you going to take your swim first?"

"No."

She busied herself putting away the records, determined not to ask why he was so late. But her palms were wet and her feet swollen, and she had to sit down.

He sat across from her, sipping his martini, looking as uneasy and uncomfortable as he had the day he returned from New York.

"Say it, Hubbell."

"Say what?"

"Whatever it is."

He fished out the olive. "Who is Frankie McVeigh?"

"Frankie McVeigh!" She laughed in relief. "We went to college with him. Well, *I* went to college with him. To our Senior Prom, as a matter of fact."

"And?"

And we did it behind the gym. "And nothing very

much. Oh." She smoothed her hair. "We were in the YCL together."

"Did you ever see him after college?"

"No. Why?"

"He informed on you."

"The little rat." She couldn't help grinning. "So he got even."

"It's not funny, Katie."

"But I left the Party during the war, you know that."

"*I* know; they don't."

He looked so worried, so serious, but she felt so relieved, so light-headed, even happy. "To hell with them!"

"Katie, they say you tried to get the studio to make a subversive movie."

"I what?"

"You recommended a book they claim was propaganda for Red China."

"Now that is pure, unadulterated—oh, Jesus. *'Shivouth!'*" She had to giggle. "Hubbell, the Chinese kibbutz! The Communist rice patties!"

"The matzohs, I know."

He didn't laugh, he didn't even smile. She knew him, and suddenly knew it wasn't funny, knew it was very serious and was going to be very bad for her.

"They really are insane, Hubbell. But I guess that's not the point."

"No, it isn't."

Her hands were cold now. "Who told you?"

"J.J."

They had sat by J.J.'s swimming pool with the phonograph blasting away inside the house because J.J. was as paranoiac as everyone else about bugging and eavesdropping. At first Hubbell hadn't got the point. He understood that J.J. was trying to help, and was grateful, but kept saying if they didn't like Katie's politics, let them blacklist her: he didn't care and he was sure she wouldn't. J.J. sweated, fiddled with his eyeglasses, ran in and out of the house getting fresh drinks—he was afraid, it developed, that Hubbell would think his old man was a terrible shit and afraid, at the same time, that his shit-heel of an old man would find that he had tipped off Hubbell. Anyway, he finally came out with it.

"The thing is, old buddy, you're married to her. And a studio employee can't have a subversive wife."

"It's none of their frigging business."

"Hubbell, they say it is."

"So?"

"So either she names names or you get the sack."

Well, there it was, really rather simple. The Un-American charmsters weren't insane, nor were they kidding. Quack quack; there's a pumpkin in every back yard. They were out to shut everyone up.

The sun spangled the whitewashed walls of the living room with orange-red, really a lovely color. Hubbell's glass was empty.

"Do you want another drink?"

He shook his head.

"Of course, they'd throw you off this picture and blacklist you. But you wouldn't be blacklisted in Europe, would you?"

"No, I wouldn't." He cracked his knuckles. "I think I will have another drink."

She watched him mix the martini, interested in how much could be told by someone's back, in how calmly she was sinking. One reason she had learned to swim so quickly in the blue Caribbean was that she knew she would never ever go down for the third time.

"Funny how decisions are forced on you willy-nilly. On 'one,' I should say. I mean, how one can't put them off." She laughed a little at herself being grand, then straightened up and pressed her hands into the small of her back. "You don't really want to go to Europe, do you, Hubbell? You want to stay here and work here. Don't answer, take the Fifth." She rattled on quickly, to help him too. "Listen, do you think it would be terrible if I had a very weak, very small but very dry martini?"

"Just one couldn't hurt. I'll make—"

"Don't smile!" she yelled, suddenly hating him.

It was true: people really did go white. She could almost see him count to ten before he spoke in a very calm voice:

"I am not telling you to do one thing or the other, Katie. I'm not even asking."

"The hell you're not!"

"The hell I am," he said so quietly that she spoke quietly too.

"Well, we both know what you'd like me to do."

There was a hook he could wriggle off, but he didn't. "Yes, we do," he said. "It's all out of control and snowballing downhill. It's senseless—to me, anyway—to wreck your life for a principle nobody gives a damn about any more. It won't prove anything or help anyone."

"It could hurt someone."

"Not any more."

"Just how do you figure that?"

268

"I don't think there are any names left for you to give them that they don't already have."

"Oh, I can think of one or two. Pony Dunbar, for example."

"Pony Dunbar has nothing to do with the movie industry. You wouldn't have to mention her."

"Well, there's someone else I *would* have to mention."

"Who?"

"Katie Morosky. Known as Kate Gardiner. Possibly someday as Katherine Gardiner—or is Vicki coming back? Or is she here?"

"Katie." He had the drink for her in his hand, but he set it down on the bar. "Will you believe one thing, please? What's wrong between us is not because of Vicki or any other girl."

Now she understood why some people went down for the third time and elected to stay down in the cool dark. "Oh," she said. "Well. Could I have that drink, please?"

"Oh, I'm sorry."

"Thank you." She tasted it, wished it were stronger. "Well, sir, Miss Bankhead, let's be objective or something. First things first, etc. I don't—what was I going to say? Isn't that ridiculous?"

"Katie—"

"Oh, yes. First things first. I don't know of any justification for informing. None; the opposite, in fact. There's something really wrong with any country that grows informers. And the people who promote informing are as evil and disgusting as the people who do it. On the other hand, there are the innocent bystanders

—like you." She tried to smile and lost control. "Oh God, Hubbell, say what you want me to do!"

He was shaking his head violently. "Run for your life, Katie! Heads you lose, tails I lose. We were both wrong. Run for your life!"

He walked quickly to the door leading to the beach and the dark ocean. She put her glass down without finishing her drink. He didn't open the door, just stood there, staring out.

"Once," she said, "oh, months and months ago, we went to bed and it wasn't good, not at all, and I was glad. For both of us. But it was only that once. Listen, Hubbell—"

"What?"

"If we got a divorce, you wouldn't have a subversive wife."

She waited, but he didn't move from the door, didn't speak.

"That would solve everything, wouldn't it?" she asked.

Now he came over and knelt by her and took her hand. "No," he said sadly, "it wouldn't."

"Got any better suggestions?"

He shook his head slowly. "No," he said, and squeezed her hand very tightly.

It was a good room, she was glad of that. He had told the hospital he wanted her to have a very good room and it was: a good size with a big window and a big tree outside which intercepted the sunlight. She had not been in labor too long, the baby was a healthy girl, and she was glad of that too.

She looked at Hubbell standing at the foot of the

bed, almost as thin as Bissinger, who stood next to him.

"Well," she said with a rueful smile, "I guess we should have had a horse."

She saw tears flood Hubbell's eyes, but it was Bissinger who came around to the side of the bed and took her hand.

fourteen

THE SALESWOMAN at Saks resembled Paula Reisner. Or maybe Katie just thought so because of the letter in her bag from Vienna, where Paula was happily translating and angrily protesting all the Nazis whom the Austrian government sheltered and embraced. The saleswoman did have an unplaceable accent and sardonic humor, but unlike Paula and like everybody in the Men's Department, she could not be hurried, and now Katie would be late. She snatched her charge plate and rushed out of the store.

Even the traffic on Fifth Avenue was beautiful, and the people had their own faces. It was late spring but early enough in the afternoon for a few to sit on the steps of St. Patrick's and use the sun for warming, not tanning. She tried to hurry but the weather, more than the shoppers, refused to let her walk very fast. In Central Park people were probably napping on the grass.

Somewhere Eisenhower was sure to be playing golf. And John Foster Dulles dominoes. She would stop in at F. A. O. Schwarz later and get her genius daughter a set, if she had time.

The face of one of the big clocks took the smile off hers: she *had* to walk faster. By 56th Street, her calf muscles were tightening: high heels, and she hadn't played tennis in four years. The light was against her and she hesitated: she could cross the Avenue but she did want just a look at Bonwit's windows.

Then she saw him, walking past the windows, coming to a halt at the curb directly opposite. Clinging shyly to his arm was Vicki—no, the hair was paler, the figure more angular, and Vicki never wore beige. His clothes and his tan said he was still living in Southern California; and when he looked up from the girl and found her, she saw that his grin hadn't changed either.

She grinned back. They stood there, grinning at each other through the traffic, shaking their heads, laughing. The light turned green, they started to cross at the same instant, but she waved him back to his corner.

He looked at her, took her hands, kissed her, introduced her to his girl—Katie didn't hear her name—looked at her again, put his arms around her, kissed her. They grinned and laughed and told each other how marvelous they looked, how they hadn't changed a bit. She was delighted she was wearing her new suit, was easy and confident because she knew she looked so well in it. He looked older, older than he should have.

"How's the baby?" he asked.

"She isn't a baby any more, she's practically four years old! Oh, Hubbell, come see her!"

He shook his head. "Chicken." He grinned, and explained to the girl—Laurie, her name was—that he'd never seen the baby out of her bassinet. And when Katie remarried, her husband had adopted the baby, so she really wasn't his.

"Still married?" he joked, and the embarrassment or pain or whatever it was left his eyes, and they were that blue again.

"Yep," she said. The girl wore a ring, but not on that finger.

"Then I guess it was all for the best."

She wasn't certain whether he was asking, but "Yes, it was," she said.

He focused on a new foreign car that had stopped in front of them, then returned to her, laughing. "Guess who else is in town: George Bissinger!"

"My God!"

"We're going to Africa."

"You're kidding!"

"No! To make a flick. Oh, Katie, it's going to be a complete, glorious, unadulterated disaster! J.J.'s producing and he's scared shitless of animals!"

"And George. And you. And whoever his girl may be."

"His wife."

"Now you are kidding!"

"Cross my heart."

"Does she wear shoes?"

"You don't know her. She thinks she's going to do the costumes for the movie, but Bissinger's making elaborate plans for her to get constant dysentery. It's all crazy! But it should make a marvelous comic novel. That's really why I'm going."

274

"Oh, Hubbell, that's wonderful," she said, unable to make her voice bubble, and suddenly there was a gap neither of them could fill.

The girl took Hubbell's hand: Katie always underestimated those girls.

"Listen, Hubbell," she said, "I'm awfully late. When are you leaving?"

"Day after tomorrow."

"Will you call and come for a drink? Please. It's the only David X. Cohen in the book."

"What's the X for?"

"The only David X. Cohen in the book," she said, and they laughed, even his girl laughed, and Katie hurried up the street, past Bonwit's windows.

At 58th Street she dodged cars effortlessly as she ran across to the Fountain in the plaza. The tables were set up, the sign—BAN THE BOMB NOW!—was tacked in place, but it was lettered too discreetly. Evie, wearing her sensible shoes and that damn brown suit, was unpacking the leaflets and the brochures and the petitions.

"I'm sorry I'm late," Katie apologized.

"Better late than never," said Evie, being Evie, and they embraced briefly, each kissing air.

Fortunately there were quite a few passersby who were interested and wanted just a little encouragement before signing their names. Katie gratefully closed down the other layers of her mind and concentrated on the petitions and handing out leaflets until Evie said:

"Someone is cruising one of us, and I doubt if it's me."

On the other side of the Avenue Hubbell was leaning

275

out of a taxi, waving to get Katie's attention. She waved back. He shouted something but she couldn't hear, so she just shook her head and held up her hand and went on with her work.

The taxi went up the Avenue to where it could turn around the entrance to the Park and come back down her side of the street. She wasn't aware that it had drawn up to the curb directly in front of her until the door opened and Hubbell got out. He just stood there, looking at her, not smiling at all. Slowly she walked over to him and because she had to do something and couldn't think of anything else, held out a leaflet.

"You never give up, do you?" he said.

"Only when I'm absolutely forced to," she said gaily. "But I'm a terribly good loser."

"Better than I am," he said.

"Oh, well, I've had more practice." She smiled. "Your girl's lovely, Hubbell. Bring her for a drink when you come. And George."

"Oh, Katie," Hubbell said. "I can't come. I can't."

In the sunlight she could see flecks of gray in that very blond hair. She wanted to touch where it was gray.

"I know," she said.

He took her hand and they looked at each other, and then his arms were tight around her and his cheek was tight against hers. Just a moment; then he released her, stepped back, took her free hand in both of his.

"Is he a good father?" he asked.

She nodded, her eyes blinking for a second. "Very."

"Good."

He shook her hand as though in gratitude, then took the leaflet and grinned. "See you, Katie."

He turned quickly and walked back to the taxi. He even got into a taxi gracefully. She saw his hand pull the door shut, saw the taxi drive off, saw leaves flutter in the sunshine.

From far, far away she heard his voice call:

"Hey, Katie!"

And there she was, frizzy hair and lumpy brown skirt, standing under her sycamore, hawking her leaflets. And there he was, laughing in the white-and-red convertible, reaching out his hand.

"Hey, Katie! What're you selling?"

She turned away and walked slowly to her stand, and once again began handing out her doomsday brochures.

About the Author

Arthur Laurents lives on the beach in Quogue, Long Island. He likes to ski. Most of his writing has been for the theatre and includes such plays as *Home of the Brave, The Time of the Cuckoo, A Clearing in the Woods, Invitation to a March,* and musicals such as *West Side Story, Gypsy, Anyone Can Whistle,* and *Hallelujah, Baby!* He has also written for the films *The Snake Pit, Rope,* and *Anastasia* among others.